CHARLIE PERKINS

By Terry L. Shaffer

Copyright © Terry L. Shaffer, 2014
ISBN-13: 9781507783207
ISBN-10: 1507783205

This is a work of fiction. Names, characters, locations, and incidents are either the product of the author's imagination or are used fictitiously. Any resemblance to actual events locales, organizations, or persons, living or dead is entirely coincidental and beyond the intent of either the author or the publisher.

CHAPTER 1

Charlie Perkins had a secret and, like a poker player with more aces than he'd ever had, he was trying not to let it show. Secrets were hard to keep in a small town like Truth or Consequences, New Mexico, and since Charlie had never kept a secret this big before; he wasn't exactly sure what to do.

He dressed in his regular clothes - cowboy boots, a plaid work shirt with rolled up sleeves over a dirty, yellowed long underwear top and a pair of Levis held up with his regular belt and cowboy buckle – thinking that wouldn't draw attention to himself. Other than that, keeping his mouth shut was the only other thing he could think of to do.

It would be hard for a stranger to guess Charlie's age; he had spent so much time in the New Mexico sun that his face was tanned dark and lined with creases from squinting so much. The lines made him look older than his twenty-five years. At five feet ten, a hundred and seventy pounds, he was wiry, and if his arms were bare, corded muscle showed whenever he moved them. He had an honest-looking face, and people tended to trust him on sight.

He pushed his "New Mexico, Land of Entrapment" ball cap up slightly on his forehead then drained the last third of his bottle of Bud. "Well, time to get to work," he announced with forced casualness to no one in particular, which was good because no one else was around in the Plugged Nickel Saloon except the bartender and she was busy refilling the beer coolers.

He rose and sauntered out of the tavern into the midday New Mexico sun. Trying to act like he hadn't a care in the world, Charlie wandered over to his faded blue Jeep Cherokee, got in, and started it up. He did a U-turn and headed back toward I-25 through Truth or Consequences. The hardest thing he had done so far to maintain his "cover" was to obey the damned forty mile an hour speed zone through Williamsburg. While he was going so slowly, he reached over and made sure a metal ammo box was still secure on the passenger floorboard.

Once he merged onto I-25, he kicked the Jeep's speed up to seventy-five and maintained it until he got to the Hillsboro/Silver City exit at Highway 152. Turning west at the stop sign, he glanced in his rear view mirrors to make sure no one was following. The Jeep remained in passing gear as he pushed it up into the winding foothills of the Black Range west into Hillsboro and beyond toward Kingston.

His excitement began to build as he passed the narrow bridge between the two towns, then turned left onto a rough dirt trail that had probably been a mining exploration road. He looked carefully for other tracks – tires, footprints or even horse hoofs, but saw nothing to suggest anyone had been in here since yesterday. Less than three miles up the road, Perkins turned off the road into the mouth of a wash and, in four-wheel low, began grinding his way around boulders, sandbars, and stagnant pools of tire-sucking mud as he slowly eased the Jeep further and further up the wash. If he had not had his seatbelt buckled, his head would have hit the ceiling several times due to the violent jostling of the vehicle as it made its way over smaller rocks and downed trees. Even the contents of the ammo box had begun to rattle. Finally, the wash narrowed, and boulders as big as the Jeep prevented the tough little vehicle from making any more forward progress.

Perkins was happier with his parking place, since when he was here yesterday, the Jeep had sat all the way out at the mouth of the wash. Now he was at least a half a mile closer and out of sight of the old road he had come in on. He gathered up his backpack, slung his metal detector over his shoulder, pulled out a straight steel pry bar, then stopped as his eyes fell on the ammo box. Should he take it? There wasn't another soul within miles so he decided to hide it under some blankets on the back seat.

*****

Charlie Perkins was a prospector. He didn't start out that way; he started out in high school handling cattle and horses and the myriad of chores that went with it. He was pretty good at it too. He could gentle a skittish colt and, on horseback, could turn a recalcitrant cow and calf as well as anyone. Charlie's biggest problem was that he didn't like school, and, after dropping out at the beginning of his junior year, he never went back. There was plenty of work on the ranches in the area and Charlie made the rounds, picking up a few weeks' work here and there. All told, he made a reasonably good living at it.

But then, on a day off, he agreed to "burro" for a buddy who was placer mining a claim in the Caballo Mountains. It was back breaking work, digging, screening, dry-washing, and finally panning what was left but suddenly it was all worth it when he saw those little chunks of gold at the bottom of the pan, then they joined their brothers in the little-finger-sized vial. That first day they netted almost half an ounce of gold – gold just out there for the taking. It didn't occur to him that they had processed in excess of two cubic yards of rocks and soil to extract that gold. The bug bit Charlie deep and hard and his career path started to veer off course.

Gradually, as his knowledge grew and he acquired the necessary equipment, Charlie's days as a cowboy came to an end, and he began trying to make his living searching for the mother lode, the strike to end all strikes. The Caballos and the Black Range were historically rich in minerals, including generous deposits of gold and silver. There were times when he did pretty well, but there were dry spells when he had to fall back on his cowboy skills or borrow from other prospectors who were flush for the moment. He never made enough to save any money, but he discovered the best place to learn his trade was in the taverns after the sun went down. There, over a few beers, especially if he was buying, the old timers would tell of fabulously wealthy veins and streams where one could pluck the nuggets out like pecans from under a tree after it had been shaken. They spoke of the best techniques for extracting the precious metal from the earth and of hoards of Spanish gold secreted in the Caballos centuries ago. Many seemed to know someone who had seen the evidence of these rich strikes, but none seemed to have made one himself.

Undaunted, Charlie persevered. He had three or four decent claims that produced on occasion but when a good rain came – a good gully washer, not just a shower – he liked to hike some of the more remote washes in the Black Range, hoping for that big nugget or a nice piece of quartz shot through with veins of gold. He found lots of rocks shot through with iron pyrite (fool's gold), but he was still waiting for his golden ship to come in.

Like yesterday, enough of a weather front had come through over the last couple of days to cause some of the street drains in town to back up and when the clouds finally rolled on through and the sun came out just before noon, Charlie Perkins decided it was time for one of those kinds of hikes.

Charlie had not made anything like a systematic search of the washes in the mountains near Kingston – there were too many of them – but he did keep track of where he had been and tried to spread himself out so he didn't hike the same wash twice. The one he chose for yesterday's hike was in the vicinity of some he had been in before but he was sure he'd never set foot in this one.

He had parked the Jeep up off the main part of the road and started casting back and forth across the mouth of a wash with his metal detector. He couldn't understand why more old timers didn't use detectors. They were a great adjunct to just looking at the ground as he slowly worked his way up the wash.

The sun had dropped below the summit of the Continental Divide by the time Charlie reached a place in the wash where it narrowed to about fifteen feet. Large boulders partially blocked the passage, and the top part of a tree had washed up against them, further blocking his way. He decided to just scan the upstream faces of the rocks – a good place for gold to settle – then call it a day, since by then he could barely see the end of the metal detector.

He had thrust the metal detector ahead of him, through a gap between the rocks, and was trying to squeeze through between two boulders when the detector's audible warble went off scaring Charlie half to death. The head was at least eighteen inches above the surface of the wash, so whatever had set it off was either on the surface or close to it, but it was too dark now for Charlie to see what was triggering the instrument. He let the detector warble as he finished squeezing between the rocks. He could barely make out, below the head of the metal detector, a square object partially buried in river rock and sand and wedged against the upstream side of the boulder. Charlie knelt down and discovered a handle folded over on the top of the object. He straightened the handle out and gave it a tug. It reluctantly came free, leaving a dark, damp, rectangular indentation in the rocks and sand.

In the dim light, Charlie could see that it looked like a metal ammo box, and it felt abnormally heavy. He could see a padlock on the hasp end. He looked around at the deepening gloom and decided he was done detecting for the day. Squeezing back between the rocks, Charlie could hear the contents of the box sloshing and realized that part of the weight was water that had washed in during the storm.

He made it back to the Jeep without turning an ankle in the river rocks and opened the rear hatch. He had to clear away a shovel and some plastic buckets before he could set the box down beneath the dome light in the rear of the Jeep. He looked the box over, finding no name or means to identify its owner, and decided he'd have to cut the lock, but he couldn't do it here since his bolt cutters were at home.

The drive back home to Elephant Butte was a study in burning curiosity. The sloshing notwithstanding, what could be so important that someone would lock it in a perfectly transportable ammo box? The boxes were common enough, mostly military surplus, and Charlie had two or three of them that he kept small items in – but he didn't lock them. He tried not to even think of what might be in the mysterious metal box.

Once he got the box into his house, Charlie wasted no time clearing the dirty dishes out of the sink and laying a piece of cheesecloth over the drain. If there was gold in the box, he didn't want to pour it down the drain. He cut the lock and opened the top. It was full of water, which was no surprise, but before he poured it out, he felt around in the box for broken glass or anything else that might suggest there was gold loose in the water. He found nothing, so began to dribble the water through the cheesecloth. Nothing appeared in the makeshift filter.

Charlie set the box on the counter, after shoving over the mass of dirty dishes a little farther. The first object he removed was a small weight scale, which raised his hopes for the presence of silver or gold. There were three eyedroppers and a handful of empty little-finger-sized vials commonly used for storing gold in water. Finally, at the bottom was a sodden blue-with-gold-trim drawstring bag tied in a bow. It was heavier than anything else in the box, but he attributed that to the water in the fabric.

Shaking fingers made whatever was inside tinkle almost like small bells as he untied the drawstring of the bag. He pulled the mouth open wide, and involuntarily took a deep breath and held it, when he saw the vials inside, each of which was full of what looked like gold. There had to be ten or twelve glass vials – twelve when he sat them all out on the counter in rows like little soldiers. It was generally held that each vial, when full, contained very close to an ounce of gold. He had come across someone's stash! Finally he exhaled as he stared at the vials. They represented more gold than he had ever seen at one time, and probably more than he had extracted from the mountains in all the time he had been prospecting. Suddenly he looked in the box again, checking for some kind of identification, but found only a damp interior.

Charlie was torn between never returning to that draw and rushing back to it at the crack of dawn, and that conundrum haunted him all evening long and far into the night. Early on, he decided that he was about average honest, and if someone came knocking on his door asking for his ammo box and gold back, he'd probably surrender it, but short of that, he was keeping it. No, the question was, should he risk running into the owner by returning to the draw or not? If he did run into the owner, it would sure eliminate any chance of finding more gold. Would the owner have put all his gold in the one box or had he spread it around . . . what was the word the investor guys used? Diversify! Don't keep all your eggs in one basket. With a start, Charlie realized that applied to him now, so he spent the next hour finding three different hiding places for "his" gold. Finally, after his sixth beer, he fell into a restless sleep.

The next morning, Charlie awoke and his decision was clear. He would return to the wash. His big concern now was staying casual and not attracting any attention from his prospecting associates. To a man (and occasional woman), they were all extraordinarily paranoid about where their claims were and where they were seeing color. Charlie was no different, and the bullshit he had heard in the taverns was reason enough not to trust a one of them. He decided the best thing to do was to make today a carbon copy of yesterday. That way no one would look twice at him.

The cold air had moved out of the region overnight and it was warmer than yesterday. Charlie noticed that as soon as he emerged from the Jeep, and after he squeezed between the same two rocks he noticed something else – the smell of something dead. He also saw why there was a top of a tree cluttering the passages between the rocks in the narrows. A huge cottonwood tree partially embedded in the left bank had uprooted about fifty yards upstream, and part of the tree had fallen into the wash. It would make scanning with the metal detector that much harder, but Charlie was motivated.

Almost immediately, he started getting hits with the detector and his pulsed raced. *Could these actually be nuggets?* He slung the metal detector again and started scuffing through the rocks in the wash with his bar. The first thing he spotted was a spoon followed in short order by a fork, a pancake turner and, further upstream, a twelve-inch griddle. Puzzled, Charlie tried to work the detector in between the leafy branches of the tree but met with little success, so he moved slowly upstream along the tree's trunk. The smell got worse, and so did Charlie's feeling of foreboding.

The metal detector hits seemed more concentrated at or under the tree limbs, but Charlie was having a lot of trouble alternately running the instrument over an area then stopping to scuff through the rocks and sand with the bar. And the smell kept getting stronger. By the time he had worked his way near to the base of the tree, he didn't need the metal detector to tell him that the tree had fallen right on someone's camp. Mashed between the branches of the tree was an aluminum stand and a two burner Coleman stove. Beyond he could see part of a towel and a bit of cloth that could have been a hot pad. Fully half the width of the wash was covered by the tree.

By now, Charlie's apprehension had turned to dread. Someone had tried to tunnel under the tree in three locations, but each time was thwarted by rocks half the size of a Volkwagen. He could also see where someone had tried to hack through some of the tree branches to get nearer the larger trunks, but that was obstructed by limbs ten or more inches in diameter.

He hiked upstream around the tree trunk to the massive hole created by the root ball. It didn't look like anyone had tried to work any of the newly exposed material. He circled around to the other side of the fallen tree where part of the main trunk rested on the bank of the wash. Between the leaves, he could see flashes of orange, and even one tent stake still driven into the ground. Among the branches of the tree, he could see what looked like an army fatigue jacket impaled by branches driven into the ground on the bank. There was a branch of the cottonwood two feet in diameter resting directly over what he was pretty sure was someone's tent, and he hoped fervently that the smell came from someone's unfortunate dog, but he knew better. In three more places, someone had tried to dig under the tree to get to the tent, but it didn't look like any attempt had succeeded.

Charlie worked the detector around the branches of the tree as closely as he could on the bank of the wash, but came away with nothing. If this was a prospector, most of his gear must be between where he had spotted the stove and the bank of the wash; in other words, under the tree. Or he had left his gear at his dig, wherever that was. Clearly someone had been here before Charlie and had tried to get under the tree either to help someone who was trapped or to retrieve something. That posed the question of whether the shadow partner would return with a chainsaw and/or the authorities.

Charlie's first impulse was to get the hell out of there. Take what he had found and call it good. But the prospector in him rebelled at the idea of leaving a paying claim. He decided to explore a little further upstream to see if he could find any claim poles. He left his detector and the bar at the tree and hiked further up the wash. Not a hundred yards further up was a fresh dig site located on the left bank under what looked like a huge slab of rock. The rock had been undercut at least four feet, and Charlie saw no shoring to keep the rock horizontal.

There was a whole mining set-up, including screens, a dry washer, a gas-engine-powered vacuum and even two five-gallon containers of what Charlie assumed was water. There was a tub half full of water and two green plastic gold pans nearby. There had to be a partner. There was too much equipment for one person to use, there just *had* to be a partner.

He noticed a five gallon bucket of fine material sitting near the tub and, for the hell of it, scooped some into one of the panners, added some water and started swishing it around the upper surfaces of the pan. He saw color right away before he had washed out even half the detritus, and the more dirt and sand he washed out into the tub, the more color he saw. He lost track of where he was as he continued to swirl the water around in the pan, washing away more and more dirt and sand. Finally, he could wash away no more without risking throwing out the gold with the water, Abruptly he remembered where he was and that the means for extracting of the gold – the eye droppers – was in the ammo box in his Jeep.

Charlie shook his head and carefully laid the pan down on the ground. More than anything, he wanted to continue to work this dig, but he was afraid the partner might come back. If he was lucky, the partner had panicked and was halfway to Argentina by now.

He just couldn't resist as he turned and stared into the dig. It was then that he noticed the overhanging rock wasn't a rock at all, but something smooth and dull black where he could see the surface through the adhering dirt. He reached out and brushed away some more clinging dirt and rubbed his hand across the surface. It was smooth like a river rock, but didn't feel like metal or even fiberglass. He pushed up on it, but it didn't give at all. He knocked on it. It didn't have the solid sound he expected, but it wasn't really a hollow sound either.

As long as it doesn't come down on my head. He rose to his feet and looked all around him, seeing nothing but the wash and banks littered with greasewood and prickly pear cactus. He could see why they had made their camp down by the cottonwood. There was more shade there, and they would be up out of the bottom of the wash in case more rain came. As he walked downstream to the campsite, he retrieved his detector and bar. *I won't be needing these for a while.* By the time he reached the Jeep, he had decided to bring back his own extraction kit. That way if the partner caught him, all he'd have to give up was what he had already panned.

Back at the dig site, he used his eyedropper to suck up the bits of gold from the bottom of the pan and deposited them – still in water – into a vial. He was impressed how much gold lay in the bottom of the vial after just one pan. Charlie worked steadily on the contents of the bucket until it was empty. He had been on his knees in front of the tub panning material from the bucket for the past three hours, and when he stood up, he had to stretch the kinks out. By then, the sun was behind the mountains and it was time to get out before it was too dark to see. He was pleased to see that the vial was nearly half full.

As he hiked back to the Jeep, he pondered that he had neither heard nor seen any sign of another human being anywhere around, and that if a vehicle had gone by on the dirt road, he would have heard it. He was more confident now that the partner wouldn't bring back the law, and the threat of the law being around was probably why the partner wasn't around – at least that Charlie could detect.

As he drove back through Hillsboro, he debated the pros and cons of maintaining his present schedule or coming up here early in the morning and working until it was too late to see. He didn't know how much time he had before the partner returned, but if he had been the partner, he wouldn't abandon such a dig. Sooner or later the man would return, and Charlie would just as soon be gone when that happened. As long as he was working the site, he didn't want any of his cohorts to get suspicious, so he probably ought to stop by the Plugged Nickel for a while, just to keep things normal. It was coming rent time and he'd have to go to Las Cruces to sell a vial or two of gold, but that wasn't out of the ordinary. So long as he only sold a couple, no eyebrows would be raised. Gold buyers were a close-mouthed lot. They had to be. If a seller – especially a prospector - learned that his buyer was telling tales, that buyer would soon be out of business.

Such were his thoughts and activities over the next seventeen days. Once in a while he would vary his routine a little just for show, but each afternoon would find him extracting material from deeper and deeper under whatever the thing was above him, processing the material, and panning out the rich deposit of gold. He went so far as to try to drive a couple of posts under the furthest overhanging edges of the object above the dig, but the edges of the thing were so rounded that he couldn't get a post to stay in position. He debated nailing some cleats into what he thought of as the hull, but decided against it, fearing the vibration would loosen the whole structure's grip in the dirt and bring it down on top him.

On the eighteenth day, in a manner of speaking, that's pretty much what happened.

CHAPTER 2

Charlie's day started out regularly; he was up and at the Plugged Nickel by about eleven. As a matter of fact, he ran into a couple of fellow prospectors and even bought them a beer. He was on his way up the mountain by twelve-thirty and on site by one forty-five after stopping at the old KOA campground for gas and more coffee. Still maintaining his casual demeanor, he stood there and jawed with Jim, the proprietor for a few minutes before heading up Highway 152 toward Hillsboro. When he got to the dirt road off the highway, he carefully checked the section of the dirt road on which he daily carefully brushed away any tire tracks in the powdery dirt but found no evidence that a vehicle had passed this way. He drove the Jeep up to his usual spot, grabbed his equipment, and headed up the wash.

The smell wasn't quite so pronounced anymore and time had ameliorated his guilt at not calling in the authorities. He had promised himself that when the gold petered out, he would call just before he left for the last time.

As he approached the dig, he sensed that something wasn't right. His equipment seemed to be in the regular places but something . . . there! Under the hull, something was hanging down that wasn't there yesterday. He slowed his pace almost to a halt and carefully crept up on the scene. At first he thought the hull had settled but it was positioned as it always had been; something like a scoop or a ramp was now extended from the bottom of the hull to the surface of the wash, a distance of about four feet. Charlie didn't have a flashlight with him so all he could see at the top of the ramp was dark. He thought there was a flashlight in the Jeep so he put down his gear and returned at a half trot to the Jeep. He found the flashlight under the passenger seat but grimaced when he saw that the batteries were getting low. Still, dim light was better than no light so he high tailed it back up to the site.

As he approached the hull, it occurred to Charlie for the first time that maybe he ought to reconsider. Was going into that thing with barely a light and no weapon such a good idea? No one on the planet would know where he was. The more he looked at the ramp, the stronger his curiosity became. He finally grabbed a rock hammer and slipped it down the back of his jeans, and started to climb up the ramp. He had to hunker down to even get to the ramp, but it was open enough that he could ascend easily enough on his hands and knees. The ramp was just a little short of four feet wide and smooth, but Charlie had no difficulty getting traction on the surface as he climbed slowly up into the thing.

Coming from bright sunlight into darkness was blinding, even using a slowly dying flashlight. "Hello?" he called out, "anyone in here?" There was no response except a slight echo of his voice inside the hull. When his hands got to the top of the ramp, all Charlie could see was that the ramp led onto a platform of some sort. He stopped there and shone the flashlight all around the interior, but the blackness was complete and the weak beam couldn't cut through it.

Finally, seeing or hearing no movement, Charlie edged up onto the platform. Still no reaction, and he still couldn't see anything that concerned him. He took a "step" on all fours, then another. Now he appeared to be close to the middle of the platform and without warning a beam bathed him in a bluish light. When he tried to back out of the thing, Charlie found that he could no longer move. He couldn't budge an arm or a leg, say a word, or move his head. He noticed that he could still flex muscles although he couldn't move them, and he was still able to breathe and blink normally, though his respiration and heartbeat had taken off like a frightened quail. Then a bright blue, pulsing ring appeared before him and began moving very slowly toward him. As it reached the crown of his head, he felt a slight tingling, but no real discomfort.

He could see that the pulsing ring was large enough in diameter to fit completely around his body. It paused at his head and the pulsing increased rapidly. It seemed like it took at least an hour for it to pass by his head to his neck, at which time the pulsing slowed down to just about Charlie's heart rate – which was far above normal. For a few seconds, he felt like he had inhaled either pure oxygen or nitrous oxide but the sensation quickly subsided.

The ring continued its journey down the length of Charlie's body, then retraced its track just as slowly until it cleared his head, then it went dark. The blue beam of light continued to hold him long after the ring had darkened. Charlie could see where the ring had stopped, but saw no apparatus that would have supported it. Suddenly the light beam went out and Charlie found that he could use his arms and legs again. He scrambled down the ramp as fast as he could, stopping several feet away where he thought he was safe. Within moments the ramp retracted into the hull and the joint between hull and ramp disappeared.

Charlie didn't know whether to sit down, fall down, or stand there swaying. His head was in an awful turmoil, but as near as he could tell, everything else seemed okay. Finally, he shakily turned over one of the five-gallon buckets and sat down. His head didn't hurt so much as feel like little fireballs were zipping around all over behind his eyes. Now that he was sitting, closing his eyes didn't seem to help, so he put his head down between his knees, thinking he might black out, but the little fireballs just kept zipping around inside his head. Finally he eased down onto the ground and eventually fell asleep.

When he woke up the sun was over the mountains and dusk was falling fast. The fireballs were gone, but his head still felt weird, like someone had aired it out. Actually, he realized that he felt pretty good. He sat up and looked at the hull. It had not changed. The ramp was still up and his shovel, bar, and buckets were still underneath. He didn't know how he knew, but Charlie was sure that he had been scanned while he was inside that hull and was still alive because his brain met a certain criteria. Whose criteria he didn't know, but he *knew* other animals had gone up that ramp and not come back out because they didn't measure up, whatever that meant. He had passed some kind of test.

As he drove home, he debated what he should do next. He didn't think he should go on mining the material beneath the hull. The feeling that it wasn't far from collapsing into the hole beneath was strong. He had dug in as far as he should go. When he asked himself how he knew that, he had no answer. Now that he was done, he debated how to report the body to the police. He had originally planned to make an anonymous call to the Sierra County Sheriff's Office telling them where to look after placing rock cairns at strategic spots so they wouldn't get lost. He didn't like that idea much anymore. It now seemed a higher priority to tell someone about the hull and what it had done to him.

What *had* it done to him? He felt different, but he still couldn't put his finger on what exactly wasn't right. He shrugged off the feeling and went to the refrigerator for a beer, but as he opened the appliance's door, suddenly he wasn't interested in drinking a beer or anything else that threatened to anesthetize his ability to think straight. Now that was different. There hadn't been too many times in recent memory when he didn't feel like a beer, or even a shot of whiskey.

To whom should he report the hull and how much should he tell them about what it did to him? Like everyone else, he had joked about people who claimed to have been taken up into spaceships and probed, and how outlandish it all sounded, but this happened, this was true! So who would believe him? Who would at least come out and look at the hull. Pictures! If he had pictures they'd believe him. They'd have to. He didn't have a camera, but he could pick one up at WalMart easy enough and then they couldn't laugh at him. They'd have to come with him and see the hull for themselves.

The next day Charlie acquired a camera, shot his pictures, and had prints made. Now he had to decide where to take them. White Sands Missile Range sounded like the right place, but it was run by the Army and he didn't figure they'd have much interest in something like this that might be a UFO. He decided on Holloman Air Force Base in Alamogordo, because it was next closest.

About two hours later he turned into the First Street gate, and was stopped by the sentry.

"Good morning Sir," said the sharply appointed gate guard. "How can I help you?"

"Yeah, good morning," Charlie replied, suddenly tongue-tied. "I'd like to see someone about something I found up in the Black Range Mountains."

"Sir, can you be more specific?"

"I found something up there that might . . . well, might belong to the Air Force."

"What makes you think so, Sir?" said the sentry, looking up and noticing that a queue was starting to form behind Charlie's Jeep.

Charlie noticed it too. "It's like nothing I ever seen, not like an airplane or nothing, but it sure don't belong up in the mountains. I think it might be a UFO!" he blurted. "I have pictures!" He started to reach into his shirt pocket to show them, but the sentry took a step back.

"Sir, please keep your hands in plain sight for me, okay?"

Charlie knew he was blowing it, so he took a deep breath and tried again. "Sorry, um, Airman, but if I could just get someone to look at my pictures, I think they'd understand better."

"Okay. Sir? Would you pull your Jeep over into that parking lot and just wait in your vehicle while I call someone to come see your pictures?"

With a sigh of relief and frustration, Charlie turned his Jeep into the parking lot as indicated by the sentry, put it in park, and waited. It seemed like he had waited hours before he saw a young man in a blue uniform walk out to the sentry, who then pointed at Charlie. The young man waited for a car to go by, then walked over to where Charlie was parked.

"Good morning, Sir, I'm Lieutenant Castleman. I understand you have some pictures you want to show someone and think it might be a UFO?"

"That's right," said Charlie, reaching into his shirt pocket and handing about half a dozen photos to the young second lieutenant.

The officer took his time looking at each photo. Finally he looked at Charlie. "What is it?"

"That's the thing, I don't know. I do know it has a ramp in its belly that opens up and there's some kind a of scanning thingamajiggy in there."

"How do you know that?"

"Well, it opened up and I went inside . . ."

"You went *inside* that thing?"

"Well, yeah. That's the only way I know about what's in there. Anyway, some kind of a beam held me down while a blue circle scanned me. Then I got the hell out of there!"

"I see. Were you injured?"

"No. Felt a little light-headed for a while, but I weren't hurt no place."

"And you think it's a UFO because . . . ?"

"Well I don't *know* that it's a UFO. It might belong to you folks for all I know, but it's mighty high tech to be laying out in the mountains."

"I see your point. Whereabouts is it?"

"It's up in the Black Range Mountains between Hillsboro and Kingston. Do you know that country at all?"

"No sir, I just arrived from Colorado a month ago."

"Ok, well, I'd be willing to lead someone up there. This afternoon even."

"Ah . . . I don't think we can respond quite that quickly. Would you mind if I get some information on how to contact you, and keep the photos so I can show some other people?"

"That's fine. When do you want to go up there?"

"That'll have to be decided by my boss," said Lieutenant Castleman, "but hopefully not too long. Do you think it's still there?"

"I should think so. It looks like it's been there for quite a spell. There's dirt and plants and rocks all over the top of it, and the only way I know'd the ramp opened up in the belly is because I been digging under there."

"Digging? What for?"

A wary look came into Charlie's eyes. "Oh, just prospectin'."

"I see. Well, I'll take these photos right in to my boss and we'll be in touch. That okay with you? Oh, have you shown these pictures to anyone else?"

"No but I can make some more prints if I need them, in case I have to show them to somebody else."

"I'd appreciate it if you didn't have any more prints made and, for that matter, didn't discuss this with anyone until you hear from us, okay?"

"Okay, but don't wait too long."

"Thank you for coming by, ah . . . Mr. Perkins, we'll be in touch."

On the way back to T or C, Charlie wasn't sure if he had been patronized or not. The young lieutenant seemed sincere enough, but once the pictures got kicked upstairs, who knew what might happen? Anyway, if the kid wasn't feeding him a line of bullshit, the whole thing went much better than he expected. He was prepared to face some ridicule, but he was also ready to take his pictures to the Army if the flyboys laughed at him.

Charlie had bizarre dreams that night. Aliens coming and going in a variety of interstellar vehicles, seeding planets with probes to search for intelligent life. Technology so advanced Charlie could hardly comprehend. Alien forms so un-human-like, they were beyond science fiction. But what scared him most were the "close-to-home" dreams, where scanners were opening previously unused areas of his brain, turning on the lights, and implanting knowledge where there had been only emptiness. Was he under the control of whomever had built that hull? Was he even now perceiving one thing, but doing another? He woke up sweating and shaking and didn't even bother trying to go back to sleep. He didn't want to dream anymore.

In the days that followed, Charlie began to notice that he was different than he used to be. He would finish the sentences of newscasters on the television, and know ahead of time what the weatherman was going to predict. As the days passed, he even found himself getting bored with his old friends. They never said anything Charlie didn't already know was coming, and most of it seemed inane or trite. It was as if Charlie was outgrowing his friends who were still in kindergarten and he was advancing at a furious pace to . . . somewhere else.

The changes were driven home when his cell phone rang on the fourth day after he had been to Holloman Air Force Base. He knew it would be Lieutenant Castleman, and that Castleman wanted Charlie to lead an investigative team to the hull.

"Was there anything you did that caused the ramp to open?" Castleman asked.

"No. Matter of fact, I wasn't even there when it opened. It was already open when I got there."

"Do you think it might open again while we're up there?"

"I have no idea what the thing might do."

"Are you sure it's unoccupied?"

"No. I didn't see anyone or anything in the small area of the hull I was in, but I can't speak for the rest of the thing. I don't even know what the whole thing looks like."

There was a pause, as if Castleman was listening to someone in the background. "Do you know if anyone else has seen this hull?"

Charlie had been dreading that question. "I have reason to believe that at least one other person – maybe two – have seen the hull, but I can explain that better when we get up to the site. Oh, and Lieutenant? Have them bring a chainsaw."

CHAPTER 3

Promptly at 0800 hours the next morning, two blue Air Force Suburbans rolled into the parking lot at the old KOA. Lieutenant Castleman jumped out of the first Suburban and walked over to greet Charlie, who had emerged from his Jeep.

"Good morning, Mr. Perkins," the young officer said, "how are you doing this morning?"

"Well, okay, I reckon," Charlie replied, eyeing the two Air Force vehicles. "Come with a small army, I see."

"They're really in charge," he said with a shrug, "I've brought a whole OSI team with me."

"OSI, what's that?"

"Office of Special Investigations. They have teams that respond to situations like this, and they have the equipment and training to investigate every facet of the scene."

"Oh, okay. Did you bring a camera and a chainsaw?"

Lieutenant Castleman laughed. "Yes, the camera is standard. Everyone was wondering about the chainsaw."

"It'll make sense when we get up there." With that, Charlie returned to his Jeep and led the small procession up Highway 152 toward Hillsboro.

Forty minutes later, he turned off on the dirt road leading down to the site. He had misgivings. What if they arrested him for murder? For digging on Bureau of Land Management or Forest Service land that didn't have a claim? Deep down he didn't believe that would happen but a lot of things could go wrong, getting the military involved.

He shifted into four low and turned up the wash. After a little wheel spinning, the four-wheel drive Suburbans followed. He parked in his usual spot, got out of the Jeep, and waited for the Suburbans to disgorge their passengers.

Lieutenant Castleman walked over with another man who bore two bars on the collar points of his fatigue jacket. "Mr. Perkins, this is Captain Webber. He's in charge of this OSI team and will actually be running the investigation. Actually, this is kind of beyond my bailiwick. I sort of invited myself along for the ride and, since I work at the Public Information Office, the boss thought it a good idea."

Charlie shook hands with Captain Webber and their eyes locked. He was probably in his late twenties or early thirties, six feet tall, and muscular. His dark brown hair was close cropped from what Charlie could see below his fatigue cap, but it was the Captain's eyes that warned Charlie not to mess with him.

Five men walked up behind Captain Webber, each carrying either boxes or bags of equipment, and they all had a bright, interested, and capable look about them.

Charlie didn't hesitate but led them through the narrows and the hundred yards up to the dig site. The hull was still as Charlie had left it - with the ramp up.

"Hold up, Mr. Perkins," said Captain Webber. "Why don't we do some tests to see if this thing is emitting anything before we get too familiar with it?"

As the men set about unloading and setting up their equipment, Charlie walked over to Captain Webber, who was talking with Lieutenant Castleman. "How about I walk you two fellers down to that uprooted tree. I think there's something there you should see."

"Yeah, I thought I smelled something when we walked by."

Charlie pointed out the paths someone had made through the branches in an attempt to get to the tent from both the wash and the bank. When they saw the tent beneath the trunk of the tree, the request for the chainsaw became obvious.

"Mr. Perkins, you understand that a death investigation, even one so overtly accidental as this one, has to be handled by the civilian authorities? The Air Force can't be involved in that unless the victim or a perpetrator is actually in the service."

"So you can't cut the tree away and see what's been making that God-awful stink?"

"No Sir, we can't. It makes sense now why you think someone other than yourself has seen the, uh . . . hull, as you call it."

"I figure there was a partner who tried to get into the tent either to help the guy inside or to get something of value. There's enough equipment at the dig site for two men, and there were no other vehicles around when I first came up here."

"When was that?"

"About three weeks ago."

"So you've been mining the area under the hull for three weeks with probably a body no more than three hundred feet away? I'm surprised you didn't call the local authorities."

"I thought about it more times than you can imagine, but it would have ruined my prospecting, and it was showing a lot of color."

"By color you mean gold?"

"Yep. I wasn't hurting this person and there was nobody else around. I figured the cops would dig out the body then, when they saw the hull, they'd call you and you'd dig that out, and I'd be left with nothing."

"You're probably correct, but it still seems a little cold to work a man's claim after he died."

"Well, it wasn't doing him any good."

"What about the partner?"

"What about him? I haven't seen hide nor hair of anyone up in this country since I started, and I've been checking every day."

"I'm glad you called us first," said Captain Webber. "It gives us a chance to do our thing without being interrupted by the locals."

Just then one of Webber's troops walked up. "No emanations detected, Captain."

Webber nodded. "Good, proceed."

"What're you going to do with that thing?" Charlie asked.

"Pretty much what you thought. Very carefully dig it out and haul it to someplace where we can study it."

"Well, watch out if that ramp opens up. I've been feeling peculiar ever since I crawled in that thing and have been having some really weird dreams."

"Yes, we need to get into that," said Captain Webber. "I'd like to tape your statement about what you know about this thing, from the first moment on. Would that be okay?"

A red flag went up in Charlie's head. "Here? Now? Am I under arrest for something?"

"No, no, nothing like that," said the Captain with a smile, "it's just that you know more about this thing than anyone, because you've been inside it, right?"

"Well, yeah . . ."

"We just want to know what to expect if the thing opens up again. You're certainly not in trouble; as a matter of fact, we're grateful for your assistance."

That sounded pretty good to Charlie, but he knew he didn't dare tell them about the gold he had extracted unless he wanted to donate it to the U.S. Government. But there was more. He *knew* things he shouldn't about this craft and probably knew more about the circumstances of it being here than any human alive or dead. It had all come to him subconsciously in what he thought were dreams, but he now knew that the blue ring had imparted knowledge about the craft and how it came to be here. He was becoming aware of more knowledge all the time, and it was a little disturbing that he could tell what people were thinking before they said anything. He knew when he opened his mouth about being in trouble that Captain Webber had no motive behind the interview, but wanted to learn what Charlie knew about the craft. It was also disturbing that he could sometimes move things by just thinking about them. He knew he had to tell them about what the ring had taught him but he didn't think telling them about being telepathic and telekinetic was such a good idea.

"When do you want to do the recording, Captain?" Charlie asked, knowing that the officer would try to persuade him to come back to the base. He also knew that in the back of Webber's mind was the idea that if things panned out with Charlie, they might want to take him to Nellis Air Force Base in Nevada, where they could do far more comprehensive medical tests on him. He wasn't too thrilled about that, but would play it by ear.

"We're pretty busy here right now. Do you think you could come back to the office in a few days? We're all set up there to take statements, and I want to be sure the whole team listens in, because we get better questions that way."

Charlie lost track of what Webber was saying about halfway through his explanation. He was more interested in what the OSI team was doing around the craft. Two men were putting away what he thought might be multi-channel radiation sensors, one was still shooting photos, and the other two were digging over the top of the craft.

As he watched, Charlie spoke over his shoulder to Captain Webber and Lieutenant Castleman: "There is only about two and a half meters of the craft yet uncovered by my digging. The craft is about two point five meters wide at the widest point and it is being held off the ground by an antigravity field that you probably could not detect. It is harmless, but has kept me from being crushed for the last three weeks."

Charlie turned to look at the officers and saw that they were both staring at him.

"How do you know that?" asked Castleman.

"I don't know," said Charlie, "it's just some of the stuff that's been in my dreams. Hell, it might not even be accurate but there it is."

"So it's not going to collapse to the ground the minute we finish digging it out?" asked Webber.

"That is my belief, besides it would have already fallen."

"Can it be moved?"

"The anti-grav field merely keeps it above the surface of the planet. You can move it laterally any way you want."

"How long has it been here?" Webber asked.

"Why don't we save that for the interview at your office, Captain? There is a lot of information regarding how the craft came to be here, and it would probably be better if we got it down all at one time. As to how to move it, I suggest you arrange for a flatbed trailer to meet us at the highway. Once free of the ground friction, the craft can be moved rather easily."

"You mean like a balloon that won't get any lower to or higher from the ground?" asked Lieutanant Castleman.

"That's a pretty good analogy, Lieutenant. You could just pull the craft over above the trailer, then tie it down in such a way that it won't drift off, then cover it with a conventional tarp."

"I'll get one heading this way," said Webber as he pulled out his cell phone.

"There's no reception up here," said Charlie. "You'll probably have to be in line of sight to the Caballo Mountains to get a signal."

"Yeah," said Webber as he looked over at his men. "Sergeant Glisan, can you spare one of your men to drive back toward Caballo to arrange transport for this thing?"

"Yes Sir," said a stocky, black man wearing the stripes of a master sergeant. He turned to one of the men putting away equipment. "Corporal Downey, you know how to reach the motor pool, right?"

"Yes."

"Take the Captain's phone down to where you can get a signal and call into the motor pool and ask for Master Sergeant Naab. Tell him what we need, then arrange to lead him up here. Be sure they bring enough tarps to cover the whole thing."

"Okay, Sarge, on the way."

Master Sergeant Glisan had heard Charlie telling his Captain about how to move the craft and almost immediately started his men digging out the borders to free it from the grip of the earth and rocks that had clearly accumulated over a substantial period of time.

By the time Corporal Downey returned leading a tractor and lowboy, the craft had been completely uncovered and moved with surprising ease down to the mouth of the wash. The driver of the tractor skillfully backed his trailer onto the dirt road almost to the wash, and loading the craft was simply a matter of pushing it over the lowboy and securing it so it wouldn't drift away. Before covering it with the tarps, Captain Webber had more photographs taken of the craft which had no sharp corners and was shaped like a wedge with a squared off bow similar in configuration to a jon boat with a rounded cover over the bow. The hull was flat black and failed every test for metal, be it ferrous, aluminum, titanium, or some alloy. If it was a composite, it was comprised of materials unknown to man, since every effort to breach it short of gunshot or explosion had failed. There were no seams, lifting points, or hard points on the hull, and the OSI crew had to fashion a web out of ropes to keep it "on" the trailer.

Just as they were preparing to depart, Charlie approached Captain Webber and asked: "If I'm driving back with you to Alamogordo, could you see your way clear to help me out with some gas money? I obviously haven't been working and when I don't work, no money comes in."

Webber handed him fifty dollars and said: "We probably won't get around to our interview until sometime tomorrow. How about meeting us at the First Street Gate at noon, and we'll escort you onto the base?"

"That would be just fine and, Captain? Is there any problem with me continuin' to work that area where your boys dug out this craft?"

"No, but we will be notifying the Sierra County Sheriff's Office of a possible body under that tree, and will recommend they contact you to lead them up to it. As a matter of fact, it would be better if you just made the report yourself and kept the Air Force out of it altogether."

"I'd be glad to do that, Captain," said Charlie though he didn't say exactly when he would make the call. "I'll just be at the main gate at the base at noon tomorrow, and we can have our little chat."

Webber nodded and when the opportunity presented itself, Charlie drove around the small procession and made his way back to the old KOA for gas and a chat with Jim.

"Say Jim," said Charlie after pumping his gas and coming in for his change, "have you heard anything about there being a lost prospector up Hillsboro way recently?"

"Nope, not for a long time. Most of the time, no one knows where those guys go anyway," said the big man, ringing up the sale. "Why, did you find somebody?"

"Naw, I just heard some fellers talking over a beer the other day and was just wonderin' if there was any truth to it."

"Well there might be, but you couldn't prove it by me."

CHAPTER 4

It was closer to twelve thirty by the time Charlie got to the main gate at Holloman the next day. He had been busy since he had parted with the Air Force the previous day. First he had gathered up all his little vials of gold from their hiding places throughout his house and put them all in a canvas bag that he put in a three-pound coffee can, then buried it under a pile of rocks about a hundred yards off Highway 152 on the dirt road leading to the site. He re-checked where the craft had been and, with a little modification with a shovel, was satisfied that it looked more like someone had been mining there and less like something had been removed.

Then he went back to the KOA and called the sheriff's office from the pay phone. They reacted as he expected, and it took nearly an hour for a car to come out to meet him. He led the officer up to the site and explained that he had been prospecting and found the downed tree, smashed tent, and detected the smell of what he thought was something dead. He didn't know anything more about it than that. The deputy took his name and turned him loose just in time – or close enough - for Charlie to make his appointment at Holloman Air Force Base.

Corporal Downey showed him where to park his Jeep, then drove him to the other side of the base to what appeared to be a hangar, where he parked in an "OSI Personnel Only" space in front. At the front counter, he and the receptionist fitted Charlie with a visitor's pass, and Downey led him through a door and up a flight of stairs. They came to an unlabeled door. Downey knocked, then opened the door. "Mr. Perkins, Sir," he said to Captain Webber.

"Mr. Perkins, thank you for coming in today. No trouble getting through the gate and all?"

"Nope, not with your man's help," said Charlie as Webber pointed him to a chair across the table.

"This is an interview room, Mr. Perkins. It is wired for sound and video so we don't have to fool with portable equipment on the table. I tell you that because I want to make sure you know you're being tape recorded and video-taped. Is that okay?"

"Sure, that's fine."

"Can I get you something to drink, coffee, tea, water?"

"Coffee is fine."

Less than three minutes later, there was a knock at the door, and Downey brought in coffee on a tray with sweetener and creamer.

When Charlie had doctored the coffee to his taste, Webber began: "Okay, today is August twelfth. The time is fourteen oh seven and I, Captain Peter Webber, am about to interview Charlie Perkins regarding a recovery made in the Black Range between Hillsboro and Kingston near Highway 152."

Captain Webber led Charlie through the first part of the interview in detail, starting from the beginning when Charlie walked up the wash and discovered the uprooted tree. Charlie was careful not to mention the ammo box but the rest of it was easy. It was the truth. Very slowly, Webber walked Charlie through his discovery when the ramp was open and his experience inside the craft.

"Now, you've mentioned that you've had weird dreams since that day, is that right?"

"Yep, still do."

"Can you tell me anything about the dreams?"

"Well, I've given this a lot of thought and now I think whoever left that thing up in the Black Range was using it to locate an intelligent species on this planet. The door periodically opened, sort of like a live trap, and several wild animals had been curious and went inside. Once the blue scanner determined the animal did not have the intelligence they were looking for, it was vaporized, and they kept looking."

"You say the animal that had been caught was not set free, but killed?"

"Pretty much. I don't know where the animals went once they disappeared off that platform but I got the impression they just ceased to exist. They didn't come back out."

"Any idea how they did that?"

"Not a clue."

"Okay. What else have you gleaned from the dreams?"

"Apparently humans are of sufficient intelligence with the potential to understand the message this alien species is sending."

"And what species is that?"

"Well, I'm not sure. I went to the library and looked up the area of the sky this craft came from and as close as I can figure, it came from the fourth planet orbiting Alpha Centauri A, also known as Rigel Kentaurus, a G-type Main Sequence Star similar to our sun in the Centaurus constellation. It is four point three light years from here. Everyone has heard about Alpha Centauri and the fact that it's the closest star to our solar system, but in fact it is actually three stars and Alpha is the third brightest star in the sky."

Webber sat back in his chair. "That's pretty technical talk for prospector."

"Yeah, I know. That's part of the deal. I read all that stuff in the library and I can remember it almost like I was reading it to you."

Webber pondered that for several moments before continuing: "Does this species have a name that you know of?"

"I can't pronounce their name, I just call them Rigelians."

"Okay, what was their message, based on your dream?"

"That they are from where I told you, and they seek communication with other intelligent species advanced enough to unravel the secrets of this probe. Probes like this were launched to the terrestrial planets in habitable zones in several hundred solar systems between here and their home planet."

"Did they say what kind of communication they desired?"

"No, but I suppose that depends on what you find out about that probe. Where is it, by the way?"

"Further back in the hangar. So you don't know how to activate the probe?"

"Nope, the ramp was just hanging open that one morning, and stupid me walked right in."

"I don't think they considered you stupid, or you probably wouldn't be here," Webber said dryly.

"Probably not."

"How long has the probe been here?"

" I don't know, you saw the amount of material piled on top and around it, maybe hundreds of years?"

"Yeah, that's probably something we won't determine until we get the probe working."

"So you're going to try to open it again?"

"Sure, why not?"

"Who knows what might happen next time. Maybe they'll expect someone more advanced than their first specimen. Then again, maybe its job is done and it won't open again until you guys figure it out."

"Any other information from your dreams?"

"Not that comes to mind."

"As you probably have figured out on your own, this project has been classified TOP SECRET, and we ask that you don't discuss it with anyone, including your spouse, girlfriend or whomever. Are you comfortable with that?"

"I suppose I have to be; too bad though, it would have made for some dandy tales to tell over a beer."

"We'd also like to give you a complete physical, with some other stuff thrown in. I wish we had a baseline physical to start with, but that will have to be this one. We want to see if any part of your body is acting differently than normal as a result of your contact with the probe. Is that all right with you?"

"You mean today?"

"Well, they'll start it today, but it might take two or three days."

"That's a lot of gas between here and T or C."

"We were hoping we could convince you to stay here and let us put you up. The only downside would be no beer until the tests are over. It might skew the results."

"Two or three days, huh? I guess I could manage that."

"One last thing on the agenda. We'd like you to walk out to the probe with us and sort of outline if you can where the ramp opened up in the body. As you know, we can find no seams or anything that might suggest a joint. Maybe outlining the ramp on the body of the thing will help somehow."

As they walked out into the hangar proper, Charlie looked at the probe. "This doesn't seem so intimidating now that I can see the whole thing, but what it done to me still gives me the willies."

That chore done, Corporal Downey drove Charlie over to the Forty-ninth Group Medical Treatment Facility, where he was admitted and set up in a private room. An hour later, an orderly came in to make sure he was comfortable, but more to take a medical history from him including diseases he had had, surgeries, and broken bones. Then it was wait around for dinner and watch television until lights out. By then, Charlie was starting to have some doubts about what a good idea this medical stuff was.

At 0700 hours the next morning, a nurse walked in and took his vital signs, then told him she was going to bathe him and change his bed. "Excuse me, Ma'am, but there's nothing wrong with me, and I can take a shower by myself just as easy as not."

The nurse, busily recording his vitals on his chart, told him that would be fine and went to find him a razor to go along with his soap and toothbrush, since he had his usual three or four day's growth of stubble on his face.

While the nurse changed his bed, Charlie took a shower and shaved. He had to admit he felt better when he was done and had donned a clean gown. The nurse was gone and his breakfast was there when he came out of the bathroom.

At about ten thirty, a middle-aged man about five foot ten with salt and pepper hair walked in dressed in a lab coat with a name tag identifying him as Norris. He also had spread eagles on his collar points. He introduced himself as Colonel Norris, the commander of the medical facility, and a doctor.

"I understand we're going to do some tests on you to see what kind of shape you're in."

"I reckon, though I don't feel any different now than I did before this happened."

"That's good. We'll make this as painless and as fast as possible, but sometimes we can't do one test after the other and sometimes, someone else is in line ahead of you. Please just keep in mind that we're doing the best we can, and your health is our number one priority."

"Well, that's very nice, thank you for stopping by." They shook hands and the Colonel walked out.

Within an hour, an orderly came in pushing a wheelchair.

"What's that for?" Charlie asked, with trepidation.

"You're scheduled for some x-rays, a cat scan, and an MRI, in that order."

"Are they gonna cause me not to walk?"

"No. You won't feel a thing, and they won't do anything to you."

"Well then, I'd rather walk."

"Suit yourself."

Three hours later Charlie almost wished he had a wheelchair. They had run him through all three scans, taken blood, made him pee in a bottle, and were just now taking him back to his room.

His lunch was waiting for him when he walked in and sat down on the bed.

Promptly at two o'clock, the Colonel came back.

"How're you doing, Mr. Perkins?" he asked.

"You folks sure know how to run a fella through the ringer," Charlie said tiredly.

"They've been pretty hard on you, huh?" the doctor asked.

"Oh hell, not bad, just long and . . . boring."

"I'm sorry about that, but it can't be helped. Most people have to wait weeks to have an MRI or even a Cat scan, but we were told you're kind of a high priority."

"That right? I wonder why?"

"I'm not privy to the details, Mr. Perkins, but to the OSI, you're pretty hot stuff."

Charlie snorted. "Imagine that."

"Now I need to poke and prod you one more time and we'll be done with the testing, but we'll have to wait for some results, which might take until tomorrow."

Charlie nodded and the doctor went to work examining his ears, nose and throat, palpating his abdomen, listening to his heart, and all the other things that went along with a thorough physical exam.

When he was through and snapped off the rubber gloves, Colonel Norris patted Charlie on the back and said: "You look to be in fine shape, Mr. Perkins, but we'll know more when the test results come back."

"Well, that's just fine, Doctor. When do you reckon I'll get out of here?"

"I'll have to talk to the OSI about that, but as far as we're concerned, probably sometime tomorrow. I'm sure I'll see you again before you leave, but I think you have the rest of the afternoon off."

As Colonel Norris walked out of the room, Captain Webber walked in.

"They working you over pretty good, Mr. Perkins?" he asked solicitously.

"They've done a pretty thorough job, if you know what I mean," Charlie said, looking meaningfully at the captain.

"Since we have you here, we'd like to run you through a series of psychological tests too. They're not as boring as the physical exam, but they give us an idea what, if any, changes have occurred in your psychological makeup since you were inside that craft. Think you can hold out another day or so?"

"What kind of psychological tests?" Charlie asked warily. He was concerned that if this bunch discovered how well he could read minds and move things with his thoughts, he'd never get out of here. So far no one knew that his eyesight and hearing were substantially improved, and even Charlie didn't know yet how much physically stronger he was.

"Oh, just a couple of standard intelligence tests, one called a general aptitude battery, and a personality index that tells us what kind of personality factors you have. None of them are in and of themselves conclusive, but when taken together, they provide a surprisingly comprehensive profile of who Charlie Perkins is."

The next morning, Colonel Norris stopped by just after breakfast. "Good morning, Mr. Perkins, did you sleep well?"

"Oh, can't complain. Are you here for more tests?"

Norris laughed. "No, I just wanted to let you know that we'll be reading the results of your tests today and they'll be ready probably this afternoon or tomorrow morning at the latest."

"So far, did you find anything out of the ordinary?"

"No, but the lab tests will take a little longer, and we won't hold you in here while we're waiting for them."

Charlie smiled. "Then I guess that's good news, huh?"

The doctor smiled back at him as he turned to go. "I'll see you in the morning," he said over his shoulder as he pushed the door open.

Charlie's enhanced hearing noted that the Colonel didn't get far before he was accosted by another man who sounded like Captain Webber. Webber told the Colonel that he wasn't too worried about Charlie's physical health, but had some concerns about what was going on in his head. He explained about Charlie's extraordinary memory and the high technical level at which he answered some of the questions the day before. He wasn't sure if

Charlie's latent intelligence was manifesting itself, or if the experience inside the craft had done something to his brain.

"If you're looking for enhanced brain activity, you're at the wrong medical facility, Captain. Measuring brain function requires some very sophisticated equipment that we just don't have, and probably never will. We did x-rays, an MRI – Magnetic Resonance Imaging – and a CT – Computed Tomography – but that's about as far as we can go. You'd have to take him to someplace like the O'Callaghan Federal Medical Center at Nellis to have more sophisticated tests done."

"Whew, that sounds expensive."

"It is – on the outside. Hell, just an MRI will run fifteen hundred dollars or more but since your project may affect national security, if the tests are done at a military hospital there's, of course, no charge."

"Okay. We're going to run him through a battery of psychological tests while I make arrangements to move him to Nellis."

"I think that would be the smart thing for today. Mr. Perkins isn't all that enthusiastic, but he's hanging in there pretty well."

As the two men walked away, Charlie knew that it was his turn to walk away too. Being cooperative while they did a physical was one thing, but shipping him someplace else like a cow for sale didn't sit well with him. Once he was there, they had their thumb on him, and he wasn't interested in being stranded in a strange place where he didn't know his way around or how to get home. He found his clothes in a locker and got dressed. He decided the best way to get out of this place was to act normal and just walk out like he had been a visitor or something. If he was lucky, no one would recognize him. If not, he'd have to make a run for it.

He slipped out of his room after closing the bathroom door, thinking someone coming in to do something with him would assume he was in the can. He saw no one he had seen before and casually walked down the hall toward the front entrance. His luck held until he was almost at the front lobby, when the nurse who had changed his bedding nearly ran into him.

"What . . . what are you doing dressed? I thought we were going to be doing another series of tests . . . ?"

Charlie's greatly enhanced brain kicked in: *"You don't see me, you've never seen me before, and you don't care what I do anyway."*

The nurse shrugged her shoulders and walked away.

Charlie knew the medical facility was on the same street as the entrance gate so he headed that way, trying to walk through parking lots instead of along the sidewalk. He made it to his Jeep without incident, and drove through the gate and out of the base without anyone giving him a second look.

The question was what to do now? Sure as hell they'd come looking for him, so he couldn't go back home, at least not longer than necessary to gather up a few possessions. He didn't have much cash and very little in the bank, but he had several thousand dollars in gold that he could easily lay his hands on. Go home first or go get the gold? He decided that the sooner he was in and out of his little house in Elephant Butte the better. Sure as hell the Air Force would be looking for him there.

He drove home from Alamogordo feeling paranoid. He was sure there were covert cars, or even jet fighters, following him. He finally turned onto his street with no one following him and pulled up next to the house. He had thought about what he should take, and it didn't amount to much. When he unlocked the front door and looked in, his heart sank. Someone had been in the house and had ransacked it. What few possessions he had were strewn on the living room floor. Tables were knocked over, his mattress was upside down on the floor, and the contents of his drawers were thrown all over the bedroom. The same had been done in the kitchen. Dishes, silverware and the contents of the cupboards littered the floor. The back door jamb was shattered, and the door was standing open.

Charlie didn't even take the time to put things right. He stuffed a couple of extra pairs of jeans, three shirts, some underclothes, and an extra pair of boots into a pillow case, then threw in what camping gear wasn't already in the Jeep. He decided he didn't need the rest and left. He was disappointed in the Air Force. He thought that if they were going to search his house, they would be a little more civilized about it.

He tried to stay within the speed limit as he drove back to T or C from Elephant Butte, and was relieved when he got out on I-25 and could open it up a little. Watching in the rearview mirror made time go faster, he discovered, and it seemed like in no time at all, he was turning onto Highway 152 and heading up through the foothills to his stash. When he arrived, out of curiosity, he drove to the narrows and looked upstream beyond the boulder bottleneck. There was yellow "Police line do not cross" tape festooned on various branches of what was left of the tree, but the section over the tent was moved and the tent and its contents gone. So was most of the smell. The sheriff's office had done their job. For a moment, he wondered who the unfortunate prospector had been, but he quickly shifted back to escape mode and drove back to where he had the gold stashed.

He headed back down the mountain, destination Las Cruces, where his gold buyer was. He only hoped old Sam could handle as much gold as Charlie had to sell all at one time. He had been dealing with Sam Odgers for years, and Sam had proven he could keep his mouth shut. Now if he just had enough cash to buy Charlie out.

There was no one parked in front of Sam's Gold Emporium when Charlie drove up. Sam's was a former gas station and the single island still stood, but the pumps were long gone. It was situated in an old strip mall where more shops had "For Rent" signs than occupants. Lugging the canvas bag, he went into the store and directly to the back counter where Sam did his buying transactions.

"Well, well, Charlie Perkins, long time no see. I thought you were out of the business, it's been so long."

"Nope, just real busy, Sam. But I have quite a bit of product for you if you're interested."

"As always, my friend, as always."

Even Charlie was surprised at how many little vials he stacked on the old leather desk pad. Thirty vials was a lot of gold.

"Looks like you hit a big one, Charlie! Let's see there's twenty-nine – no, thirty vials."

"That's my count too, Sam," Charlie offered, then waited as Sam began weighing the vials, then setting them aside. When he was done, he punched some numbers into a calculator, added some more figures, then finally looked up.

"I make it twenty-eight point four troy ounces, Charlie," said Sam. "Is that about what you figured?"

"Yep, that's pretty close. What's the price of gold today anyway?"

"It took a bit of a dip today since the stock market did so well. Right now spot price is $1218.20. That gives you $34,596.88. If you sell it all today, I have to have you fill out one of those government forms because it's over sixteen ounces."

"Can we break it into two or three transactions so I don't have to worry about the forms?"

"Sure, I'll date one today, one yesterday, and one tomorrow. How would that be?"

"And that's not too much for you to buy all at once?"

"No. I have to cut you a check – three checks – but I can cover it, no problem."

"Well, why don't we do it like that and I'll get out of here."

"You in a rush?"

"Sort of. I have to be somewhere pretty soon," Charlie said with an easy smile. *Like gone!*

"Okay, hold on a minute, and I'll go do the checks."

Charlie looked behind him out the front door as if expecting to see blue Air Force Suburbans pulling into the lot, but the only car out there was his Jeep. When he tried to think of where he would run, he drew a blank. He'd lived around T or C his whole life, and he didn't know anywhere else, certainly not well enough to hide. Maybe he'd just hide out up in the mountains for a few days until a better idea came to him.

Sam appeared a few minutes later carrying three slips of paper. "Here you go, Charlie; they're good for ninety days, so cash 'em before too long, okay?"

Charlie looked at the checks and for the first time realized that he was richer by over thirty-four thousand dollars. That also meant he had to go back to T or C to deposit these in his credit union account. That was okay. He had to pick up some supplies anyway, and T or C was as good as anyplace else.

"Thanks, Sam, see you next time."

"You bet, Charlie, stay safe."

Charlie got back in the Jeep and backed out of the parking lot, heading east on Lohman toward I-25 north back to T or C. He paid no attention to the blue Chevy pickup with the loud exhaust that pulled into Sam's just after he turned the corner. Three men got out of the truck and went into Sam's. They were of a kind: skinny, filthy, dark-tanned faces wearing jeans, work shirts, ball caps, and boots. The tallest of the three took the lead and walked to the back where Sam had just finished locking Charlie's gold and paperwork in the vault.

"Gentlemen, what can I do for you?"

"I guess you could say we're looking for some information. See, the fella that just walked out of here is an acquaintance of ours and he owes us some money. We was just wondering if he sold some gold or . . .?"

Sam smiled thinly. *This man could be trouble. Guys like him usually came in to sell gold, not to buy it, and certainly not for information.* "I'm afraid that's about all I can tell you gentlemen. Transactions are confidential."

"So he did sell some gold. How much? See, he owes us a sizeable sum."

"Like I said, the transactions are confidential."

"That's not a very friendly attitude to have," said the tallest one, suddenly slamming his palm down hard on the counter.

"I think you fellas better mosey on out of here. I don't want any trouble, and there's nothing here for you."

The tall one's face turned mean as he leaned over the counter almost into Sam's face. "Maybe I didn't make myself clear," he hissed. "We came a long way for that information, and aren't leaving without it."

"You just get out of here right now, or I'll call the cops." As he reached down behind the counter for the phone, the mean one punched him in the temple, sending him to his knees and his head into the cabinet behind the counter. The one who hit him then vaulted the counter and grabbed a dazed Sam by the shirt collar, slapping him back and forth across the face twice and bloodying his nose.

"How much did you buy, old man?"

"You better get your asses out of here," cried Sam. "I already done hit the alarm."

"Oh Goddamn, Glen," yelled one of his associates. "Let's get the hell out of here. The last thing we want is the cops."

"Shut up," Glen snarled over his shoulder, "this old man has something to tell me and I want to hear it. What do you say old man, you want some more of this?" He punched the old man in the face twice in quick succession. "What about it?"

"I told you," Sam moaned, "transactions are confidential. I ain't telling you squat."

Glen slammed Sam's head into the rear cabinet and stood up. "Shit. All right, let's get out of here."

He didn't have to tell his associates twice. They were already running for the door. They piled into the pickup and it started with a roar. The squealing of tires was added to the roar as the pickup left the parking lot in a cloud of blue smoke.

*****

As Charlie left Sam's, he also didn't see the two blue Air Force Suburbans parked further to the west down Lohman.

"He's on the move, sir. We can take him anytime you say," said a voice over of the radio.

"No," said Captain Webber, "let's just see where he goes. We'll have to come back and see what that was all about in the store but right now just tag along. Besides, we don't really have a reason to detain him, other than my hunch that he's more than what he appears to be. When he stops next time, I'll go up and have a chat with him. That's about all we can do right now."

Charlie led them directly to his credit union and they watched him walk inside. When he came out, Captain Webber was leaning against the fender of his Jeep. Charlie's shoulders drooped as he walked up to the fatigue-clad Air Force officer.

"Damn, I knew I made one trip too many in to town."

"What do you mean by that, Charlie?" said Webber, taking a chance that using his first name might loosen the man up just a little.

"Well, hell, now I'm goin' ta jail, right?"

"No. Why would you be going to jail?"

"For one thing I snuck off the base, and I don't imagine you were through with me."

"You're right, we weren't through with you, not by a long shot, but you did nothing illegal. Remember? We asked you to come to the base. You weren't in custody."

"I'm not going to jail?"

"Nope."

"Well, I'll be damned. Here I've been running around keeping an eye on my backside expecting you to haul me in any minute."

"We're not going to do that, Charlie. What we'd like to do though is conduct some more tests to see if that thing had any long lasting effect on you. I thought that was something you'd kind of like to know too."

"Sure it is, but I heard you and the doctor talking about sending me to Nevada for a bunch of tests, and I sort of got cold feet. I started feeling like I wasn't going to make it back home. Besides I'm not so sure I want to be poked and prodded any more than I already have been."

"I understand, and I sympathize with you, but the fact that you were exposed to this thing won't go away. The tests in Nevada won't take more than two or three days tops, and then you'll be back home doing what you want to do. And it won't cost you a thing. The Air Force will pick up the tab for everything."

"Well, can I think about it for a few days without having you following me all over?"

Webber stood up and reached into his pocket. He retrieved a business card and handed it to Charlie. "No more following, Charlie, but here's my card. All my phone numbers are on it, and you can call me anytime if you have questions before you make up your mind."

Charlie accepted the card, looked it over, then put it in his shirt pocket. He squinted at Webber against the bright sunshine and asked: "So I'm free to go? No strings?"

"That's right. I really hope you call, Charlie, knowing the results of the tests will set your mind at ease and, quite frankly, ours too."

"By the way, I don't appreciate your tearing up my place the way you did. You left it in a helluva mess."

Webber's face went blank. "Tearing up your place? Charlie, I've never been to your place and neither have any of my men. We didn't tear up anything. Honest."

Charlie squinted at him, then concentrated on what the man was thinking. He was satisfied that this was the truth. "Well somebody surely did."

They shook hands and Webber gave a "wind 'em up" gesture to his men. Both Suburbans eased into the parking lot from around the block.

Charlie wasn't nearly as relieved as what Captain Webber might think he was. He knew the craft had done more to him than merely given him some bad dreams and he was still far from sure that he wanted the Air Force knowing about it. Now he had to worry about someone else who was after something he had, and he had a pretty good idea who that someone was.

Charlie woke up the next morning feeling pretty good until he remembered the mess someone made of his house. Since the Air Force was no longer chasing him, he had come home, cleaned up, and repaired the back door as best he could. He was worried about the burglars coming back, but had convinced himself that it was only neighbor kids and not the dead prospector's partner. Then he remembered that he had over thirty thousand dollars in the bank, and that went a long way toward making him feel better. Inexplicably, he also woke up knowing it was time to change the direction of his life. It was time to look beyond a tenth grade education, because now he knew he could understand and remember what was being taught to him and, what's more, he was interested.

Charlie decided he would go back and work the wash for as long as it lasted, because he could make good money there. When it petered out, he would live on the money, get his GED, then re-evaluate how he felt about going to school. He knew that he was tired of the cowboy/prospector gig, and wanted more of a challenge in his life. Surprising no one, he didn't call Captain Webber back and hoped that their interest in him would fade with time.

He didn't even bother going to the Plugged Nickel that morning, instead driving straight up to the wash. He started right where he left off, excavating material out of the bank, screening it, dry washing and panning the gold out of the sand and small rocks. He was used to the hard work and didn't mind, especially since he was seeing so much color in what he was panning. Every particle went into the vials, and it didn't take long to build up another sizeable stash.

Periodically, he would haul a number of full vials down to Sam, who told him about the three men and what they had done. Sam then converted Charlie's gold to checks which Charlie promptly deposited in the credit union. He was living on far less than he was making, and building up a substantial nest egg. But he was worried about the fact that someone had beat Sam up just to get information about him. He didn't owe anyone any money that he knew of, and no one had appeared demanding payment.

A day didn't go by that he didn't wonder about the man who had died in the tent and what became of his partner. In a way that was reassuring, but he found himself always waiting for the other shoe to drop. Why hadn't the partner returned or even turned in the accidental death anonymously? These questions he asked himself over and over, but never came up with a plausible explanation. And what of the Air Force? Had they forgotten about him, or were they just biding their time?

As he knew it would, the day finally came when he had to concede he was wasting his time trying to wrest more gold out of the dig. The yield had been diminishing for several days, and lately there were pans full of just grit with no glittering particles of gold. In a way he was glad. Mining had begun to try his patience, and it was time to move on.

The day after he had moved his equipment out of the wash, he went to the Dona Ana Community College in Las Cruces and obtained a GED preparation book. While he was at it, he picked up a school catalogue. In one afternoon he skimmed through the GED prep book and found nothing that challenged his current knowledge. He made arrangements for the nearly eight-hour exam and finished early, confident that he had passed with high marks. Three weeks later the test results, a transcript and the GED diploma arrived in the mail, he had aced the test.

Charlie had already reviewed the community college catalogue and decided on following the recommended curriculum recommended by the college. He bought the required books, and skimmed through them easily, again not finding anything outside his ability to comprehend and certainly not outside his ability to retain.

Charlie knew that his newfound talent was a direct result of his time aboard the probe. He had never had the patience to read an entire book, much less textbooks, and retention was a joke. He didn't do well, so he just quit caring. Then, that blue scanner did something to his head, and now he was different. He didn't think he was any smarter, he was just able to retain everything, as if he had eidetic memory abilities usually only found in small children. He looked up photographic memory at the library one time and read that such a memory has no relation to intelligence and there was much controversy about it actually existing at all. Charlie didn't know what to believe, only that once he read something, he could remember it nearly verbatim and it didn't go away.

He didn't mind if people thought him brainy just because he could remember things so well. He did mind if they discovered that he was also able to intercept another's thoughts and move things with his mind and those abilities were still getting stronger. Sometimes it was hard to keep those attributes hidden when in company but thus far he had covered his lapses.

Information technology would be his first specialized field of study. He was convinced that computers were the thing of the future and he knew virtually nothing about them. He'd be taking the classes out of self-defense because he knew so little, but he was interested in what computers were doing in the world these days, and what was on the drawing boards for the future. Once he had mastered this field, he could move on and always review the textbook of a particular curriculum if he wasn't sure it was for him. Things were coming together nicely and his future was looking up.

He was looking forward to starting the semester at Dona Ana Community College.

Charlie woke up on Tuesday with a sense foreboding, and it reminded him when he had the feeling last – when he concluded there was a body under the tree in the wash. He just couldn't shake the feeling something bad was looming just below the horizon. Out of curiosity, he called the Sierra County Sheriff's Office and inquired about the body from the wash. "Oh," said the young female switchboard operator, "you mean that homicide?"

"No, the case where the tree fell on the guy in the tent."

"Yeah, same case. The guy was dead before the tree came down; they're holding back the cause of death but he was dead before. Say, do you know something about the case?"

"I took the deputy up to the place the first time."

"Well, they want to talk to you pronto," said the girl.

"Who's 'they'?"

"Sergeant Ramirez and Detective Olsen."

"Are they there now?"

"Hold on, I'll check."

Charlie didn't like the sound of this. They'd want to question him in more detail, and he had promised the Air Force to keep them out of it. The investigators would surely want him to come in so they could sweat him, because he was their most likely suspect. Suddenly Charlie wasn't feeling so good, and hung up the phone.

Moments later, the other shoe dropped. There was a knock at the door and, expecting the cops, he was almost relieved to see Captain Webber in full Air force blues waiting for him when he peeked around the corner.

CHAPTER 5

Though the appearance of the man in uniform caused Charlie's stomach to lurch, he played the game and invited the Air Force officer into his house and offered him a seat.

"Charlie, how're you doing? Making out okay?"

"Yes, can't complain, how about you?"

"About the same, staying busy studying the probe."

"Have you made any progress? Has it opened again?"

"No on both counts. We haven't been able to penetrate the hull with any technology we have to work with, and the thing has shown no sign of opening."

"I don't imagine that's too much of a surprise, is it?"

"Not really but I'd like to ask you: Do you think it opened because of you specifically or just opened arbitrarily in an effort to capture someone like you?"

"Like I said before, Captain, I wasn't even near the damned thing when it opened. I was just dumb enough to climb in when I found it that way."

"How have you been feeling? Still having the nightmares?"

"Not so much anymore," said Charlie, becoming very guarded. He particularly didn't want the Air Force to know about his other talents.

"What have you been doing with yourself?"

"Oh, I finished mining out that dig. Did pretty well too. Lately I've just been living off what I earned."

"Something's different about you though. You seem more aware, like you're on top of things more than before."

"Well I don't know about that, but I have taken the time to get my GED, and am thinking about enrolling at Dona Ana Community College next term."

"Studying what?"

"Oh, probably general studies to begin with, but I'm looking at information technology as a starting place."

"Good choice, can't go wrong learning all you can about computers."

"Especially since I don't know anything about them."

"I notice your language skills have improved since we talked last. Any idea why?"

"I've been doing a lot of reading, something I never did much of before."

"Before what, your encounter with the probe?"

Damn it. "Yeah, I guess you could say it happened about that time."

"Charlie, I'm not going to beat around the bush. We'd like you to come over to Nevada and let us do those tests. Having better language skills might be just the tip of the iceberg of what's going on with you."

"And my memory is much better too," Charlie blurted before he could control his mouth.

Webber nodded, as if he expected that. "All the more reason to let us do some scans and see what's going on in your head."

"Well . . ."

"Didn't you say you broke your right ankle and had had a lower back surgery?"

"Yes, I fell off a roof about four years ago. I guess I got off lucky. I don't feel any pain at all from it."

"Would it surprise you to learn that there is no evidence of your ankle ever being broken and no scar from the surgery on your back?"

"Well, there must be some kind of mistake. You can go down to Sierra Vista Hospital and check their records. I was there."

"Oh, I don't doubt you, Charlie. My point is that the probe did something – maybe several somethings - to you, and in case you hadn't noticed it, you're in perfect health absolutely and perfect condition."

"That right? I just chalked it up to the fact that I quit drinking so much beer. I haven't been sick or hurt for a long time, so I don't know if that's part of it or not."

"Wouldn't you like to know what else is going on that you maybe haven't noticed yet? We might be able to warn you to be on the lookout for something that will worry you otherwise."

"Why is the Air Force so interested in my health all of a sudden?"

"Charlie, we both know it isn't just that. We've tried everything we can think of to open that probe, and have struck out every time. We're thinking that maybe it did something to you that might enable us to get back in."

"Are you sure you want to get back in? I sure as hell don't want to climb back in that thing."

Webber leaned forward and said: "And we're not asking you to. All we want to do is see how much we *can* learn about what it did to you. Maybe then we can find a clue to opening it."

"Did it ever occur to you that it might be best if it's left closed until we're a little more advanced and can handle what it is or what it can do?" asked Charlie out of the blue .

Webber sat back. "Yes, many times, but I obey orders. The orders are to activate that thing at all costs."

"I'll tell you right now, I don't plan on being one of those costs."

"No, I didn't think you would. So what do you say, will you fly with me over to Las Vegas and let the doctors see what's going on inside your head? For what it's worth, if it were me, I'd do it in a heartbeat because I'd like to know if something bad was happening inside."

*****

Reluctant to go but relieved to be away from T or C for a while, Charlie agreed to fly with Captain Webber to Las Vegas. He had never been there and he wanted to take a cab through town on his way to O'Callaghan Federal Medical Center. He wasn't impressed by the glitz and glamour but the presence of so many gambling machines made him think about what he could do with one. Webber's military ID card got them on base, and the cabbie dropped them off in front of the sprawling medical facility.

Webber walked Charlie through Admissions and to his room, where an orderly helped him into a hospital gown, then left.

"I'm already hating this place, Captain Webber," said Charlie with a grimace.

"I know you are. Let me go see if I can find a robe to go with that gown." Ten minutes later he came back with a lab coat. "This is about the best I can do. If someone tries to take it, we'll gang up on him, okay?"

"Better," Charlie gritted, "but not okay."

And it got less okay as they waited and waited and waited some more. Charlie spent much of his time staring out the window trying to think of how he could keep the tests from discovering what was really going on in his head. He didn't know enough about the various scanners to skew them in a way that wouldn't be readily apparent to the technician or the doctor reading the results. He thought about just putting his foot down and saying he had waited long enough, and now it was time to leave. But he knew Captain Webber would be suspicious, especially after he learned that Charlie was beginning to pursue some more intellectual goals.

Captain Webber alternated between fretting that Charlie would call a halt to the waiting and insist on going home, and stewing about what the snafu had been that caused this interminable wait. The military was famous for "hurry up and wait", but this was getting out of hand. Supposedly someone high up in AFOSI had called the hospital and made it clear this was a high priority project, and classified as well.

Little was said between them. They had exhausted what little they had in common on the flight from Las Cruces. They could only smile at each other occasionally when their eyes made momentary contact and utter some obtuse epithet about the wait.

Charlie's in-room lunch had been delivered, consumed, and the dishes removed, and Webber had had time to go to the cafeteria and return before a major wearing the collar caduceus of a doctor walked jauntily into the room.

"Gentlemen, I'm Major Haines. I understand we have some interesting scans laid on for you, Mr. Perkins?"

Charlie nodded and glanced at Webber but said nothing.

"Can you tell me what kind of symptoms you're having?"

"Uh, Sir? I don't know that we should be discussing this until we know your level of security clearance."

"Security clearance? For medical tests? I hardly think that the results of some tests would interest the spooks, do you?"

"Well Sir, in this case, yes. It was my understanding that only one person was to be involved in the actual scans and their subsequent evaluations. You haven't been briefed?"

The major waved his hand in dismissal. "Medical records are privileged, but not classified, Captain. Now, Mr. Perkins, as I asked, can you describe the symptoms you're having?"

"Excuse me, Sir, but I'm afraid I'm going to have to insist. Until I know you're cleared for what Mr. Perkins has to say, I'm going to have to advise him not to answer."

"In case you didn't notice, Captain," the Major said coldly, "I am a doctor, this is a hospital, and I outrank you. We will proceed."

"Charlie," Webber said to the grinning Charlie Perkins, "please don't answer until I tell you it's okay."

"Captain, this is bordering on insubordination!"

"Yes Sir. With respect, I am under orders not to let this man talk to or be examined by anyone who is not cleared for this project, and I don't believe you are."

"We'll see about this," the Major huffed and stormed out of the room.

"First it's 'hurry up and wait' then the right hand doesn't even have a notion what the left hand is doing. Welcome to the military, Charlie."

Charlie snorted. "The Major seemed a bit chagrined, Captain. What's he going to do?"

"He's probably conferring with his supervisor who will, hopefully, straighten out the snafu, and we can get on with your tests."

About ten minutes later, another officer walked into the room. He was dressed in khakis, wearing a ubiquitous unbuttoned lab coat with a stethoscope draped around his neck. A caduceus was on one collar point and the silver oak leaf of a lieutenant colonel on the other.

"I understand we have a problem here."

"Yes Sir, it appears we do. I'm Captain Webber from the Office of Special Investigations. I have escorted Mr. Perkins here to the hospital to undergo a series of medical tests, the results of which are classified as TOP SECRET. I am under orders not to let anyone without the proper clearance have anything to do with him. My understanding is that someone high up in my office called and made arrangements with someone here."

"That so? I haven't heard a word, but in the interests of not making a big deal out of this, I'll make some inquiries." He thereupon left the room.

Nearly an hour elapsed before another doctor, wearing the silver spread eagle of a full colonel, walked through the door. He smiled when he saw Webber snap to attention and said: "As you were, Captain. I hear you're giving my staff some heartburn over getting this man examined."

"Yes Sir . . . I mean no Sir, I don't mean to Sir. It's just that this is a classified project and I am under orders to allow only someone properly cleared access to this patient."

"Relax, Captain, I took the call from OSI, and I *am* cleared to conduct the tests."

Webber let out a long breath. "Glad to hear it, Sir." With a certain amount of relief, Webber handed the Colonel a sealed envelope. "These are the medical history, x-rays, CT scan, and MRI results. I was supposed to deliver them directly to the person doing the tests here."

The Colonel nodded. "Thank you. The Major was just trying to be efficient. There was a cancellation on one of the scans, and he thought he could fill in with Mr. Perkins since, he was already here. I think we have things straightened out. Mr. Perkins, I'm Colonel Weaver. I'm sorry for the mixup and for the wait. It was my mistake. I had it in my head that you were coming in tomorrow."

Without waiting for a response, Weaver continued: "In order to get these all done in a timely manner, we've scheduled them for late at night and early in the morning so as not to screw up other patients already scheduled for the same procedures. I'm glad they did a CT scan and an MRI at Holloman. We won't need to duplicate them. Your first exam, a functional magnetic resonance imaging, is scheduled for twenty-two hundred this evening. The fMRI measures brain activity by detecting associated changes in blood flow. It is predicated on the concept that cerebral blood flow and neuronal activation are conjoined. When an area of the brain is in use, blood flow to that region increases. After the fMRI we're doing a SPECT, a Single Photon Emission Computed Tomography. This one requires some harmless radioactive tracers to be injected into your bloodstream. This will use those radioactive tracers to show us blood circulation and blood volume in your brain. Other than the injection, neither scan is painful or invasive. All you have to do is lay there quietly."

"We have to wait for the tracers to dissipate so we've scheduled a PET, a Positron Emission Tomography, for twenty-two hundred hours the second night. This scan also uses harmless but different radioactive tracers to show cerebral metabolism, blood flow, oxygen use, and the formation of neural transmitters. Finally, we might do a Qeeg, a Qualitative Electro Encephalograph, if we detect any what we consider pathological results."

"All these scans together will tell us what's going on in your brain. I and one technician will actually be conducting the scans and I will personally read the results. Does that satisfy you, Captain?"

"Yes Sir, thank you Colonel."

"Has anyone talked to you about doing psychological tests as well? Doing the physiological scans only offers part of the picture; if there are irregularities, psychological tests often illustrates how the irregularities are manifested in the personality."

"Will they cause Charlie to be here longer? He isn't too thrilled about being here at all and if we have to extend his time . . . well, I don't think you'd be too happy, would you Charlie?"

"That's right. I don't mind the odd hours, but I hope you can give me those other tests during the off hours from the scans. Is that possible?"

"Yes and that's the plan. Some of them take some time but they're not going to injure you, they'll maybe be just a little tedious."

"That I can handle, so long as I don't have to stay here any longer than necessary."

"Now that we have the right person in the right place, I think things will go much more smoothly," Colonel Weaver soothed. "Do you want to know any more about the tests we're going to conduct?

"Well, what kind of psychological tests you're talking about," asked Charlie pensively.

"Depending on what the scans tell us, we had thought about using a couple of intelligence tests, then we have a varied list that measures different personality aspects and some achievement and general aptitude tests. That's a lot of testing, and it may be that not all are necessary based on what we find on the scans. We want to be thorough, but don't want to overdo it. I suspect we only get one chance at this, right?"

"You'd be right there, Doctor," said Charlie, his mouth set in a grim line.

"I think the best thing to do is to let you have your dinner in peace, then give you a couple of the psych tests before the fMRI and the SPECT. We can do the same thing tomorrow after you're had a chance to get some sleep, and if you need more time for the rest of the psych tests, we can do them on the third morning. How does that sound?"

"Colonel, you're not going to have the time to conduct all these psychological tests in addition to your regular workload if you do them during the day," Webber pointed out.

"You'd be right, Captain, but I can't see why the results of any of the psych tests need be classified unless he does something completely unexpected so I'll meet you halfway and have the same psychologist administer all the psych tests, that way, nothing gets out that shouldn't."

"Okay. Charlie, you up for this?"

"I suppose so."

They waited another half hour before a female captain walked in. She was about five eight with dark hair tied back in a severe bun. Even with the severe bun, one could tell she was a beautiful girl with large, expressive eyes hidden behind wire-rimmed glasses. She smiled when she saw the two men waiting for her.

"Good afternoon, I'm Captain Samantha Chase and I'm a psychologist. I understand from Colonel Weaver that we're going to conduct some tests?"

Charlie had jumped from the bed to stand when the lady walked into the room and she noticed and waved him back to the bed. "Let's be informal, shall we? We'll be spending quite a bit of time together; why don't you call me Sam or Samantha," she said offering her hand to Charlie.

Charlie grinned and blushed. "Just call me Charlie," he mumbled.

Next Captain Webber shook her hand and made eye contact. "You understand the, ah, circumstances of this testing?" he asked.

"Yes I do. I have a TOP SECRET clearance, but it remains to be seen if I'll need it or not."

"I guess my only concern," said Webber, "is how well he does and how long it takes for him to do the tests – if either is significant, then we'll have to classify the testing and the results."

"I understand. Mr. Perkins – Charlie - if you'd like to come with me, we'll go to the lab and get started."

Charlie hesitated long enough to don his "robe" then followed her out of the room, the sound of his cloth slippers slapping the tile floor echoing in the hallway as he departed.

Assuming he had several hours to kill, Webber took out his laptop and began researching the names of the tests Colonel Weaver had mentioned. He learned the history and the application of the two intelligence tests Captain Chase would be administering. Though he had his suspicions about Charlie's capabilities, he didn't think the prospector would overwhelm either examination. According to what Webber read, Charlie was born with just so many smarts and nothing could be done – at least from what humans knew – that would change that. He had just begun to read about Hermann Rorschach when Charlie and Captain Chase returned to the room. Webber looked at his watch. Only an hour and a half had elapsed.

"Surely you can't be done with both tests already?" Webber joked.

Charlie looked like a dog that knew he was in trouble, and Captain Chase was tight-jawed.

"Yes, as a matter of fact we are," she said without a smidgeon of her former brightness. "Charlie blazed through both tests in record time and even at that, I think he dawdled part of the time to make it look like it was taking longer. He says no, but I was watching and I know what I saw."

"Were you guessing, Charlie?" asked Webber.

"Hell no! Those questions were hard, and I had to study! The Cap – Samantha – thought I was dragging my feet, but I wasn't."

"No one has ever gone through both tests as fast as Charlie just did. Was there something about this 'project' that you haven't told me? You might as well tell me now, since I guarantee everything from this afternoon on is going to be classified."

"Charlie was exposed to something – we don't exactly know what – and it caused him to first have a series of nightmares. Since then, he got his GED by acing the test and is making plans to go to college. Charlie was a prospector and cowboy with no real aspirations to further his education past the tenth grade, but something has changed his mind about whether he can cope with the academic environment. Finally, Charlie's level of English usage has risen dramatically from the way he used to talk. Charlie, am I getting this right?"

"Pretty much. I feel like I have to explain in a little more detail to Samantha. You see, since I . . . since the exposure, I've been feeling like my brain is waking up. I understand things quicker, and I retain what I read at a glance. I never used to read much of anything, but now I skim through books in no time and retain the entire content. That's why I was able to finish your tests as quickly as I did. I only had to read the stuff once and then answer the questions, but I had to *read* the questions. I couldn't just skim them. I assume a lot of people skim the text before the questions then go back and dig out the answer, and that takes a lot more time. I don't feel like I'm any smarter. I'm just using the smarts God gave me better, if that makes any sense."

Captain Chase stared at her subject for several seconds before she looked over at Webber and said: "Unless he was playing with my tests, the results will show only his IQ. Maybe improved retention will improve his score a little, but he gets no credit for completing the tests so quickly. He still has to get the right answer to score on the test, so we'll see in an hour or so what the results are."

"I'm sorry, Samantha," Charlie said contritely. "I didn't realize that my improved retention would create a problem for you."

"Well, maybe it didn't. Let's just see what the test scores tell us." Somewhat mollified, she turned and walked out of the room.

"Way to go, champ," said Webber, "nothing like pissing off the teacher on the first day of class." He had a grin on his face, and Charlie knew he was just being ribbed a little in an attempt to break the tension. What Webber *didn't* know was that Charlie had not reached this conclusion merely by reading his body language. The minute Webber opened his mouth, Charlie was in his mind and knew precisely his intention. He desperately didn't want Captain Webber or anyone else to know that.

"Charlie, I guess I didn't realize just how well developed your retention speed and cognitive abilities were. Is there anything else you're experiencing? I know they asked about headaches and bad dreams and such, but is there anything else that just hasn't occurred to you, like your retention abilities?"

"No Sir, I've told you everything. There should be no more surprises," said Charlie with his fingers mentally crossed.

"I think it's time we dropped the 'sir', don't you? Just call me Pete from now on. I mean, we're working on the same thing here, for your sake as well as mine, so let's keep it informal."

Charlie nodded while at the same time feeling crappy for not being honest with this sincere young captain, but survival had to come before anything else.

Captain Chase was back within the hour. "Well Charlie, the results are in and I don't think you skewed the results with your retentive and cognitive abilities. The tests results say that you're a bit smarter than average but no genius. You can relax now. We're not going to put you in a bell jar."

Charlie breathed a sigh of relief. He thought the chances of not skewing the results were one in a million, and he was grateful that all was well, even if he didn't understand why.

"Do we have time for any more tests before Colonel Weaver is ready for Charlie?" asked Webber.

"I don't think so. Let Charlie rest a little. I'll have time tomorrow morning for some of the personality and aptitude tests," Captain Chase replied.

Charlie's anxiety rose again when Dr. Weaver and a technician rolled a gurney into his room at about nine-thirty that evening. "Right about now your blood pressure jumped because you don't know what to expect. Work on relaxing. There's nothing mystical or dangerous about these scans, Charlie, they'll only help us find out if something is out of whack in your head, which I think you'd already know about. These scans are just going to tell us what's different, okay?"

"Charlie did the two intelligence tests today and scored high average. The kicker was that he did them in far less time than anyone else ever has before," said Webber.

Dr. Weaver's eyebrows rose. "That's interesting. It suggests to me that things are working at a somewhat higher level than they used to. Charlie, what do you think?"

"That's sort of what I've been thinking, Doctor. I seem to pick up faster on things in general, and I sure retain what I've read a lot better than I used to. It's almost like I have a photographic memory."

"Well, if that's the case, these scans will prove it. Ready to go?"

They shifted Charlie over to the gurney and Webber patted his arm before he was wheeled out. "No worries, Charlie," he said, "I'll be in at eight tomorrow morning to help with whatever needs to be done. I'll be at the Nellis Inn - that's the on-base transient facility - so if you need me, have someone call there."

The next three hours were a combination of whirls of technology and profound periods of boredom. Charlie found out rather quickly that he wasn't claustrophobic, which would have been a real problem in the tight quarters of the scanners. As they were rolling him back to his room, Colonel Weaver told him: "You did good, Charlie, I think our results are clean, meaning you didn't move and fuzz up the pictures."

The next morning, as promised, Captain Webber walked through the door at 0800, carrying two cups of coffee. "I don't know if you've had anything to drink this morning, but I guarantee you this is better coffee than what they serve here. How did things go last night?"

"The colonel seemed to be happy with the way the tests went. He said he thought there would be clean results."

"That's good news. They won't be clamoring for you to do them again."

Captain Chase walked in just before 0900. "Good morning, gentlemen. Charlie, are you ready for some interesting tests?"

"Yes ma'am, I believe I am."

"Good, let's go get started." She looked at Webber before adding: "I'll probably have him until late afternoon, Captain. I'll take care of getting him lunch and dinner if necessary, unless he needs to take a break. Considering what we know now that we didn't know last night, I don't think that will be a problem."

Captain Chase escorted Charlie to the door and they were gone, leaving Webber by himself. He got back on the laptop to finish researching the various tests that were being administered to his charge.

Charlie and Captain Chase returned just before dinner. Charlie was tired. "I feel like someone has stuffed my head with cotton," he grumped. "I can't think anymore."

"Small wonder, Charlie," said Samantha Chase, "you just waded through more testing than anyone in history has done in one session. All that's left is the general aptitude test battery and you'll be done."

"Any surprises?" Webber asked.

"No, just hard to get used to someone who can read and retain as fast and as well as he can. It's absolutely phenomenal and should be considered a factor in what happened all by itself. You're one for the books, Charlie, that's for sure. Who knows how long these results will be classified."

"I'll take that as a compliment," Charlie replied tiredly.

"Okay, now it's my turn to get to work," Captain Chase said. "I need to score and tabulate the results, and I'll be burning the midnight oil to get it all done by tomorrow. All of my findings should be reviewed by at least two or three other sources to be validated. You know that, right?"

"Let's see what the results show." Webber replied. "If they're normal, maybe we can do that, just not tell anyone how fast he did them; otherwise, we'll have to be very selective who we ask to review your findings."

As Captain Chase went out the door, Charlie and Captain Webber could hear the dinner trays being delivered. When one didn't arrive for Charlie, Webber found a floor nurse and asked why.

"The patient isn't supposed to have anything to eat or drink for four to six hours before the scan. We would have made sure he had something to eat earlier, but he was tied up with examinations."

Reluctantly, Captain Webber returned to Charlie's room and gave him the bad news. "I'll see that you get something to eat afterward, even if I have to bring something in myself, but you're going to have to tough it out until they're done tonight. In the meantime, I suspect a nap might sound pretty good, huh?"

"Yeah, Pete, it would. Those tests sucked my brain dry."

"I can't even imagine. Well, let's get you rested for tonight. Hang in there Charlie, you're almost through it."

Again at about nine thirty that evening, Colonel Weaver and the same technician arrived with a gurney and took Charlie away. Again the Colonel asked if there had been any surprises in the psychological tests, and this time Charlie answered: "Only that I got through them fast, Colonel. She's grading them right now."

"Okay, all we have on the board for tonight is the PET. Again, Charlie, we're going to inject you with some harmless radioactive tracers, then run you through another scanner, much like we did last night. Shouldn't take more than a couple of hours tops. Then you're done with the scanning, and I'll get to work reading the results."

The next morning Captain Webber arrived at about 0630 – without coffee. He had thought to take Charlie to breakfast, but he was still asleep. Instead of trying to find something to do, Webber just decided to wait quietly and let Charlie wake up on his own. He was clearly dreaming, his eyes moving rapidly and his hands outside the covers twitching. Suddenly Charlie's arm moved and the water pitcher on his table nearly slid off the edge. Had Webber not caught it, it would have fallen to the floor.

Webber was stunned. Charlie's hand had been more than three feet from the pitcher, but considering the proximity of the movements and absent any other cause, one had clearly caused the other. Webber put the pitcher back on the table, but kept his hand close by in case Charlie had another violent movement. He sat back and tried to absorb what he had just seen and what it meant. This put Charlie in a whole different classification of phenomena and maybe, just maybe, into a pigeon hole by himself.

About fifteen minutes later, Charlie started to stir. "Good morning Charlie. How're you doing this morning?" Webber asked gently.

Charlie lazily rolled toward the sound of Webber's voice, his eyes still closed. "Good mornin'. Yeah, breakfast out of here would have been good, but . . ." He froze. Then his eyes popped open and focused on Webber. The Captain could almost see the wheels turning furiously in Charlie's head. "Did you say something about breakfast?"

"Not out loud," Webber said softly.

"I must have dreamed it."

"Not likely, Charlie, you were too busy knocking the pitcher off the table without touching it."

Charlie was silent, withdrawn.

Webber let the moment pass, then asked: "How are you feeling this morning?"

Charlie hesitated only momentarily before replying: "Better. That nap before the test last night helped a lot, and they did manage to get me a sandwich and some cookies afterward."

"Good. Today, Captain Chase should finish her testing and if we're lucky, we can get some results by this afternoon. How does that sound?"

"Okay, as long as I'm out of here by tomorrow."

Promptly at 0900, Samantha Chase arrived. "Good morning. Charlie, we're headed down the home stretch. You ready?"

"Yep, I got some sleep and I think I can handle one more test. Which one is it?"

"It's called a General Aptitude Test Battery; it measures nine aptitudes with twelve different tests: eight written and four that are performance. Even if it doesn't tell us much about what's happening in your brain, it will give you an idea where your aptitudes lie, which might be useful when you choose a career path or a major in college."

"Okay, let's get it over with," said Charlie, considerably brighter than he had been the evening before.

Captain Webber had just settled in to writing an "after action" report on what had transpired at the medical center when Colonel Weaver walked in. As Webber started to rise, Weaver stayed the motion with his hand.

"Where's Charlie?" he asked, appearing a little perturbed that his patient was missing.

"He's taking his last psychological test, Sir, considering the speed at which he takes examinations, Captain Chase wasn't sure what time they'd be done."

"Which one?"

"I believe he's taking the General Aptitude Battery, Sir."

"That usually takes several hours. It will be interesting to see how long it takes him."

"Sir? I'm just beginning my report on Charlie's testing here. Can you give me an idea how he did on the scans?"

"In a nutshell, Captain, he was off the charts, but I'll save the details for when the four of us can confer. When they return, please call me and we'll set up a meeting ASAP."

"Yes Sir. Um, should I be concerned in any way for, perhaps, his welfare?"

"Oh, I don't think so, but he's sure one for the record book." Weaver turned and walked out, and Webber returned to his report. He wondered if he should have told the Colonel what he had witnessed earlier, but wasn't sure he had the need to know and, before he talked to anyone about it, he wanted to have a long Come to Jesus chat with Charlie.

Captain Chase brought Charlie back to the room a little before noon. Charlie seemed reserved, and didn't say much as he climbed back into bed.

"I think we're done," she said brightly. "Charlie did his usual bang-up job of wading through hours and hours of tests in no time at all."

"If you'd wait a minute, Captain," Webber said, "I'll call Colonel Weaver and set up a time for us all to meet. That's what he wanted, and that way none of us has to repeat the results."

Without waiting for a response, Webber called Colonel Weaver's extension, and Weaver called the meeting for fourteen hundred hours.

Before he hung up, Captain Webber asked: "Uh, Sir, do you have a secure place where we can talk? This will be a classified discussion."

"What? Oh, yes. We share a conference room with the security folks, I think that will suffice." He hung up without another word.

"Fourteen hundred in the conference room they share with security," Webber told Captain Chase, who nodded, then left the room.

Webber turned to Charlie. "We have to talk. I think we both know what all these tests are going to say, but they won't include anything of what I saw this morning, will they?"

Charlie looked at Webber with a hang-dog expression. "I almost ran, Pete, after Samantha was through with me. I almost ran, but I didn't know where to go."

"Like I said yesterday, Charlie, hang in there. We'll work this out together; it isn't the end of the world. Meanwhile, why don't you go take a shower and change back into your street clothes, and we'll go have lunch."

Charlie nodded and went into the bathroom.

Above all I can't make myself Charlie's enemy, both for his sake and for the sake of the country.

After lunch, they returned to the room, only to find that it had been made up and was no longer theirs. They asked around until they found the conference room, and both sat down. Charlie was avoiding eye contact as if he was ashamed of something, and Webber knew he had to take the initiative.

"Charlie, has it occurred to you that if your abilities were common knowledge, your time wouldn't be your own? Talk shows would want you to demonstrate your abilities, people off the street would be coming up asking for favors, and others would try to play whatever angle they could think of in order to make a buck off you. Wouldn't you agree that it was just a matter of time before your psionic abilities came out?"

"Is that what they're called?" Charlie asked, "I think of them more as a curse."

"Again, I can't imagine," said Webber, "but I'd appreciate it if you'd stay out of my head. I'd like my thoughts to be my own. Can you do that?"

"Sure. I don't try to listen to other people's thoughts. They just come to me on their own, and the stronger the emotion involved, the harder it is to fend them off."

"You started to see signs of these abilities at about the same time you noticed everything else?"

"No, it was a little later. First I felt the waking up in my head, then later I started noticing that I could anticipate what people were going to say. Then, little by little, I started to realize that I could move things without touching them."

"We have no way of knowing if your abilities are fully developed now, but I guarantee there are those who are going to want to find out."

"That's what I'm afraid of. They won't let me go once they find out what I can do." He cast a pleading look at Webber.

"Going back to what I said earlier, your life wouldn't be your own if people knew about what you can do. At least this way you can be assured of some privacy."

Charlie thought about that for a long time before he answered. "What are they going to do with me?"

"That's a decision that has to be made at a pay grade much higher than mine," said Webber. "The best we can do is come up with a suggestion they're going to like that they'll go along with which will also be good for you."

"Well, I'm not going to jail," Charlie said firmly, looking right into Webber's eyes. "I haven't done anything wrong, and they're going to have to kill me if they try to lock me up. I don't think there's a lock made I can't get out of, and it'll take more than one or two cops to hold me down too."

"Charlie, that's the last outcome we want to see. Of course you're not going to jail because you're right, you have done nothing wrong. But there are those in government who will look at you as a national defense asset, and others who will look at you as a threat if you fall into the wrong hands. I can't help how other people think and neither can you. All we can do is try to stay low-key and appear cooperative."

"I know you mean that 'we' as us against them, Pete, but I don't want to get in the way of your career."

"I suspect that you have just become my career, Mr. Perkins," Webber said with a laugh, "and I will insinuate myself into every program that remotely touches you so that I stay joined with you at the hip, okay?"

Charlie looked a little relieved. Just then, Colonel Weaver and Captain Chase walked in. Webber jumped to his feet and Charlie hesitantly joined him.

"Stay seated, gentlemen," said the Colonel. "Shall we get down to business? I guess I should lead off."

"Mr. Perkins, I'm not going to read off values and scores, because they won't mean anything. What I will tell you is that, as you already know, your brain is significantly more active - by a factor of at least ten - than anyone I've ever examined. The reason for that is not completely clear yet but I found some very good clues. Blood circulation, oxygen levels and general metabolism in your cerebrum are extraordinarily high. The cerebrum is where most of the higher-level brain functions occur and all these readings are a sure sign that more of your brain is functioning – and far more vigorously - than anyone I've ever tested."

"All this may sound intimidating but I think our brains were designed to run at higher capacity, and that's just what yours is doing. I don't think you need to worry about one day having a meltdown of some sort. Captain, what did Mr. Perkins's psych tests reveal?"

"As I told Charlie and Captain Webber the other day, Charlie's intelligence – his IQ – is in normal parameters. He's more intelligent than the average person but not a genius in terms of his smarts. The Rorschach was normal, and so was the Thematic Apperception, except he seemed somewhat reserved in some of his responses, as if there was something he was trying not to make apparent. The MMPI suggests that Charlie is a completely normal personality with no psychopathology concerns."

"Charlie's achievement tests suggest that he is not well-educated – yet – but his General Aptitude Test Battery indicates that he has a strong ability to learn and, at present, his strongest areas of aptitude involve motor coordination, finger dexterity, and manual dexterity. In summary, Charlie appears to be a relatively normal, well-adjusted man with an extraordinarily high aptitude for learning, and he tends to be more of a doer than a thinker."

"Were his scores high enough to need to classify the results?" the Colonel asked.

"The scores were not, Sir, but the speed at which he completed them certainly would raise eyebrows if not classified."

"Very well. I think that about does it. What now, Captain Webber?"

"That's for higher ups in OSI or the Air Force to say, Colonel. My orders were to get him tested and to ensure that the results are classified and either kept in a classified storage facility here or sent to Holloman for now, where we have a secure vault."

"What's to become of our friend, Mr. Perkins?" Colonel Weaver asked, looking at Charlie for the first time.

"As far as I'm concerned, Sir, I'm to take him home to Alamogordo and turn him loose."

"Don't you think you'd better ask for direction before you do that?"

"That would probably be wise, Sir. I'll check with my superiors before we kick Charlie loose."

"That's it then. Charlie, it has been a pleasure working with you, and a real treat to be the one who administered your tests. If you ever find yourself in the Las Vegas area, please be sure to look me up."

"That begs a question, Sir," said Webber. "If Charlie volunteered himself for further testing, what else would you like to do with him?"

"Let me think about that one for a while, Captain. Personally, I'd like to see how his 'condition' evolves over the next year then test him again."

"I'll be sure to pass that on. Captain, how about you?"

"Charlie," said Captain Chase, looking right at Charlie, "I think it's important that most people don't know about what's happened to you because it could conceivably put you at risk."

"We've already had that chat, Captain," said Webber, breaking in. "Charlie has signed a non-disclosure agreement as a precaution, but also understands it is in his best interest if people don't know what he can do."

Charlie nodded as Captain Chase continued: "I agree with Colonel Weaver. I'd love to do more tests in a year or so, because I'm pretty sure Charlie hasn't plateaued yet. He's still growing, so to speak, and there's going to be more behind those eyes than there is now."

"I guess that wraps it up. Thanks, everyone, for your cooperation, and maybe we'll do this again sometime," said Colonel Weaver, adjourning the meeting.

Charlie had little to say as they were driven to the airport and boarded their flight. Once airborne, he turned to Webber and asked: "Now what?"

"Can you stand to put up with me for a while longer while I check with my boss, or do you need to get away?"

Charlie thought of his cold, lonely house and what was probably waiting for him in Sierra County, and decided maybe this wasn't such a bad deal after all. "I'll stick around if you want me to." *I really don't want to go back to T or C and face those cops or worse, whomever broke into my house.*

"Well, the fact of the matter is that it's going to take a while to get through the chain of command and get a ruling about what to do with you. I'm sure they're going to want you for further study. If it was up to me I'd have you stashed in the Holloman Inn here on base or in a motel in town, but I'd need authorization for that. Why don't you go on home for now, and I'll see how fast I can cut through the bullshit."

That's not what I want to hear.

CHAPTER 6

Charlie decided to wait until after dark, then make a run by his house to see what was happening, He wanted some more clothes and he had forgotten a small metal box that held what papers were important to him. He thought that if the coast was clear, he could be in and out in a matter of minutes, and the cops would never know he had been there. He hoped that the little bastards who had ransacked his place hadn't been back and made a mess of it again. It would make it harder to pick out what clothes he wanted and the box of papers might not even be there.

It was just after nine o'clock in the evening when Charlie turned onto his street. As he drove by, he saw nothing out of the ordinary, except for the "Crime Scene Do Not Cross" tape draped across the entrance to his porch. Its presence made him hesitate. What if they were really waiting for him to come home? He went around the next block and pulled over to think. It was possible that cops were waiting for him in his house right now, but that would mean they had been there every night since they first showed up. They'd get tired. More likely, no department, including the Sierra County Sheriff's Office, could afford to pay overtime night after night with nothing tangible to suggest he was even coming back.

Finally, he decided to take the chance. He continued around the block to his street, then pulled into his driveway. He got out of the Jeep and stood there listening to the night sounds from the neighborhood: someone's television on too loud, a dog barking down the block, an argument that was not yet quite out of hand, and the million and one other ambient sounds one paid no attention to in his neighborhood. He opened the front door with his key and crept into the living room without turning on a light. The street light two houses down gave him some illumination, and he saw that his living room and kitchen had been ransacked again.

He eased down the hallway toward his bedroom and, just after he passed the open bathroom door, two arms snaked around his waist and tackled him to the floor. The body attached to the arms landed directly on top of Charlie, knocking the wind out of him. For a few moments, he was helpless as he struggled to catch a breath. By then another body was standing over him, then put a knee on Charlie's neck. On his knees, the tackler straddled Charlie's hips and roughly ratcheted a set of handcuffs onto his wrists from behind.

"I told you the bastard would come back, didn't I?" said the one with his knee on Charlie's neck. "Let's get 'im up and get the hell out of here. Chip, you get his keys and drive the Jeep." Charlie, still struggling to normalize his breath, was yanked upright, and a hand patted his front pockets until it found the one with his keys in it and pulled them out.

"Okay, I got 'em," said another voice. "Let's get out of here."

With a pair of hands on each bicep, the two men hustled Charlie back down the hall to the living room and out the front door. No one noticed him drop his wallet in the front yard. Someone opened the back door of the Jeep and shoved Charlie inside, then got in beside him and pushed his head down to his knees. Both front doors opened, and Charlie could feel two more bodies get in. One of them started the Jeep and spun gravel as it backed out of the driveway and onto the street.

"Swing by and I'll get the pickup," said a third voice. The Jeep turned at the end of the block and pulled over long enough to let the front passenger out. Moments later, Charlie heard a V-8 engine with a bad exhaust leak start up and pull away, with the Jeep following.

Charlie tried to keep track of the turns to figure out where they were, but he was lost in short order and just concentrated on getting his wind back. The Jeep was driven slowly for a while, then picked up speed as, presumably, they drove out of Elephant Butte, but he was at a loss to determine which direction. Charlie could tell they had merged onto the freeway when the speed increased and steadied out.

"What the hell is this all about?" Charlie asked in a muffled voice, since the man sitting next to him still held his head down between his knees.

"Shut up, you'll find out soon enough."

Charlie held off trying to force his way up and to overpower the man next to him. He didn't know if these men were armed, and he didn't know if he had the ability to take on two or three grown men at once. He knew he could easily escape the handcuffs, but overpowering two men, especially while the Jeep was rolling, was an unknown. He settled for tapping into the driver's mind to get an idea of where they were going. He got more than he bargained for.

He knew this guy! Not well, but well enough to nod when they walked by each other. His name was Chip, and Charlie knew him to hang around with another man he knew slightly, Darrell. They were both prospectors and treasure hunters who were always on the periphery of any discussion over beer, but never the ones telling the story. Now that he thought about it, Charlie remembered that Darrell drove an old beat up Chevy pickup with a bad exhaust leak. He didn't know where the men lived, or how they lived for that matter, but knew they were not men he wanted anything to do with.

He gently probed the man's mind beside him on the back seat, but didn't recognize him. It was clear he was after the gold from the wash. They knew Charlie had worked the dig and had extracted gold, but they didn't know how much. They had beaten Sam Odgers in an effort to find out how much, but regardless, they wanted it. The man beside Charlie also unknowingly told him that he had murdered the man in the tent and he intended to do the same to Charlie after he got what he wanted. This was not a man to trifle with and at the first opportunity, Charlie knew he would have to make his move. Chip and Darrell were followers, no question, and it wouldn't surprise Charlie if, when this stranger was done with them, they would meet the same end.

Through Chip, Charlie could tell when they turned off I-25 and headed west on Highway 152 toward Hillsboro. When they entered the town, Chip slowed down and eased about halfway through the near-ghost town before making a left turn and driving up the hill away from the main part of town. He made a couple more turns, then stopped when he turned abruptly off the road and parked. Charlie was amazed at how clearly he could see what was going on through the two men in the Jeep. It gave him confidence, and he badly needed it, because he had no idea how potent his telekinesis would be against the three men.

He heard the pickup with the exhaust leak stop and shut down. Almost immediately Chip and the stranger hustled Charlie through a gate and into a ramshackle structure that might have, at some time in the past, been a miner's cabin. Chip hurried to light a Coleman lantern, and Charlie saw that the cabin's interior was of rough-sawn studs with no interior finish, consisting of a living room/kitchen area and a separate bedroom. There was a badly worn couch in one corner, and a table with three wooden chairs nearby. As they walked him through the door, Charlie again asked what they were doing and why. The stranger slammed him down onto one of the wooden chairs, then slapped him on the ear.

"I told you to shut up!" he yelled, more confident now that he was on his home turf. "Where's that duct tape? I know how to shut him up." Through the ringing in his ear, Charlie could hear a length of duct tape being stripped off a roll, then felt it roughly applied over his mouth. "There, now you can jabber all you want. I'll tell you when you can talk."

Out of the corner of his eye, Charlie saw Darrell walk into the cabin and quietly close the door, then lean back against it. He could feel Darrell's misgivings about this whole thing, and thought he might be the weak link, if there was one.

"You two take him into the other room and handcuff him to one of those bunk posts. He sure as hell isn't going to break free from one of them," said the stranger Charlie now knew was named

Glen Ritchey. "And since you're such good buddies with him, see if you can talk some sense into him, before we have to get rough."

Chip and Darrel immediately grabbed Charlie by his biceps and walked him into the next room, which was little more than a boarded up lean to, with a roof over a dirt floor and no window. It was stuffy in the room, and every step they took kicked up clouds of dust. There was a two man bunk built into one corner, and the corner posts were six-inch logs extending from the floor into the roof. They set another chair next to one of the posts, and Chip unlocked one of Charlie's wrists long enough to push it around the post and rehandcuff him. It was a stretch, and Charlie had to lean way back in the chair for his arms to reach. It was uncomfortable, but no one seemed to care.

After they had him recuffed, Darrell knelt down and looked at Charlie. "Listen dude," he said softly, "you gotta cooperate with this guy or he'll kill you. He's done it before."

"Yeah," said Chip with a grin, "turns out he wasted a bullet on that guy in the tent. We didn't know the tree was going to come down on him."

"Shut up, Chip," Darrell growled. "This is serious shit. Charlie, this is about the gold that guy had. Where is it?"

His mouth still taped, all Charlie could do was raise his eyebrows.

"C'mon, it was in a metal ammo box. Where did you stash it? Your life depends on it."

Charlie knew Darrell believed what he was saying, and it chilled him. Darrell was clearly afraid of Glen Ritchey, but it looked like Chip was too stupid to recognize the danger. Charlie started to grimace and work his face muscles in an effort to convince Darrell he needed the tape removed.

"Glen? Can I take the tape off his mouth?"

"I don't give a shit what you do with him, as long as I don't have to listen to him lying about the gold."

Darrell urged Charlie with his own upraised eyebrows and Charlie nodded. As gently as he could, Darrell pulled the tape loose from Charlie's mouth, then wadded it into a ball, and dropped it on the floor.

"Okay Charlie, you can talk," snarled Chip. "Where's the gold?"

"I never saw an ammo box, you guys! I worked the dig, yeah, but I didn't find any ammo box. You sure it isn't under the tree or in the tent? Maybe the Sheriff's Office found it."

Darrell paused for a moment to consider Charlie's answer.

"Charlie, if you claim you don't have the gold, Glen is going to be all kinds of pissed."

"I can't give you what I don't have!"

"What about the gold you took out of the wash? Don't say you don't know about that. We watched you working it, and followed you. Glen roughed Sam up pretty bad before Sam admitted he had bought gold from you. We told him we had followed you to him, but he wouldn't say how much. So where's the money from the gold?"

"There wasn't all that much, and I used it to pay off some bills. I owed Jim at the KOA two months' worth of gas, and I borrowed money from a few people. There isn't much left; what there is is in my wallet." Charlie was relieved that his savings pass book was in his pack, which he had left in the Air Force's car. At least they wouldn't find that and know he was lying about the money he had received for the gold.

Chip shoved Charlie over to one side and felt for his wallet, then yanked him over to the other side and did the same thing.

"He doesn't even have a wallet on him!" he growled then rose to go tell Glen. Charlie tried a subtle suggestion that he wait, and Chip started to say something, then shut his mouth and just stood there.

"I told you I paid off bills with it. If my wallet isn't in my back pocket, then I must have dropped it when we were at my house."

"Glen ain't gonna like this, Charlie. I hope you're telling the truth. He has ways of making sure you're not lyin'."

"Like I said, Darrell, I can't give you what I don't have. Can I get a drink of water? And I have to take a leak."

"Just wait right here. I'll go ask Glen what to do."

Darrell, followed by Chip, walked out of the room into the main cabin. Charlie could hear Darrell's voice as he explained what Charlie had said. Glen's response sounded angry but under control.

Darrell came back in by himself. "He's working himself up into a rage, Charlie. He's drinkin' straight whiskey, and when he gets a buzz on, he gets mean as hell. He said this time, he wasn't going to beat you up like he did Sam or the guy in the tent. He says you can kiss any water or food goodbye, and piss your pants for all he cares. C'mon Charlie," Darrell said almost desperately, "work with me here."

"Darrell, I would if I could, but I can't give you what I don't have."

"Lock the fucker in the dark. See how he likes that!" bellowed Glen from the other room.

Darrell scrambled to comply, and moments later, Charlie found himself alone in pitch blackness, thirsty, and needing to piss real bad.

*****

"You told him to do WHAT?" came the voice over the scrambled phone. "So he's just out there loose?" asked Lieutenant Colonel Jeffries, duty officer at OSI Headquarters in Quantico, Virginia.

"Sir, I couldn't get an answer from anyone here at the base. No one wanted to take responsibility for making a decision like that. I might be able to find him again, what do you want me to do with him?" asked Captain Webber.

"Captain, from your description, this guy sounds like the Bionic Man and is either a national security asset or a liability we can't afford another nation to have. You should have made sure he was securely in our control – one way or the other."

"Yes Sir. He didn't seem that eager to leave, but I knew it was going to take me a while to get direction as to what to do with him, I was afraid he'd get impatient and and not want to come back."

"If you don't understand anything else I'm telling you, Captain, understand this: by becoming a national security issue, this man has lost all his Constitutional rights – at least until we can get the matter straightened out. Go find him, right now! If he objects, arrest him and put him in detention, but do it NOW!"

Webber could see all kinds of bad coming from this phone call. Colonel Jeffries was overreacting, and would send it up the chain of command with his spin on it. Sooner or later, someone from Quantico would be barging through the door, wanting to take over.

He decided he'd go find Charlie and put him up for the night at a decent motel in Alamogordo. He'd deal with the headquarters flap in the morning. It was well past ten o'clock at night by the time Captain Webber got into Elephant Butte. He drove straight to Charlie's house, hoping to find him watching television and sipping a beer. When he pulled up in front of the house, his hopes faded quickly. The house was dark and there was crime scene tape across the front.

Webber sat in front of the house for a moment deciding what to do. Finally he got out of his car and walked up past the tape to the front door. His knock on the front door went unheeded but the door swung open a little way. The hair on the back of his neck stood up. *What's going on here?* He backed off and went back to his car, where he retrieved a five-cell flashlight. As he walked back up the sidewalk, the flashlight led the way, and the beam fell on a wallet lying partly open on the walk in front of him.

It was Charlie's wallet and it contained several hundred dollars, his ID, and miscellaneous slips of paper. He slipped the wallet into his pocket and continued up the steps. He knocked again at the door and called out Charlie's name, but the greeting met stone cold silence and darkness. Webber shone the light into the living room, and saw that it had been ransacked, making him wish he had a sidearm. He pushed on into the room, being careful not to disturb anything and trying to flash the light in all directions at once. There was no blood that Webber could see, but it was hard to know if the disarray came from ransacking or a struggle.

He worked his way through the rest of the house, finding it all the same way but, thank God, there were no bodies. On the kitchen counter he found a copy of a search warrant and a short list of evidence that had been seized. At least now he knew it was the Sierra County Sheriff's Office that had left the documents and the crime scene tape. As offended as it left him, he hoped the police had made the mess, and had taken his man into custody for one reason or another, but surely someone would have noticed the wallet on the walkway?

Webber drove over to the Sierra County Courthouse and parked in back where the Sheriff's Office was located. At eleven o'clock at night, he didn't expect much help or cooperation, but he had to try. He pushed the button at the back door and after a several second delay, a metallic voice answered.

"I'm Captain Peter Webber of the U.S. Air Force. Is there a chance someone who participated in the search warrant at 205 Chama Drive in Elephant Butte is around? That's the home of Charlie Perkins."

"That would have been the detectives, and they've all gone home."

"Can you at least give me the name of someone who was involved?"

"Try Detective Sergeant Ramirez, he'd know."

"When does he come in?"

"He's usually here between seven-thirty and eight o'clock in the morning."

"Okay, thank you."

"You want to leave a message?"

"No, but there's one thing – can you see if you have a Charlie Perkins in the jail?"

"Hold on a minute. No, no one named Perkins."

"Okay, thanks."

Webber returned to his car and sat there for a minute, thinking. If Charlie wasn't in jail, maybe he was in the hospital. He called Sierra Vista Hospital – no one named Charlie Perkins had been admitted.

Webber was at the Sierra County Sheriff's Office first thing in the morning asking for Sergeant Ramirez. A stocky middle-aged man with a mustache emerged from the security door and identified himself as Ramirez. They shook hands, and Webber showed him his OSI identification. Ramirez escorted him into the building and to a closet-sized office containing a filing cabinet, a standard metal desk, and two chairs. He motioned the Air Force officer to the chair on the other side of the desk.

"Can I get you some coffee or something?"

"No, thanks, I'm almost to toxic level on coffee already."

"What can I do for you?"

"This has to do with a guy named Charlie Perkins."

Ramirez's face showed surprise. "What's he done that the Air Force wants him?"

"He hasn't done anything, *per se,* but he has been very instrumental in a case we're working."

"What kind of case?"

"I'm afraid that's classified," said Webber with a grimace. "Sorry about that, but all I can say is that we really need to find Charlie."

"Is he in trouble with you folks?"

"I wouldn't say in trouble. We just need his services for a while longer."

"So he's not going to Air Force lock-up?"

"No. Were you involved in the search warrant at his house?"

"Yes. We're looking at Charlie Perkins as a person of interest in a homicide investigation that occurred a while back."

Now it was Webber's turn to be surprised. "You think he committed a murder?"

"Well, we don't know. He led us to a body under a tree that had uprooted up above Hillsboro, if you know where that is."

"Yes, I do."

"Anyway when we cut away the tree, we found the remains of Mr. Moss Richter, white male, thirty-seven years old. He had been shot in the back of the head with a large caliber weapon, probably a handgun since we found him inside his tent. Richter is - rather, was - a prospector from around this area known by most of the old timers. Sometimes he partnered up with another prospector by the name of Glen Ritchey, and we can't find him either. He has a failure to appear warrant out for him out of Doña Ana County, and he might have left for parts unknown."

"So he might be good for the murder too?" Webber asked.

"Yes, he's as viable a suspect as Perkins is. Thing is, Richter had been bragging a little about hitting a rich strike up in the Black Range, and we can't find any gold anywhere around the crime scene. And we looked – hard. Ritchey could have done him in and walked off with the gold, or Perkins could have heard him bragging and gone up and killed him for his stash."

"I see. Ah, did your people ransack Perkins's house?"

"We might have messed it up a little more than how we found it but someone had already gone through it like a tornado, pulling out drawers, tipping over furniture, that kind of stuff."

"So it was a mess when you got there?"

"You could certainly say that. Matter of fact, we took pictures before we started just to prove that we hadn't made such a mess."

"When did you execute the warrant?"

"Yesterday afternoon, about one-thirty."

"Could we look through those pictures?"

"Yeah, I imagine they're printed out by now. Anything in particular?"

"Yes, the front of the house. Did you come through the front door?"

"No, it was locked, but the back door had already been kicked in, so we went in that way."

"I was there last night at about ten or ten-fifteen and found the front door ajar, and it didn't look like it had been forced. I also found this," Webber said as he laid Charlie's wallet on the desk.

"Damn, how did we miss that?" said Ramirez in disgust.

"I'm not sure you did. I found it outside on the front walk, and I doubt it was there when your people were searching. That makes me think Charlie was back there between your search and when I got there."

"Sounds reasonable."

"And he probably unlocked the front door when he got there."

"That's probably right. It's a keyed deadbolt on both sides on the front door. We had to haul the evidence out through the back, because we couldn't get the front door unlocked and didn't want to mess up anything else."

"That's why I wondered about looking at the pictures. They would show if the wallet was there or not."

"Sit still a minute, I'll go get them."

Ramirez was back in under five minutes and carrying several proof sheets of photographs. He handed some to Webber and began scanning some himself. Moments later he said: "There," and pointed to one of the prints. It was a photo of the front of the house from the street, and showed the entire front sidewalk. There was no wallet in the photograph.

"Well, that's settled, anyway," grunted Ramirez.

"Sergeant, Charlie Perkins has been with me for the last three days. We've been out of town. We just got back late yesterday afternoon. I sent him home with the agreement that we'd hook up again today, but I haven't heard from him."

"So you think he's missing?"

"I don't know what to think, except I know he's not at his house, and he's not with his wallet. His Jeep is gone too."

"What kind of Jeep does he drive?"

"It's a faded blue Jeep Cherokee. I think I have the plate number back at my office."

"You're out of Holloman?"

"That's right. You should also know that Charlie told me about the body under the tree – actually he said it smelled like a dead body – and that he was working the dig that the victim apparently started. I insisted he report it, but I don't know when he did. I don't know anything about a stash of gold that he might have found, but I'm assuming he was finding gold, or he wouldn't have kept working the site."

"That's probably right. The thing that makes us so interested in Perkins is that he's been selling gold to a dealer in Las Cruces over the past five weeks. Know anything about that?"

"Only that Charlie said he was seeing 'color' and I assume that meant he was getting gold out of where he was digging. Did the victim have a vehicle of some sort?"

"Yeah, he had a beat-up old black and silver S-10 Blazer, but it wasn't registered in his name, so we don't have a license plate for it."

"Do you have some kind of alert out on Perkins, or a warrant - anything?"

"Not yet, but I thought I should put out an ATL, Attempt to Locate, and I can put in it that Mr. Perkins is also a subject of interest to the Air Force and include your name and phone number."

"That would be very helpful, Sergeant, thank you."

"If you get him first, is he eventually going to be free to go?"

"Eventually as in a few days, or as in years? I can't answer that until I've had a chance to confer with my superiors. Right now my marching orders are to find him at any cost and bring him in. Beyond that, your guess is as good as mine. If we find him first, we'll give you full access to him."

They exchanged business cards, and Webber went back to his car. Where to start looking for a desert rat that doesn't want to be found, or someone who has been abducted? How can you look when you don't know the players? He guessed he'd better get back to the base and inform headquarters that Charlie Perkins was officially a missing (and very wanted) person.

CHAPTER 7

Glen Ritchey woke up with a crick in his neck from being folded up on the ratty couch, and a raging hangover from the cheap whiskey he had drunk the night before. He was in no mood for anything to go wrong and when he saw Chip asleep in a chair tilted back against the bedroom door, he almost lost it.

"God DAMN it, you lazy piece of shit!" he bellowed as he kicked the chair legs out from under the sleeping man. Chip landed in a heap, trying to make sense out of what was happening to him.

"Get up you lazy bastard. Do you even know if our prisoner is still a prisoner?"

"Well damn, Glen, how could he get out? I was right against the door the whole time."

"I don't care. You were supposed to stay awake after you relieved Darrell. That's what guarding means, you dumb ass."

Chip got up and scraped the chair away from the door, and peeked into the bedroom. Charlie, eyes closed and looking extremely uncomfortable, was still handcuffed to the chair.

"He's still there," said Chip. Relieved, he started rubbing the back of his head where it had collided with the door.

"It's a damned good thing. Now stay awake, or you might not wake up next time," said Glen as he stormed out the door and around the cabin to the outhouse.

"It's a damned good thing," Chip mocked after making sure Glen was out of hearing. What wasn't out of hearing – for Charlie – was the whole conversation and the noise Glen made leaving the cabin and slamming the door of the outhouse.

When Glen came back in, Darrell, who had slept on the front seat of his truck, was with him.

"We're going into T or C to see if we can find that asshole's wallet. You stay here and guard – and I mean GUARD – the prisoner like you're supposed to." With that, Glen and Darrell walked out of the cabin and moments later, Chip heard the truck start up and idle noisily away.

"And I mean GUARD the prisoner," Chip mocked. He looked in at Charlie again and found he hadn't moved or awakened. "At least I can go take a dump in peace," he said to himself. Charlie heard the door slam as Chip left the cabin and the door close as he entered the outhouse.

Charlie knew this was his chance to escape. Unlocking the handcuffs was hardly an effort for a telekinetic and Charlie was up on his feet – and almost fell down. His butt and legs were cramped, and he had to work the stiffness out before he could even walk. The crotch of his pants was also wet, which felt cold and clammy, but Charlie put that aside for now.

He went to the door and listened, hearing nothing. He opened it and, finding no one in the cabin, looked around for his keys. He grabbed them from the table then gently eased open the door. His Jeep was parked next to an S-10 Blazer and unlocked. He quietly opened the driver's door and slipped into the seat. As he leaned forward to insert the key into the ignition, he heard the familiar rumble of a V-8 with an exhaust leak and before he could react, the blue Chevy pulled up behind the Jeep.

Charlie scrambled out of the Jeep and made a dash around the side of the cabin, running smack into Chip coming back from the outhouse. They went down in a heap and by the time Charlie could untangle himself, Glen and Darrell were on him and had his arms pinned behind his back.

Chip took the opportunity to punch Charlie viciously in the stomach as he snarled: "Where do you think you're going asshole?" then slugged him again, this time in the mouth.

Charlie was dazed as he felt himself being manhandled back into the cabin and into the bedroom.

"It's a good thing we came back for the keys or this bird would have been long gone," Glen gritted as he and Darrell dragged Charlie back into the bedroom chair where the cuffs lay on the corner of the bunk. He picked them up and examined them. "Just as I thought," snarled Glen, "the cuffs were too loose and he squeezed out of them. I told you dumb bastards to make sure they were on tight."

"They were on tight," Darrell protested, pointing at the imprints on Charlie's wrists.

"That's just from trying to get out of them," said Glen as he personally reattached the cuffs around the pole and onto Charlie's wrists, clamping them down hard. He slapped and backslapped Charlie, leaned in close, and said: "I'm tired of waiting on you, asshole. When I get back, you'd better be ready to talk, or I'm gonna make you wish you was dead." He backhanded him one more time and asked: "Got it?"

Glen then turned on Chip. "And what were you doing while this asshole was waltzing out the front door?" He slugged Chip in the mouth, and Chip stumbled backward over a chair and went down beneath the table. He scrambled further under the table.

"Get out from under there, you're coming with me. I can't trust you alone with this asshole, asshole."

Moments later, Charlie heard the truck start and pull away. This time it didn't come back.

*****

Captain Webber turned onto Charlie's street and looked anxiously for Charlie's Jeep but wasn't surprised when it wasn't there. He pulled up in front of the house, got out, and walked around the building, entering through the rear. He didn't pay any attention to the angry sound of a truck with an exhaust leak drive by. Webber walked through the house calling Charlie's name, but knew it was hopeless. As he turned the corner driving away, he didn't see the loud pickup pull up to the front of the house.

"That looked like an Air Force car," said Chip. "Wonder what he's doing around here."

"The fucker probably already found the wallet if there ever was one. Let's go ahead and check it out anyway, just in case he missed it."

*****

"Charlie?" Darrell called softly as he slowly opened the bedroom door until he could see Charlie was still handcuffed to the post. He pulled up a chair so he was facing Charlie. "You have to tell him where the gold or the money is when he comes back or he'll kill you just like he did Moss. He's got a crazy hot temper and if he doesn't get what he wants, somebody dies."

"Darrell," Charlie said more calmly than he felt. "Glen is going to kill me no matter what. Can't you see that?"

"Yeah, I reckon I do. But you can't just sit there and let him!"

"I don't plan to," said Charlie as he released the locking mechanisms on the handcuffs once again and tipped the chair back onto four legs.

"How'd you do that? You must have a key hidden somewhere."

"No key, Darrell, but I don't have time to explain. You going to get in my way, stay here or go with me? You know when Glen finds me gone, your life is worthless too; hell, for that matter, once he gets his hands on the gold or the money, you *both* are history. I hope you realize that."

"No . . . no, he said we was partners and we'd split it up even like."

"And you believed him? Aside from that, you gonna fight me or let me go?"

"Aw hell, Charlie, I never wanted in on this killin' stuff from the beginnin' an' . . ."

"Where's my cell phone?" Charlie stood up and shook the kinks out then walked toward Darrell. Suddenly Darrell and his chair began sliding backward across the floor of the cabin out of Charlie's way.

"What the hell?" cried Darrell.

"That's more of what I don't have time to explain. You got the keys to that Blazer out there?"

"Nah, Glen don't want us driving it. It belonged to Moss, and he's afraid some cop would stop us and we'd get in trouble. Glen has all the keys."

"Okay, I'm hot-footin' it out of here, Darrell. Last chance. Are you coming or staying?" He spotted his cell phone on the table and grabbed it as he walked by.

"I reckon I better go with you. You're right about one thing: Glen is gonna be plenty pissed when he finds you gone. Where we gonna go?"

"Let's hustle down to the General Store Café and see if anyone is headed toward the freeway."

As luck would have it a local older couple was just finishing their breakfast, knew Charlie, and were willing to give them both a ride, at least to the KOA. They started out doing the thirty-mile-an-hour speed limit and Charlie took a deep breath but didn't say anything. As they left town and started up into the curves, the driver was very cautious and braked for each coming curve, slowing down far below the recommended safe speed. Both Charlie and Darrell were sitting on the edge of the back seat, expecting to see Darrell's pickup come roaring around the next curve. Finally they reached straighter road and the man opened it up to about sixty. As they neared Copper Flats, Charlie suddenly pushed Darrell's head down and ducked down himself. When he heard the bellowing pickup drive by in the other direction, Darrell didn't ask any questions.

The couple in the front seat serenely rode down the road, blissfully ignorant of how close to real danger they were. Charlie wanted to strangle the driver to make him go faster but the man would only nudge it up to sixty-two and that was because they were going downhill. The thirty-minute drive seemed to take hours before they finally crossed the cattle guard and coasted down to the KOA.

Charlie's thank yous were rather terse then he grabbed Darrell and dragged him inside the store.

"Jim!" Charlie said, out of breath from the dash from the corner, "I'm in bad trouble."

Jim stood up from where he had been seated behind the counter and moved over to a chair in the corner, on which lay a padded bag. Charlie knew he had guns in there, and the thought calmed him a little.

"What's going on, Charlie?"

"Got some guys chasing us, and if they catch us, they're going to kill us."

"Well, let's call the police."

"They won't get here fast enough. We gotta get out of here! This is the first place they'll look once they find us gone. Can I borrow 'Old Blue'?"

Jim didn't much like that idea, but he finally said yes and tossed Charlie the keys. "Now don't go leavin' it all beat up on a street corner, or I'll come after you myself!" he yelled as Charlie and Darrell dashed out the back door.

"Old Blue" was a 1979 Ford one ton four-wheel-drive pickup with toolboxes in the bed. Jim had bought it new and though the sun had faded the blue paint, and one fender had been replaced and was now black, he was very fond of the beast and took meticulous care of it. As a result, it ran like a noisy Swiss watch.

It fired first thing and Charlie shifted into first, forgetting first was a "granny" gear for heavy duty pickups that old. He quickly shifted into second, spun a little gravel, drove around the front of the store, and saw Jim watching out the window. He waved, then quickly headed the pickup back up to the on-ramps onto I-25.

When he nosed the pickup south, Darrell asked, "Where we goin'? I thought we were headed for T or C."

"I have a better place for us to go. Besides, he won't expect us to go south."

*****

When Glen Ritchey found both Darrell and Charlie gone, he felt the first tremors of fear – of being caught. He hadn't felt fear since his days when as a young child he had been left alone at home in his mother's ramshackle hovel in Presidio, Texas. The town wasn't much, never had been, just a dusty southwest Texas border town. His mother worked as a cocktail waitress, in Presidio and sometimes across the border in Ojinaga, Chihuahua. Sometimes she would bring a customer home to make a little extra money and without fail, the customer would be unhappy that there was a snot-nosed child squalling for its mother when they got there.

A swat or two would usually shut young Glen up, but he never forgot, and his mother never comforted him when it happened. She had other things to worry about. Sometimes, when she was home alone, usually drunk, she would show him kindness, but he had always been the kid she hadn't wanted and it showed. Glen learned early not to expect anything but bad from other people, and he became self-reliant at a young age. So self-reliant, in fact, that he found himself in trouble with the law at the ripe old age of eleven. He had been caught inside a neighbor's house with his pockets full of things that did not belong to him. His only regret – though he kept that to himself – was that he had been caught. In the future he was more careful, and when he got big enough it didn't matter anymore. He matured early and quit growing at a rawboned six foot one, two hundred pounds, with a bass voice that bellowed like a bull when he was angry, which was often.

After gaining his size, Glen realized that as he was bigger than most, and that the majority of people would do just about anything to avoid a confrontation with a bigger opponent. He found he could get his way just by bellowing and blustering most of the time. He learned to bully people to get what he wanted. When that didn't work, he resorted to his fists or any weapon that was handy. The law caught up with him again at sixteen when he beat a man so severely with a pipe, the victim lost sight in one eye. Glen was remanded to adult court and sentenced to seven and a half years in the custody of the Texas Department of Criminal Justice, Fort Stockton Unit. But he never learned how to control his temper as he demonstrated when he broke the jaw of his cellmate in three places for "flirting" with another inmate. During a subsequent incident, he broke the nose of an assistant librarian over the issue of an overdue book. These two incidents cost him, and he wound up doing the full seven and a half years.

When he got out of prison he was barely twenty-four years old, and swore he'd never go back. That didn't mean he was through with crime, just that he'd rather die than be incarcerated again. Presidio County's finest made it clear early on after Ritchey's release that he was no longer welcome in the county and it would behoove him to seek greener pastures elsewhere, this after a brawl in a Presidio bar where everyone conveniently could not remember what happened. When the suggestion was emphasized at the point of a gun, Ritchey took it to heart and moved on.

He had a former cellmate - whom he had not assaulted - living in El Paso who invited him to stay for a while, and Ritchey accepted. They apparently had different ideas about what was polite behavior from a house guest, and when the cellmate caught his girlfriend in bed with Ritchey, it was time for Ritchey to move on again.

He migrated to La Cruces, thinking that maybe a change of state would be a good thing, but when his little enterprise of robbing ATM customers got too hot, it was time to leave the city at the base of the Organ Mountains.

He caught a ride going north on I-25, and that ride took him all the way to T or C. He wandered into the Plugged Nickel Saloon, where he struck up an acquaintance with an older prospector by the name of Moss Richter. Moss took a shine to Ritchey and invited him to come help him work a promising claim for twenty-five percent of the gold. It would mean camping out in the mountains much of the time, and some hard work, but the profits were very promising. Ritchey decided the isolation outweighed the hard work and accepted. The pair began working together with Richter showing him the ins and outs of placer mining.

For about two weeks they worked well together. Ritchey was sharp enough to pick up what Moss was trying to teach him, and was willing to do a lot of the butt work in exchange for a place to stay, something to eat, and beer to drink. Besides, they were into one of the best placer sites Richter had ever seen.

It was early in the second week of their partnership, after Richter had gone to town for supplies, that Ritchey discovered the ramp down on the thing hanging over their dig. He too was lured into the hull and scanned, just as Charlie Perkins later described, and came out feeling weird and different. He kept it to himself, not wanting to admit to Richter he was scared until he began noticing the manifestations of the scan which ultimately convinced him that he was somehow becoming something more than other humans. He became more brash and confident, and started questioning the way Richter was running the dig. Richter didn't say much, but made no effort to hide his thoughts that this partnership was nearing its natural end. He had been fair with Ritchey, weekly splitting the amount of gold they had extracted. Invariably, Ritchey almost immediately made his way into town to sell his gold and party. He became a regular at the Plugged Nickel, and a regular of one of the meth dealers nearby who frequented the tavern.

Ritchey knew that Richter had been hoarding his share of the gold in a metal ammo box on which he had put a padlock. He kept the key on a chain around his neck and the box was always nearby.

One night, Ritchey came back to camp about half drunk and higher than an orbiting satellite on meth. On the way up the mountain from town, he decided that Richter was definitely holding out on him and was getting ready to dump him and keep the gold for himself. Being the aggrieved party, Ritchey wasn't going to stand for it, and had acquired a less than legal Colt Python .357 magnum to make sure his point of view was expressed in full.

When Ritchey got back to camp, the two quarreled and Ritchey's temper got the better of him, but instead of turning violent, he stomped out of the tent and went back to Richter's Blazer for another beer and a smoke, which turned into nearly half a case of beer and a whole pack of cigarettes, and when he saw the light go out in Richter's tent, Ritchey waited two hours. Then he made his way back to the tent and executed Richter by putting the muzzle of the revolver to the back of his partner's head and pulling the trigger. No one can know if Richter had had a premonition that something like this was going to happen but he had hidden his stash. Ritchey searched the tent and could not find the metal ammo box. The more he searched, the more frantic he became, sure that someone would come to investigate the sound of the shot still ringing in his ears. Finally he couldn't wait any longer and fled, leaving a dead man among the bedding in the tent.

Thanks to the meth, Ritchey drove around all night long scheming and planning. The first thing on his mind was the gold. Where could it have gone? Had he missed it in his hurried search of the tent and surroundings? Had Richter buried it somewhere? He would have had ample time while Ritchey was in town, but where? Even in death, the bastard had cheated him!

Then it started to rain, and soon it was coming down so hard even Ritchey knew he dare not go back up to where Richter's body still lay in the tent. There was bound to be a flood, and most of the camp would be washed away, since it was set up right in the wash. Finally the Plugged Nickel opened for the day and Ritchey found a sanctuary of sorts. He was on his second pitcher of beer when Chip Lakin and Darrell Cunningham wandered in and spotted him sitting alone at a corner table, slumped down as if he had been there a while. They had met a couple of times when Ritchey and Richter were together, but they hesitated coming over to the table.

The sight of the two prospectors gave Ritchey an idea, and he motioned them over. Seeing his full pitcher of beer, they hesitated no longer and sat down facing Ritchey with their backs to the door.

"Got rained out, huh?" asked Darrell, settling in and pouring a glass for himself and his partner.

"No shit," Ritchey replied in his *basso profundo* voice, letting the conversation find its own way. Reading their thoughts, he could tell that the duo was short on cash and long on thirst, which fit nicely into his plans.

"Where's Moss?"

"Oh, he didn't want to come into town. He gets kinda moody sometimes, and prefers to stay by himself. Hope he isn't a drowned rat by now."

"Boy that's no kidding. It's really coming down out there," said Lakin. "How are you two doing?"

"No complaint, we're seeing color most days. Sometimes more, sometimes less, but it still looks real promising."

"Well that's good, ain't it? Me and Darrell here are kind of between strikes right now, and when it turns wet and shitty like this, there ain't much to do," said Chip.

"So you guys are looking for work?"

"Yeah. Depends on the work, of course, but yeah."

"Well I might have something opening up. Moss and I ain't gettin' along too well – between you and me, I think he's cheating me, skimming on the price of the gold when we sell it - and I'm about ready to buy him out of this claim. You interested in working it with me for half?"

The look between them told Ritchey everything he needed to know, but he let them come around on their own.

"Sure, that'd be fine," said Lakin tentatively.

"Hell yes," said Darrell. "You won't be sorry; we're hard workers."

The tension was relieved at the table just as Ritchey knew it would, and they all grinned and took big gulps of their beer. Now that he had help to mine out the rest of the gold, all he had left to do was either figure out a way to cheat them out of their share or find a place where their bodies wouldn't be found.

The first day after the rain stopped, Ritchey went back up to the site to search it again before he brought his two laborers up. He found the tree on top of Richter's tent and try as he might, he couldn't force his way in to look for the gold and check on what he knew to be a corpse.

Three days later the sun was back out, and Ritchey found his new employees at the Plugged Nickel. He invited them up the mountain to look at the site. He parked Richter's Blazer at the mouth of the draw, deciding that trying to get Darrell's two-wheel-drive pickup in close to the narrows would only get it stuck and they'd have to waste a bunch of time freeing it.

When Ritchey caught sight of the tree on the tent, he yelled: "Oh my God!" and ran around the crater where the root ball used to be, getting as close to the tent as he could. "Moss!" he bellowed in a voice that almost carried back to Hillsboro. Making sure the others were watching, he made a big show of trying to fight his way in among the branches to the tent. Frustrated in his first attempt, he backed off, then looked at the two men standing there dumbly.

"Don't just stand there, find a way into the tent. Moss must still be in there, and he might be alive!" he ordered in an agitated voice. Then he dove back in among the branches in another attempt to get to the tent The size of the branches and the rocks beneath them made it impossible to progress more than a few feet before he was stymied again so he backed out again and noted with satisfaction that both Chip and Darrell were trying to burrow their way to the tent as well, but having no more luck than he was. As a last resort, Ritchey ran around to the wash side of the tree and once again tried burrowing in under the tree through the branches and the rocks. He finally realized there was no way he was going to search the campsite with the tree on top of it.

"You sure he's in there?" asked Lakin.

"Where else would he be?"

"If he's in there, he's probably dead, and even if he's not, we gotta get some help. You know, call the Sheriff's Office."

"I can't do that," said Ritchey, putting as much distress into his voice as he could.

"Just call them up and tell them there's been an accident."

"I can't. I'm wanted in Cruces. I'd wind up in jail, and I'm not going back to jail."

"Then call them anonymously and just tell them where to find him."

"I can't do that either. Moss and I got in an argument. I shot him."

"Did you kill him?"

"I don't think so, but I'm pretty sure the tree did."

Both Cunningham and Lakin were silent for several minutes.

"I just want to work the dig until it runs out. Then I'll have money for an attorney and I'll report what happened," said Ritchey, casting a furtive glance toward the other two, already knowing they would go along with his plan. "We'll start tomorrow and work it until it peters out, okay?"

"I dunno, Glen . . ." Cunningham began.

He was cut off by his partner, who saw a chance to get in on some sure money. "We can't do nothing for ol' Moss, Darrell. We might as well work the dig in his memory. I think he'd like that, don't you?"

"I don't even have a place to stay now," said Ritchey. "Where are you guys hanging your hats?"

"Oh," said Lakin, "we fixed up an old miner's cabin in Hillsboro. It ain't much, but at least there's a roof over our head. I guess you could stay there, right, Darrell?"

Cunningham was silent for several long seconds before he folded. "Yeah, sure."

They hiked back to the vehicles and drove to the shack. They spent the rest of the day drinking beer and talking about what a great guy Moss had been and how it was a shame he had to go out the way he did.

The next morning, Ritchey was up early. "I'm going up to the site to make sure nobody's been up there. If the coast is clear, I'll come back and get you."

In truth, Ritchey wanted one more shot to look around for Richter's stash of gold without the two dumb-asses tagging along. When he got close to the mouth of the wash, he saw a faded blue Jeep Cherokee parked partway off the road. He eased back out as quietly as the Blazer would let him and returned to the cabin.

"There's somebody up there," he told his partners grimly.

"You mean somebody is jumping your claim?" asked Chip.

"Ah hell, we never filed a claim. We just been digging up there for a while."

"Still, he can't just barge in there and start working the dig," Chip pointed out.

"The law's on his side," said Ritchey. "Short of going up there and shooting him, there's not much we can do about it . . . now." An idea had formed in his head. Why not let the stranger do all the work and extract all the gold, then relieve *him* of the proceeds? All it would take was to keep an eye on him and make sure they knew when he was done. He related his plans to the others, and no one could find fault with it. Predictably though, Darrell was a little hesitant.

*****

Ritchey was incensed that Darrell had turned on them and let Perkins go, and he would kill the bastard in a flash but now he had to maintain control and figure out what they should do. First thing on the list was to get the hell away from this cabin, because if Darrell and Charlie made it to the cops, this would be the first thing they'd tell them about.

Where could the pair have gone? They were on foot, Glen had seen to that, and the logical thing for them to do was try to get a ride back down the hill. They would likely be hitchhiking, and must have caught a ride, or had hidden somewhere in town when he drove by.

"You'd better take whatever shit you left in the cabin, because we gotta go. The cops'll be coming up here sooner or later, and I ain't gonna be here when they arrive. Where would Darrell go to hide out?" he asked Chip.

Chip thought for a minute before answering: "I can't think of any place right off. Darrell just hangs out with different folks unless he's up in the hills prospecting."

"Let's go. I don't want to wait around here any longer."

"Before we go, we'd better put some more oil in Darrell's pickup. It burns a lot of oil, and if we let it get too low, it might seize up."

"We don't have time for that. Get in the truck."

They peeled away from the cabin and instead of turning right toward the freeway, Glen turned left.

"Where we goin'?" asked Chip.

"I'm gonna check at the café, see if they've been there."

He parked partway in the road in front of the General Store Café and stuck his head in, looking for some of the old timers who perpetually sat at the first table inside the door, next to the old wood-burning stove.

"Any of you boys seen Charlie Perkins this morning?"

"Yep, he was in here about an hour ago with some other fella. They caught a ride to the KOA with Ben and Nancy Jamison."

"You say an hour ago?"

The man looked at his companions and each one muttered something different. "Well, maybe half an hour or forty minutes ago."

Glen nodded and returned to the idling pickup.

"They caught a ride down the hill to the KOA," said Glen, as he put the pickup in gear and floored it. He didn't let up on the gas until they crossed the cattle guard above the KOA. Then he slowed down and eased into the parking lot on the north side of the store, where no one from inside could see.

101

"You go around the back, and I'll come in through the front. If they're inside, we'll have 'em."

The only person inside was Jim's wife, Bev. A former Marine, she didn't like the looks of these two at all.

"Charlie Perkins been by today?" asked Glen.

"Not that I know of," said Bev, looking Glen straight in the eye. She knew full well these two were looking for trouble, and she wasn't going to help them in the least. Besides, she liked Charlie and didn't want to see these two catch up with him. She sure as hell wasn't going to tell them that Charlie had borrowed "Old Blue".

Glen nodded, and he and Chip returned to the pickup.

"Now what?" asked Chip.

"They must have caught a ride. Stands to reason they'd have tried to go north to T or C and the Sheriff's Office. I'm going south, got friends in Cruces and El Paso. What do you want to do?"

"I'll tag along if you don't mind."

"Suit yourself," said Glen as he turned back up toward the freeway and headed south.

*****

"Old Blue" was geared really low, and at sixty-five miles an hour sounded like they were going to push a rod through the side of the engine block, not to mention the temperature gauge needle really wanted to drift over to the "H". Charlie kept anxiously looking in the rear view mirrors, on the lookout for the Chevy pickup, but so far the coast was clear. As they drove, he keyed up Captain Webber's phone number and pushed "send".

"Webber," was all the Captain said.

"Pete! I'm in trouble and I need some help!"

"Charlie? Is that you? What's going on? Where are you? What's wrong?"

Charlie took a deep breath before he started to explain. When he ran out of breath, Webber broke in: "I know some of this, Charlie. I've been talking to the Sheriff's Office. They're out looking for you, and some guy name Glen Ritchey too."

"That's who's chasing us. If he catches us, he'll shoot us both."

"Okay, calm down. Where are you?"

"We're almost to Hatch, but we can only go about sixty-five miles an hour because this old truck is geared so low. I'm headed your way as fast as this thing will let me. Tell them at the gate I'm coming, 'cause I'm not stopping until I'm inside the gate. This Ritchey guy is crazy and he'll be mad as hell that Darrell and I took off."

"Who's Darrell?"

"He's one of the guys who was with Ritchey when they grabbed me – oh hell, Pete, I'll explain it all when we get there."

"Okay," said Webber, "just keep coming, and they'll be waiting for you at the front gate. Park in the same lot as last time. I'm going to call the detectives from the Sheriff's Office and they'll meet us here. Are you driving your Jeep?"

"No, I borrowed a pickup. It's an old faded blue Ford four wheel drive crew cab."

"Do you want me to try to arrange an escort with the state police?"

"Just let 'em know we're coming through Cruces, then up to Alamogordo."

"Okay, what is Ritchey driving?"

Charlie looked over at Darrell. "What year is your pickup?"

"Eighty-five."

"He's driving a dark blue beat up eighty-five Chevy pickup. You can't miss it. It has a loud exhaust leak and blows a lot of smoke."

"Yeah," said Darrell, "it has a cracked exhaust manifold. I always meant to fix that."

"What's the plate number?" Webber asked.

"What's the plate number?" Charlie asked Darrell.

"Jeez, I don't know. Sorry man."

"He doesn't know."

"Okay. Well just keep heading this way, and I'll see you when you get here."

Charlie hung up the phone and glanced again in the rearview mirror. He could see three or four vehicles behind him, but two of them were too far away yet to determine what they were. He tried pushing the old Ford a little harder, but the rattling and shimmying, and the temperature needle, held him back. Suddenly the steering wheel tried to yank itself out of Charlie's hands and, failing that, began pulling mightily to the left.

Just as they passed the Hatch exit, Charlie exclaimed: "Aw crap, that's just what we need." He pounded on the steering wheel as he fought it to the shoulder.

"What? What's wrong?"

"I think the left front tire just went flat. I don't even know if Jim keeps a spare on this rig since he mostly uses it around the campground. I've gotta pull over. We can't drive on a flat tire."

"We can if somebody's trying to kill us," said Darrell, his anxiety ratcheting up.

"Stay cool, Darrell. Let me get this thing pulled over and see if there's a spare."

Charlie nursed the limping pickup as far over on the shoulder as he dared, then jumped out and went to the rear. There in the bed was a spare tire but where was the jack and lug wrench?

"Darrell!" Charlie yelled, "get out here and help me find a jack and a lug wrench."

They started going through the various tool boxes until it occurred to Charlie to look under the hood – where he found both the jack and the handle.

"Now we just need a . . ." he said as Darrell extracted a four-way lug wrench from one of the tool boxes.

"Okay, you keep an eye out for Glen and Chip. I'll change the tire," Charlie said as he knelt with the lug wrench to loosen the nuts.

The cars Charlie couldn't initially recognize whizzed by, but others were coming, and Charlie had never changed a tire as fast as he did that one. Darrell stood by the corner of the pickup where Charlie worked and kept looking anxiously back up the road, knowing any minute his noisy Chevy pickup would appear. When it did, he could hardly believe his eyes.

"Unless you want to get stranded out here, you'd better stop and put some oil in this thing. Look at the temperature gauge!" said Chip.

With a disgusted grunt, Glen saw that Chip was right and reluctantly turned off the freeway at Hatch, ignoring the faded blue pickup pulled to the side of the freeway a hundred yards ahead of them, and steered down the road into town. There he pulled off the road, got out, and opened the hood. Waves of heat and smoke emanating from the engine compartment made him take a step backward.

"Where's the oil?" he yelled to Chip, who got out, reached in the bed, and retrieved three quarts of oil and a rag.

"Let it cool down for a couple of minutes before you even try to open the oil cap. This bitch is hot as hell."

Glen stood there impatiently for all of forty-five seconds before, with the rag, he unscrewed the oil filler cap and started dumping oil into the crankcase. He dumped all three quarts in then checked the dipstick, finding it right at the "Add" mark, so he added one more quart.

"Maybe we ought to slow down a little. We won't have to add oil so often, and we aren't calling attention to ourselves with the smoke this thing is blowing."

Neither Charlie nor Darrell could believe their eyes when they saw the pickup behind them take the exit into Hatch. They didn't dawdle, however, and Charlie had the old Ford in gear and heading south on I-25 as fast as he could coax it to go. He kept an apprehensive eye on the rear view mirror and almost held his breath until they reached the Alamogordo exit.

Turning east onto Highway 70, their vigilance didn't waver as they sped toward Alamogordo and, hopefully, safe haven. About an hour later, they reached the outskirts to the town without seeing anything alarming in the mirrors.

When Charlie pulled in at the main gate into Holloman, he breathed a sigh of relief. Had he known what he was about to face, he might have kept on going.

CHAPTER 8

The gate guards were expecting them and Charlie noticed both were wearing sidearms. He couldn't imagine Glen taking on a military base to get to them but, as the trip over showed, with a meth head like Glen, anything could happen.

Captain Webber arrived a few minutes later and they parked "Old Blue" in the visitor's lot. He drove them over to the same office Charlie had been in before. Introductions were made, and Webber told them Sierra County detectives were on their way.

"They are very interested in talking to both of you, and asked if we could put you in separate interview rooms. I'm not sure why, but that was their request." Webber damn sure knew why. Even though the pair had had time to cook up a whale of a tale between them, interviewing them separately could poke holes in an impromptu story.

"By the way," Webber said, "we went down and talked to Sam Odgers. He's in the hospital in Las Cruces. Seems he has a concussion, among other things, from the roughing up he got from Glen Ritchey."

Charlie wondered at the time how the authorities had known about Sam, but didn't pay it much mind.

Finally the detectives arrived, and Sergeant Ramirez, Detective Olson and Captain Webber compared notes before interviewing Charlie first. Based on what Odgers had said, it was pretty clear that Charlie was in the clear for any crimes. Still, his statement was very important, because it would either confirm or deny much of what Darrell had to say.

"Captain, I appreciate your cooperation in this matter, but I think Detective Olson and I can handle it from here."

I'm not trying to get in the way of what's clearly a civilian criminal case, but at the same time I have classified information to protect."

"Okay, let's see how it goes. Just let us ask the questions, and only intervene if we get perilously close to the classified edge. Can you live with that?"

"My lips are sealed unless he's close to divulging something classified."

They walked in to Charlie's interview room, and Webber made the introductions. Ramirez was lead interrogator, and walked Charlie through the whole story from the time he first walked up the wash until he arrived at Holloman Air Force Base just a couple of hours ago. Webber didn't have to interrupt Charlie even once. A look of warning was all it took.

"What's Darrell's involvement with Glen and Chip?"

"Darrell was one of Glen's gofers, but didn't like getting involved in robbery and murder. The first chance he had to walk away, he did, he's here willing to cooperate."

"That's commendable," said Ramirez dryly. "How involved was he in the actual killing of the victim in the tent?"

"I don't know. We never got around to talking about that, but my impression was that the man was already dead when Ritchey brought them in."

"What makes you think that?"

"He has never talked about the victim as if he saw him alive; you know, talked with him, watched him work, that sort of thing."

"Okay, Mr. Perkins, do you mind waiting here while we chat with Darrell?"

"Oh no Sir, Glen Ritchey and Chip are still out there somewhere and I'm very pleased to stay right here, believe me."

The three men went next door and Ramirez began the interview in a different tone than he had used with Charlie. He advised Darrell of his rights and had him sign a form acknowledging the rights admonishment, then acquired all the vital statistics for Darrel Roger Cunningham.

Darrell was eager to cooperate. He told them the whole story of meeting Ritchey at the Plugged Nickel and agreeing to throw in with him after he got rid of his partner. He confirmed that when they first went up to the dig, they found the tree on top of Richter's tent, but didn't know anything about there being a body inside until Ritchey told them. He conceded that there was a smell around the tent but that was all.

"What was Ritchey driving?" asked Ramirez.

"He was in an older faded black and silver Chevy S-10 Blazer."

"Did that belong to him or to Richter?"

"I don't know, but if I had to guess I'd say it was Moss's Blazer."

Darrell continued, telling how they watched Charlie working the site and followed him to Las Cruces, where he appeared to sell some gold at Sam's Gold Emporium. When Sam wouldn't tell Ritchey what he wanted to know, Ritchey roughed him up.

Darrell admitted that he and Chip had helped Glen abduct Charlie from his house and that by the time they got to the cabin with their prisoner, Glen was in such a rage that he was talking about killing Charlie whether he talked or produced the gold or not.

When Glen left Darrell to guard Charlie, he knew he couldn't let Charlie be murdered. Beating a guy up was one thing but killing was a different critter altogether. Darrell had tried to get Charlie to give up what Ritchey wanted, but Charlie kept denying he had any money left. When Charlie slipped the handcuffs, Darrell made his decision to leave too, and let Charlie go. All Darrell wanted was to get away from Glen and Chip and get on with his life. Yes, he would cooperate fully and testify, as long as he was protected from Glen Ritchey.

After they left the interview room, Ramirez said: "We're going to have to hold them both as material witnesses. Hell, we can hold Cunningham for kidnapping, burglary, and a whole host of other charges. Perkins doesn't look to be criminally culpable, but you never know until you hear what those other two have to say. Either way, we can't let him go."

"I agree," said Webber. "You can take Cunningham but I need to hold on to Charlie due to the urgency of the project in which he's involved. I don't know if we could get rid of him right now if we wanted to, but I can assure you, he won't be leaving Air Force custody."

"The prosecutor isn't going to like that. Will you make him available to testify if they set up a Grand Jury for this case?"

"We'll honor all subpoenas for Charlie Perkins but try to give us a little lead time if you can."

"Craig, why don't you hook up Mr. Cunningham and search him. Tell him you have to do it for police reasons, but he is being held as a material witness for his own safety more than as a suspect in this case. That should make him feel better about going to jail."

After the Sierra County Sheriff's deputies left, Webber went back into the interview room with Charlie.

He handed Charlie his wallet then said: "Well, the Sheriff's Office is gone, and they took your friend Darrell with them. I've got to keep you here as a material witness in their case until their case is resolved."

Charlie's face turned pale. "You mean I have to go to jail?"

"If you promise to stay on the base and not take off, no. If you can't promise me that, then yes. What I really want to do is take you back over to Las Vegas and have them do some more testing. Have you used your . . . ah . . . abilities since we spoke last?"

Charlie's face turned from pale to a red blush. "A little. I had to get out of the handcuffs a couple of times, and once, I kept Chip from blabbing to Glen about something."

"How did you do that?"

"I just put in a little suggestion that he didn't need to do anything but stand there, and he did."

"That's the kind of stuff I want you tested for. Things like how far away from someone can you be and still introduce a suggestion, how far away can you be and move something with your mind, and how big of an object can you control. Think you'd be up to some testing like that?"

"Only if I don't have to wear hospital clothes and eat their food."

"Deal." Webber chuckled.

After getting Charlie settled at the Holloman Inn, the base transient quarters, Webber called Captain Samantha Chase in Nevada.

"Captain Chase."

"Good afternoon, Captain Chase. This is Captain Webber from Holloman over in New Mexico."

"Oh, yes, Captain, how are things going with Charlie?"

"Interesting, to put it mildly. Do you have a minute to talk?"

"Yes, go ahead."

"What do you know about parapsychology testing?"

"Hmm, that's a tough one. I know there are ongoing studies, that there is a quite a bit of smoke but very little fire, and that officially, the Defense Department holds there is no military use for parapsychology. How am I doing so far?"

"Keep going, you're doing great."

"I know that the Air Force took over investigation into parapsychology from the CIA, specifically remote viewing, in the 1970s, but I think the study is long past. I think there might still be some active studies at Ft. Meade, Maryland, but I don't know the specifics. Why?"

"How comfortable would you be doing some preliminary testing?"

"I can probably handle a deck of Zener cards as well as anyone else. Do you think Charlie has some aptitudes in that area?"

"Let's just say we could sure use some help over here."

"It's really hard for me to get away with a full schedule of appointments. Can you bring your subject here?"

"I'll look into that and call you back."

It took a few calls and transfers around headquarters before Captain Webber had his TDY (Temporary Duty) orders to Nellis.

When Captain Webber and Charlie Perkins sat down in Captain Chase's office, they found themselves in a fairly roomy space with a conventional couch, easy chair, and recliner. Books lined one wall, and in one corner was an old oak teacher's desk that had seen a lot of use. Captain Chase had Charlie sit in the recliner, Captain Webber on the couch, and she used the other chair.

"So it is Charlie you're thinking of testing?"

"Yeah but I didn't want to out and out say it on an unsecured line."

"I see. Charlie, how do you feel about this?"

"Like I told Pete, I'm fine as long as I'm not a patient in the hospital."

Samantha smiled. "I think we can manage that." To Charlie, she asked: "So what makes you think you have parapsychological aptitudes?"

"I'm not sure exactly what the term means, Samantha. I know that I can get a pretty good idea what's in a person's mind by concentrating a little, and I can move stuff around without touching it."

"We just don't know the extent of his abilities," added Pete, "that's what we're here for."

"Charlie, can you give me an example?"

"Well, right now, you're concentrating pretty hard on what I'm saying, but in the back of your mind, you're concerned that this meeting will run over into the appointment for Airman Smithey."

Captain Webber reached up and casually scratched his ear. Charlie said: "I 'suggested' to Pete that he scratch his ear and right now you can't take notes because I have your hand pressing down on your tablet."

Captain Chase's eyes grew wide as she tried to move her hand but couldn't. Seconds later, it was free to move as usual.

"Captain," she asked Webber, "what did you feel when you scratched your ear?"

"Actually, I wasn't even paying attention and didn't really realize I was doing it."

"That's pretty convincing, Charlie. What can't you do?"

"Pete was trying to explain 'remote viewing' to me. I understand it to be, in my case, trying to send my consciousness to another place to see what or who is there, or what is happening there. If that's correct, I don't know if I can do that. He told me about Zenner cards, and I don't know if I can see the cards or just know what the image is from the card holder's mind. I don't think I can pick up things – at least big things."

"Captain Webber, what is your goal regarding the examination of Charlie for parapsychological aptitudes?"

"Well, I did a little online poking around, and learned a little about the Stargate Project which, in one form or another, ran from the middle 70s up through about 1995. A lot of different agencies did a lot of testing and studying, before they allegedly gave up the program. There clearly was a demand for someone demonstrating 'remote viewing' capabilities, but even if Charlie doesn't have that, his other abilities will be worth something to someone. I mean, he's a walking, talking lie detector if nothing else, not to mention his ability to implant a suggestion in the right head or even move the right thing to the right position. He's way past the parlor game level and someone – like the CIA – could use him."

"Charlie, what do you think about that?"

"Pete got a chewing out for not keeping me when I was here last time, although he had good reason not to. The chewer was someone back in Quantico who really had no idea what was really going on out here. I don't know that I want to make a career out of talking to different people about this stuff, but I'd be glad to help out for a while," said Charlie.

"I think what we need to do is some preliminary testing, build a foundation that would stand scrutiny, then attract the attention of people who would be interested. I agree with you, Captain Webber. Somewhere in the Defense Department, there are people who would love to take advantage of Charlie's abilities."

"Charlie, if I put you in a room by yourself and asked you to tell me which Zener card Captain Webber was holding up in another room, could you do it?" asked Captain Chase.

"Oh sure, I just don't know how far away I can do that. And remember, I'll probably be getting the images out of Pete's head, not from the card itself."

"Why don't we find out – but after my last appointment, okay?"

That evening they experimented with different variations of the Zener cards and learned that Charlie was infallible reading them from Captain Webber's mind. Previous test results had been in the five to fifteen percent above average and Charlie had blown them away at one hundred percent. Charlie found that he could detect Captain Webber's thoughts anywhere in the building and, surprising himself, could close a door remotely across the building as well. By the time they finished the door closing experiments, Charlie was tired.

After Charlie had left to go back to the Inn, Captain Chase shook her head and said: "I've never seen anyone like him. He's the real deal."

"You know that if they get him into one of those CIA or NSA-sponsored 'psychic pools', they'll wear him down to nothing. Exhaustion was one of the big problems in the Stargate Program, though few people outside the program realize it. I'd love to save him that grief but I don't know how if we call attention to him. I guess that's why they pay the generals the big bucks."

"He trusts you, that's plain to see."

"Charlie almost got himself killed while he was out on his own. There's a guy out there – two guys actually – who would gun him down just like in the old west if they had the chance. That's always on his mind and one reason he's so ready to go through all this. He figures he's safe on a military base, and he probably is. But he can't stay on base forever, so maybe it would be better for him if we gave him to the 'experts' in D.C. or at Ft. Meade. He'd be safe from a killer that way, but how safe would he be with them?"

The next morning, Captain Webber got a call from Sergeant Ramirez. They had found Charlie's Jeep in Hillsboro and the cabin he had described, but there was no sign of Glen Ritchey or Chip Lakin. The prosecutor had convened a Grand Jury, and Charlie would be needed to testify tomorrow afternoon.

Charlie was on edge when they landed in Las Cruces the next morning. He kept looking around, and his eyes were never still as they walked the concourse to the baggage claim. Neither had a bag to claim, but it was easier to meet the Air Force car there than where new passengers were arriving. Webber noticed that the driver and escort were both Air Police, in plain clothes and both were armed – the Air Police, at least, was taking the threat seriously. After picking up the two men they headed directly to the Sierra County Courthouse in Truth or Consequences where, upon arrival, the driver stayed with the car and the escort accompanied them to the prosecutor's office.

"Try to relax, Charlie," said Captain Webber as they waited outside the Grand Jury room. "Those guys are long gone. They wouldn't dare hang around here now."

"Something tells me they aren't far," Charlie replied, looking down the hallway, "I mean, it's like their comfort zone, they know the terrain and the people better here."

"Is that a hunch or a sure thing like we were working on last night?"

"Just a very strong feeling."

"You'd be the last guy I would argue with."

When finished testifying, they went to the Sheriff's Office, where Ramirez gave Charlie a release for the Jeep. "It's out back," he said. "Do you have keys for it?"

"Yeah, I have a lockout key under the back bumper."

The Jeep was a mess of disturbed mining equipment and black fingerprint powder. They wiped it off as well as they could, then Charlie got in and started it. He looked up at Captain Webber standing at the door and asked: "Okay if we go by my place and clean out whatever is left? I know everybody and his dog have been through there, but I left some clothes and equipment that I'd like to get back."

Webber looked at the two Air Policemen, who both nodded an assent, and they set off, with Charlie leading and an Air Policeman escort sitting beside him in the Jeep. The back door at the house was still broken and standing open. Apparently Glen Ritchey was the last person through the front door and for some reason had locked it, using Charlie's keys. All four men went in through the back, and Charlie looked around at the mess.

"I should clean this up some. I rented the place furnished, and I'm sure as hell not going to get my cleaning deposit back if they see it in this shape. Mind if I do a little tidying up while I'm getting the rest of my stuff?"

No one expressed opposition. Captain Webber helped where he could, but the two Air Policemen remained steadfastly vigilant for any vehicles or pedestrians coming by. Thirty minutes later found things in the tiny house back in reasonably good order. Charlie packed what clothes and possessions were left into a couple of garbage bags. While he was packing, he stood up, looked over to Webber, and asked: "You still have that pack I left in your car?"

"Yes, it's in one of my desk drawers. You probably shouldn't be leaving your savings passbook lying around like that. I didn't know who the pack belonged to at first, so I looked for ID and found the passbook. But don't worry, it's safe and locked up."

"Good, if Glen had found that, he would have shot me on the spot. He has it in his head that's his gold I sold, and nothing is going to change his mind."

As they prepared to go, Charlie asked another question, this one tightened the jaws of the policemen: "I'd like to drive around a little. Just to get a feel for what's going on. I don't necessarily need to go into anyplace, but sometimes I can get a taste for what's going on just by being nearby, and I still have that feeling Glen isn't far away."

Reluctantly, the police officers acquiesced, but one still insisted on riding shotgun in the Jeep. Charlie drove through the parking lot at Hodges Restaurant, but didn't stop. He did the same thing in two or three other locations in Elephant Butte before heading back toward T or C. There, the first place he drove to was the Plugged Nickel Saloon. He and stopped in the parking lot and his escort got out with him. They went into the tavern, but weren't in there more than five minutes.

Charlie walked over to Webber's window, which was rolled down. "He's been around here within the past few days or a week. I can sense him, kind of like an old scent, but he's not far. The bartender said he saw both of them together in there sometime last week."

Webber made sure to pass that on to the Sheriff's Office. It was the only place they checked that Charlie got a "scent", but that was enough. An hour later, they were well on their way back to Holloman.

When they returned, and Webber dismissed the Air Policemen, he asked: "Do you want to go back to Vegas this evening or tomorrow?"

"We might as well go back tomorrow, Samantha won't have time for us before tomorrow evening."

CHAPTER 9

Glen Ritchey's ire sparked around him like embers from a grinding wheel and that bastard Charlie Perkins was to blame! Ritchey swore he'd never rest until he got even with Perkins by getting his gold back and by killing the worthless piece of shit. That Perkins had escaped, turned one of his men against him, and probably called the law down on them just made it worse. Here he was holed up in another rat-infested shack – this one in Cuchillo – instead of enjoying the easy life was nearly too much to bear.

On top of that, he was almost broke. He had sent Chip into T or C with one of his last twenties in the old pickup to get some smokes, beer, and maybe something from McDonalds. The pickup was a problem too. Not only was it distinctive by being so loud, the cops probably had the license number and would grab whoever was in it at the first opportunity. That's one reason he sent Chip instead of going himself. Chip was dumber than a box of cottage cheese but at least he did what Glen told him to do without arguing like Darrell used to do. Now Glen had to come up with some scheme to get his hands on some money.

More than anything else, he had to find out where Perkins was hanging out. That would solve all his problems at once. He was pretty sure Perkins had moved out of the little house in Elephant Butte. Someone had straightened it up and taken all Perkins's clothes and mining equipment. He wasn't even sure he was in T or C and just as easily could be in Cruces or even El Paso. Glen dreamed about finding him on the road somewhere without a lot of people around where he could finish him off at his leisure.

But first things first. They had to get some money and a different set of wheels. He guessed they would have to pull some robberies. Not that he had any qualms about doing them. It was just more risky with a moron for backup. First they would hit a few houses to see if they could come up with a gun for Chip and maybe a few loose dollars. Once they were both armed, they could hit some places that had some real money and get rid of the pickup. *Damn that Charlie Perkins!* It was all his fault.

When Chip returned, they chased down Big Macs with a couple of beers, then Glen asked: "How much gas is in the truck?"

"About half a tank."

"Let's go for a drive."

Glen directed Chip to drive them out Palomas Creek. They drove slowly down the winding road until he told Chip to turn off on a side road to the left, then turn again into the first driveway. It was exactly what he was looking for: a single house, obscured from the road. Now to see if anyone was home.

They pulled up next to the concrete pad and Glen got out and went to the front door. Chip stayed in the truck with the engine running. Glen rang the bell then knocked, but no one came to the door. He tried the knob, finding it locked. He smiled, then concentrated on the lock for a moment then the door swung open. He motioned for Chip to follow him as he entered the foyer of the upper middle class dwelling.

"We don't have much time. Go find the den or wherever the desk is and go through that. Keep an eye out for a cash box or something like that but remember, we're here only for cash and a gun, okay? I don't want to have to try to fence anything else."

Chip nodded and sprinted by Glen, who just shook his head. He followed the foyer into the living room and then into a hallway, where he found the master bedroom. With practiced precision, he rifled the dresser drawers, then went to the nightstands, where he scored with a small, .38 caliber revolver, which he put in his back pocket. He skimmed through the shelves in the closet but found nothing like a stash of cash, or even a collection of coins. He headed back to the entry, calling Chip's name as he went. Chip popped his head out of another room at the far end of the house and looked questioningly at him.

"Find anything?" Glen asked as he continued toward the foyer.

"No cash or guns, but they have a great liquor selection."

"Goddamnit Chip, I said money or guns, nothing else, now let's get the hell out of here." He headed for the door then stopped and and handed Chip the revolver. "Here, put it in your pocket and don't take it out unless I tell you to."

Chip took the gun by two fingers as if it was a dead rat. Gingerly, he slid it into a back pocket, and they headed back to the pickup.

They cruised further up Palomas Creek Road and hit five more houses before finally discovering a small cache of three hundred dollars in a jewelry box in the fifth. There were pearls and several valuable-looking rings. Once again Glen had to remind Chip to leave everything but the money. On the way back to Cuchillo they stopped at McDonald's again and for some more beer.

"I know sometimes it's tempting when you see good shit, but you gotta remember that you have to find somebody you can trust to sell it to, or they'll give you up in a minute. If you can't find somebody, the stuff just sits, or you have to throw it out just to get away from it. Most guys I know keep stuff around their place, never bothering enough to try to sell or trade it, and it eventually gets them into trouble. Besides that, we have to move light. The cops have to be onto us by now, so we need to keep moving around until we find Perkins and Darrell. Once I do those two bastards and even up the score, I can take off and go someplace where the heat isn't on."

"How did you get into those houses, Glen? I can't believe they were all unlocked, but you opened the doors like they were."

"I'm not sure about, that but all I did was imagine the bolts being pushed back in the lock, and they opened. I did the same thing with that jewelry box where we found the money. Sure beats the hell out of kicking or prying."

The next day they cruised around Elephant Butte and T or C looking for easy targets to rob. "You want a place that's got some cash, or it's a waste of time and risky. You don't want to go to the big places like WalMart, because they have so many cameras and security. If you're going to take on a place like that, you need to have a crew to help you do it." He snapped his fingers. "I know just the place – no, maybe not. He's got guns and to hear him talk he's used them before."

"Where?"

"The old KOA there at the Hillsboro exit."

"Oh, you mean Jim. Yeah, I shouldn't rob him, he done me favors a couple of times."

"One thing you gotta understand, Chip. This is business, not personal. We're not robbing Jim because he'll shoot back, not because he's a friend. He has money there, but it's not worth one of us getting shot. See, the idea is to get in and get out without anyone getting hurt. You kill somebody and the stakes get a lot higher. We save the shooting for when I find that asshole, Perkins."

They settled on one of the gas stations in Williamsburg. Glen made Chip go in first and demand money. The clerk put the money in a plastic bag, but there were only a few bills.

"Where's the rest of it? I know you take in more money than this," Chip snarled, waving the handgun in the clerk's face.

"Anything over fifty dollars I have to put in the night deposit slot in the safe. If the manager found more than that in the till I'd get fired."

"Open the safe!"

"I can't, I swear!"

"Let it go, man," said Glen softly to his partner. There's no getting blood out of a turnip."

They yanked the telephone off the wall and trussed the clerk up with duct tape, then split. As they hit the freeway going north, Chip was in a snit. "Why did you give up so easy? He could have opened the safe."

"No, he couldn't. I forgot about the night deposit thing. Most of the chain stations went to that a long time ago. He didn't have anything left to give us, or he would have." Glen wondered how he knew that, but he was sure he was right; it was as if the clerk had told him.

"Well, now what? That wasn't hardly worth the effort."

"Yeah, we'll just have to hit another place."

"How about the tavern down in Arrey?"

"Nah, they hardly have any traffic except for a few locals. I don't want to do another one around T or C. Once that clerk gets loose and calls in, it'll be like we kicked over a hornet's nest. I don't want to do one in Hatch because I have other plans for there. Let's go down to Cruces and try one of those Mom and Pop mini-mart stations on the north end of town."

Chip cut across the median in a spray of gravel and pointed them south, the inside of the truck rumbled and shook so badly they couldn't talk.

They turned off at Doña Ana, just north of Las Cruces proper, and arbitrarily chose a station just off the freeway. Glen led the way this time, but didn't even draw his weapon. The clerk's eyes grew wide when he looked directly at her. She hurriedly emptied the cash register into a bag but there wasn't much more cash than the previous station. When Glen stared hard at her, she reached under the counter and brought out a bulging bank bag.

"I was going to make a bank deposit at the end of my shift," she said almost apologetically. Glen nodded, and walked out of the store with Chip trotting at his heels.

"Aren't you gonna gag her or tie her up or nothin'?"

"Don't need to. She won't call for at least twenty minutes and will have no idea of what we're driving."

By the time the twenty minutes had elapsed, they were almost to Rincon. Chip heaved a sigh of relief. "How did you do that? You didn't say a word to her."

"I don't know for sure, but she knew what I wanted and she knew I was serious. That's why she cooperated. Whatever. Let's get an eightball of crank and party!"

Chip knew of a meth dealer in Hatch, so they paused there and scored an eighth of an ounce. Both promptly shot up, using the same needle, and Chip quickly got a buzz but Glen was disappointed. "That shit didn't do anything for me," he protested angrily. "I think we got ripped off."

"No," said Chip with a stupid grin, "it was good stuff, I promise. I'm feeling great."

"Then what the hell?"

"You wanna try some stuff from someone else?" Chip asked, "I know of a couple of places in T or C."

"Hell yeah. I want to get high too."

Chip scored again, this time near the high school in T or C and Glen shot up again with the same results.

"Well Goddamn! What the hell is going on?"

"That dude's dope has always been excellent. It must be something else."

"I don't know but I do know I'd better not try a third time or I might overdose."

They drove down to the Plugged Nickel and saw the rigs of several of their acquaintances.

Just as Chip was getting ready to turn into the parking lot, Glen stopped him. "Let's drive by Perkins's place, just in case."

Chip knew it would be a mistake to argue, so he drove the speed limit through T or C, then opened it up a little between town and Elephant Butte. "It ain't no use, Glen. You know he moved out of that house."

"Yeah, I know, but you never know who might show up out of the blue, and I really want to get my hands on that bastard and your old buddy, Darrell."

"We don't know but what Charlie set Darrell up and sicced the law on him."

"Darrell never did like what we were doing with Charlie, that much is for sure, and that's enough for me to know he double-crossed us."

As expected, the driveway was empty at Charlie's old place, and the house was dark. They returned to the Plugged Nickel and went in. Several fellow prospectors nodded or said hello as they walked in. Glen went right to the bartender.

"Hey, you seen Charlie Perkins in here lately?"

"Once, about a week ago. Said he was lookin' for you."

"Is that so? Well if you see him again, tell him I'm waitin'."

"Is there some bad blood between you two? I don't want to get in the middle of something that's gonna bring trouble down on the place, know what I mean?"

"Yeah, don't worry about it. It's a matter just between him and me."

During the course of the evening, Glen managed to ask every one of their associates, but no one but the bartender had seen Charlie or Darrell.

Just before closing time, Clyde Driscoll walked in amid a few hoots and whistles. He had been doing six months in the county jail for a probation violation, and had just been released. Someone bought him a beer, and he made the rounds of the tables of prospectors and their buddies.

When he got to Glen's table he stopped and said hello. "Say, I see your partner is in the lockup."

Chip glanced at Glen, then replied: "Darrell's in jail? What for?"

"Nobody knows. They're keeping him by himself, and I only seen him twice when they had him by himself in the exercise yard. You don't know what he's in for?" asked Clyde.

"Nope. He just disappeared a week or so ago and we haven't seen or heard from him since. Guess that explains it," said Chip with a shrug.

"Any idea how long he's gonna be in there?" Glen prodded.

"No idea. Like I said, I just seen him the two times and I didn't get to talk to him."

Clyde moved on to talk to other friends, and Chip looked at Glen and said: "Well, that puts Darrell's status in a whole different perspective, don't it?"

Glen took his beer bottle by the neck and took a long swallow. "Maybe so, maybe not. I'm almost tempted to get arrested so I can get at him, except I don't want to find out the hard way this new technique I've found doesn't work on jail, doors, y'know?"

They closed up the Plugged Nickel and Chip drove them, albeit a little erratically, back toward Cuchillo. He must have had enough beer to overcome the meth, because he went right to sleep the minute his head hit the pillow.

The next morning they went into T or C and stopped at Denny's for breakfast.

"I think we'll head . . ." Glen stopped all of a sudden when the waitress came and filled their coffee cups. When she left, he continued: "I think we'll try one of the banks down in Hatch. We'll hit 'em when they first open up, when the drawers are full of cash. And maybe the vault will be open too."

"Jeez, Glen, we're talking federal time here!"

"We need more than the fifteen hundred we got last night," he said, color rising up his neck. His voice was a little more belligerent when he continued: "We need a big score, and we need to find that fucking Perkins. Then we can blow this country. I don't know where Perkins is, but I know how to score big, and that's with a bank. If you don't want in, just say so."

"No, no, I'm in, Glen," Chip placated, "it's just that I've never been in a position where I might have to do federal time."

"Hell, it ain't that different. Some of the federal prisons are all right compared to the state ones. Unless you wind up in one of the maximum security jobs, which are a bitch."

"What does it take to go to one of the maximum security places?"

"Oh hell, you have to be a repeat repeat offender – three strikes and all that – or you have to kill someone. That means if we kill someone during a bank robbery, that's where we'll likely wind up. Unless it's a death penalty case which I think killing someone during a robbery is."

"Jesus Christ! I'm not sure I want any part of that!" Chip looked around to make sure no one had heard him, then stared at Glen.

"Relax. First, you gotta get caught, and second, with the way I do a job, there's hardly a chance of even needing the guns, much less having one go off."

"Maybe I better leave my piece in the pickup."

"Wouldn't matter. If I kill somebody, you'll be charged the same as me because you were doing the job with me."

"Maybe we should just go in unarmed and fake weapons and use a note."

"I don't need a note, remember? And I'm damn sure not going into a robbery without some way to protect myself. Now, are you in or out? We gotta get going. The banks'll be opening soon."

"Okay, okay, just don't shoot nobody, all right?"

"Yeah. I'll keep that in mind," Glen said dryly.

They filled up the pickup with gas and oil and headed south on the freeway. Traffic was light – as usual. Neither man noticed that there wasn't a cloud in the sky and it would be a perfect summer day – for some.

They parked around the corner on a side street from the Citizen's Bank and walked toward the entrance. They put on their sunglasses and pulled their hats down low, then entered the bank. There were only two female tellers, but only one window was open. The other teller was on the phone. There was one other woman at a desk behind and to the right of the two windows, and she appeared to be reading a document and paying them no attention.

Glen waited for the second teller to get off the phone, then his first thought to the women was "freeze" followed by "this is a robbery. No alarms and no one gets hurt." All three women stopped any motion. He motioned for Chip to go around behind the tellers as

Glen verbally directed the women to put the money in the pillow case and emphasized: "no dye packs and no transmitters, or I'll be back, and somebody will die".

Glen told the woman behind the desk to open the vault. She got up and went to a stainless steel barred door behind her. The main vault door was standing open. She unlocked the barred door with a key and swung it open. Chip didn't hesitate to escort the woman into the vault with him and Glen could hear murmuring as Chip had the woman place several bundles of cash into the bag. When he saw no more money out in the open in the vault, Chip returned to where Glen was standing. The pillow case bulged with money. Glen's last thoughts to the women were to not call the police for twenty minutes, and that they all had no idea what, if any, vehicle the two robbers had come in.

They walked out the door as sedately as they had walked in, went around the corner, and drove off in Darrell's noisy pickup.

"I can't believe that was so easy," said Chip, "There must have been at least ten or fifteen thousand in the vault, along with what was in the tellers' drawers."

"Just keep that bag down by your feet and closed for now, in case they put a dye pack in there anyway. Take Highway 187 back up toward Salem. We'll stay off the freeway for a while. I think we now have enough cash to stay in something a little better than the shack, so where will it be?"

"How about the one where Denny's is? That looked like a nice place. Uh, shouldn't we have some luggage or something?"

"Nah, we look like prospectors, and they won't expect us to have suitcases and shit like that. I've gone in to them before, when I was flush and just paid cash. Nothing was said because I didn't have luggage. They knew I was just staying a couple of nights and wouldn't make no trouble. Stay in the truck and I'll get the room, then they probably won't even see you come in with the bag anyway."

It went down just like Glen said it would. He met Chip in the parking lot with the key to an outside room and they went in.

*****

"Pete? Before we go back to Las Vegas, do you think we could do a few experiments of our own?" Charlie asked as they were driving back to the base from T or C.

"What did you have in mind?"

"When I was sitting there in that cabin up in Hillsboro, handcuffed to the bedpost, I knew I had to at least try to escape because if I didn't, Glen would kill me as soon as he finished getting the information he wanted. Now, I'm as stout as the next man, and have been in a few scrapes in my life, but I'm no fighter. I figured I could physically handle Chip by himself, but not with the others around. I thought I could use this 'mind over matter' ability I had to unlock the handcuffs, but I didn't know what else I could do with it. I would have hated to get into a situation where I was depending on that ability to convince someone not to shoot me, only to find out it didn't work. Does that make any sense?"

"Sure it does. You want to know – ahead of time – to what extent your new abilities enhance your natural ones. Kind of like knowing how far and how accurately your gun will shoot before you need it."

"That's right. I was kind of thinking . . . well, your people, the ones who showed up with you up in the wash, don't they do regular physical training? Defensive tactics, hand-to-hand, that sort of stuff?"

"Yes, they do PT every morning. Why?"

"I was wondering if they would help me find out what I can and can't do. I don't want anyone to get hurt, of course, but it would certainly be helpful if I knew I could stop Glen from shooting me before I had to find out the hard way."

"Let me go talk to the squad and see if we can come up with some reasonable scenarios that will help you. What about your power to suggest something in order to deter someone from doing something? I assume you'd like to try that out too?"

"If they're willing. By interjecting a thought into their minds, I don't think I'm hurting anyone or permanently damaging them, am I?"

"I suppose if your ability was highly developed and you really bore down on someone, you might be able to permanently affect them, but not in the sense we're talking about. I'll call Captain Chase and get her opinion though."

When they got back to the base, Captain Webber dropped Charlie off at the Inn and drove on to his own office. He saw that he had a message from Detective Sergeant Ramirez asking him to call, and one from Captain Chase as well.

He called the psychologist first. "Captain Chase? Captain Webber. Hey, do you think we've worked together long enough to eliminate the formal 'Captain' when we're talking privately or with Charlie?"

She laughed. "I've been wondering why we've let it go so long, I suspect that we wanted to look professional in front of Charlie, but I don't think that matters. I'm Samantha or Sam, either one."

"I'm Pete. Anyway, Charlie has come up with a request and I wanted to run it by you." He explained what he and Charlie had talked about, and wondered if there was any potential for permanent damage or injury.

"I can't see how. Then again, none of us knows the extent of his abilities. How strong or overwhelming are his powers? I would say go ahead, but have him keep it in the back of his mind that he might have the potential to physically or psychically hurt someone."

"Great. The squad is already cleared for this level of security, so we won't be pushing the envelope at all. Changing the subject, we went to Grand Jury today; I have a message from Sergeant Ramirez that probably has to do with murder warrants now outstanding for Glen Ritchey and Chip Lakin."

"Well, that's a step in the right direction. To change the subject again, my bosses have developed quite an interest in Charlie and want him in DC, ASAP. I don't think that means that we need to put him in the next jet fighter heading east, but we probably shouldn't wait too long."

"I don't know whether Charlie will go for that or not. The longer Ritchey and Lakin are on the loose, the more his concern about them will ease. Eventually, I think he'll decide they've left the country and he'll want to get on with his life. And I won't blame him a bit."

"Why don't you broach the subject with him? I'm not sure he'll be coming back here but I suspect I'll be joining him in DC." Samantha suggested.

"I suspect I will be too. I understand I'm to consider myself his personal aide."

"Okay, then I'll see you whenever."

"Bye."

Webber next called his squad together. They were still working on trying to penetrate the probe and were no farther along than when they started. He explained the idea of "working out" with Charlie and the reason for it. The squad was unanimously in favor of doing it the next morning.

Next he called Sergeant Ramirez. "Hello, Captain, thanks for calling me back. I just wanted you to know the Grand Jury did indict Ritchey and Lakin on a whole fistful of charges, including murder, and the warrants are outstanding as we speak."

"Does anyone have the time to actively search for them, assuming they're still in the area?"

"We'll get the word out to the patrol people, especially since there's a vehicle involved, but we're so short on people, that's about the extent of it. Matter of fact, over the last couple of days, Sierra and Doña Ana Counties have had a spate of odd robberies that are sort of taking precedence. I personally think it's Ritchey and Lakin."

"Why odd?"

"The first one, in Williamsburg, was just a regular robbery. The shorter of the two suspects was holding a small revolver and nervous as hell. When the clerk could only produce about fifty dollars, he got really angry, until the taller one with the deep voice stepped in and confirmed what the clerk was saying about night deposits in a safe that the clerk couldn't open. They trussed the clerk up with duct tape and he didn't see a vehicle."

"The next two, another gas station/market just north of Las Cruces and a bank in Hatch the next day were the weird ones. No one can remember what the suspects looked like or what kind of vehicle they had. They just know that two men entered the premises and the clerk in the gas station handed over the money plus a night deposit bag without a word being said. It was pretty much the same at the bank, except the short one managed to get into the vault and copped about twenty thousand in cash. Nothing was said, no weapons were shown, and no one can remember what the guys looked like or what they drove. Pretty weird about nothing being said and everyone's memory being bad."

Webber's mind was racing. Could it be? "Interesting. It looks like we're probably going to have to take Charlie to Washington, D.C. pretty soon. Does that present a problem?"

"Not unless we can't get him back when this goes to trial."

"Okay, I'll keep you apprised."

*****

Since they "owned" the entire hangar, the squad put down some tumbling mats before they began their usual physical training. When Charlie and the Captain came in, they were well warmed up and waiting.

"I'd appreciate any input you guys might have about how to go about this," said Charlie. "I'd love to come away from here knowing if I can stop a gun from being fired. Not stop the bullet, I know better than that, but keep the hammer from dropping, or even prevent the gun from being drawn from a holster. Did anyone bring a weapon?"

The squad had come prepared and produced six practice handguns that would fire on empty cylinders with no firing pins. They tried a variety of ways to "shoot" Charlie and he was able to disable one, two, even three weapons at once but after that, it was too much for him to concentrate on. The same was true of hand-to-hand combat. He could control up to three of the rushing squad members, but if more tried, Charlie landed at the bottom of the pile with everyone laughing.

Finally, Charlie tried his ability to insert a suggestion into their heads. He was sure of controlling at least two of the squad, but more than that was iffy. Again he wound up on the bottom of the pile.

When it was over, Charlie felt a little more confident about what he could do and what he'd better not try. When Pete brought up the subject of going to Washington, D. C., Charlie put his foot down.

"No, I don't believe I want to go to Washington, D.C., at least under these circumstances. I'd be like a lab rat that everyone is curious about until their curiosity was satisfied. Then they'd keep me there until they 'experimented' me to death, and I don't want that. They want to come out here, or to Samantha's lab, I'm willing to go along, at least for a while, but I don't want to go to D.C."

Charlie was pleased to hear that the warrants were out on Ritchey and Lakin, and vowed to "check" for them every time he found himself in their possible territory. Webber didn't like the idea of Charlie going to T or C by himself, even if only to go to his credit union. But Charlie wanted to pay the credit union a visit before they went back to Nevada.

*****

The next morning found Ritchey and Lakin parked across Date Street from the Black Range Federal Credit Union. They were backed up to an abandoned service station, in the shade, and were watching the traffic in and out of the credit union when it first opened. There wasn't much. It was now nearly nine o'clock in the morning and only two customers had entered then left the credit union.

"This would be a good place to hit if it wasn't for the double curb in the middle of Date Street. That makes it impossible for someone to get across from our side of the highway or for someone coming out of the parking lot to turn north. It really cuts down on our ability to get out of town and away from the responding cops in a hurry," said Ritchey watching the cars drive by.

Suddenly he sat upright in the seat. "Did you see that?"

"See what?" asked Chip Lakin.

"That looked like Perkins going into the credit union."

"You sure?"

"No, or we'd be on our way over there already," said Ritchey, his agitation going from zero to sixty in less than two seconds. "Start the truck and be ready to move. If it's him, this is our chance."

Charlie Perkins sauntered out of the credit union about fifteen minutes later. He was reading a piece of paper as he walked back to Pete Webber's personal gray, late model Yukon.

"Banking all done?" asked Pete.

"Yeah, for now. Thanks for driving me over."

"Well, I don't think your Jeep should be seen over here and I didn't want you to go by yourself."

"It *is* him!" bellowed Glen. "Get over there behind them as they pull out of the lot. That rat bastard has over eighty thousand dollars of my money! He was reading a withdrawal slip what his balance was . . ."

"Glen! I can't drive over the curbs, I'd get high centered. I have to go up and make a U-turn."

"Well then hurry up and do it, they're getting away."

Webber had pulled his Yukon out onto Date heading south. He was moving leisurely, in no real hurry to get back to the base.

He reached the first left turn lane through the curbs and did a u-turn so he could go north on Date, then catch I-25 back toward Las Cruces.

Chip had made his own u-turn, so he was now southbound on Date approaching the credit union parking lot.

"There! Up ahead, making a Goddamn u-turn!" yelled Glen. "Get up there, get behind them."

The Yukon made its way through traffic and turned onto the southbound ramp onto I-25. The old Chevy pickup got caught up in traffic and had to wait to make the u-turn, driving Glen further insane. He pounded the dash in frustration. Finally Chip found a hole in traffic and cut closely in front of an oncoming car, causing the driver to lay on his horn. Glen was tempted to point his gun at the motorist, but flipped him off instead. Chip started weaving through cars, trying to catch up with the Yukon, but it was momentarily lost from view.

"Don't lose them," Glen bellowed.

"Okay, which way did they go, north or south?" asked Lakin when they neared the interstate interchange.

"Go south, go south!" yelled Glen. "There's nothing to the north. They had to have gone south."

Chip passed by the northbound onramp and squealed onto the ramp going the other direction on I-25. They had to go uphill on the ramp, so they couldn't see cars ahead of them on the freeway. Chip passed a semi on the ramp and finally made it to the top of the grade. Both men looked anxiously ahead to see if they could spot the Yukon.

"There!" exclaimed Glen pointing, "in the left lane just passing that pickup with the trailer." The Yukon didn't appear to be going any faster than the seventy-five-mile-an-hour speed limit and Chip quickly had the pickup up to eighty-five and climbing in an effort to overtake their prey.

It seemed to Glen that the gap would never close between the two vehicles. The Yukon kept passing slower traffic, then signaling back into the outside lane as the pickup slowly gained on them.

"Can't you make this thing go any faster?" yelled Glen, who by now had his gun out and was nervously spinning the cylinder.

"My foot's on the firewall and it ain't gonna last long. Look at the smoke we're blowin'."

Glen glanced behind them and saw that they were trailing a huge black-blue cloud of smoke that seemed to linger in the air until penetrated by another car.

"Just get up alongside them. I'll take care of that bastard once and for all."

"Good grief," said Webber, looking in his rear view mirror. "Someone's in a powerful hurry, look at the smoke he's blowing, cutting in and out of traffic and going like hell. That's gotta be Darrell's pickup!"

Charlie glanced around behind them then did a double take. "Damn it! That's Darrell's truck blowing the smoke all right and Glen and Chip are in it. They know we're up here!"

Pete's lips drew into a grim line as he nudged the Yukon up closer to the slower moving vehicle in front of them. "I can't go any faster until I get around these slower cars!"

They were in the inside lane behind a string of four cars following a semi-truck and trailer that was trying to pass two more semis in the outside lane. The outside lane, behind the semis was clear, but there was no way to get around them from that position either.

The truck ahead of them seemed to take forever to get around the other two trucks and none of the cars between Pete's Yukon and the passing truck seemed inclined to pull into the outside lane and let them pass.

"Can you pass them on the shoulder, Pete? "Glen and Chip are closing fast."

"Not with the semi in front of us hugging the fog line," Pete said grimly. "Once they get up into this group, they won't be able to go any faster than we are."

The gap between the two vehicles, both in the inside lane, finally narrowed to five cars.

Once Chip had tried to overtake the cars in front of him by swerving into the outside lane but the cars in the inside lane closed ranks and wouldn't let him in so he lagged back until he could cut in front of three of the five cars.

Finally the semi in front of them cleared the two trucks in the outside lane and pulled back over in front of them. Slowly, the cars in front of Pete and Charlie started to speed up and pass the line of semis. Most then pulled back over into the outside lane ahead of the lead truck.

The Yukon had passed three of the cars ahead of them as they moved into the outside lane but there was one slow poke in the fast lane that refused to get over and the Yukon had to slow down. The pickup was able to make up ground and got right on their rear bumper.

"Get around them on the right!" ordered Glen. "That's him in the passenger seat; I'll shoot him through the glass."

As they passed the Palomas Creek exit, the Yukon edged up behind the slowpoke. Space in the outside lane was opening up and Pete debated trying to pass the slower car on the right but just as he started to make the lane change, Chip did it first but then the slowpoke signaled a lane change into the outside lane in front of them. Chip came up behind him fast, and before the Yukon could accelerate away, Chip and Glen drew up almost alongside them almost rear ending the slowpoke who had just turned into the outside lane.

"Open your window!" Ritchey roared; leaning over, gun in hand, toward Chip's window.

There was a pregnant pause as everyone waited for the gunshot . . . that never came. The Yukon pulled away and kept pulling away as its digital speedometer reached one hundred.

"Why didn't you shoot?" screeched Chip.

"Why didn't he shoot?" asked Pete.

"The fucking trigger . . . I couldn't pull the trigger," yelled Glen, beside himself with rage and frustration.

"I stopped him from pulling the trigger," said Charlie calmly. "I just imagined my finger was between the back of the trigger and the trigger guard and he couldn't pull it. Just like we did in practice yesterday."

"We're not going to catch him now Glen, why didn't you shoot?"

Now Glen's mouth was a thin line. "I know why and it won't happen again."

"So you caused his gun to misfire?" asked Webber.

"No, I just wouldn't let him pull the trigger. But that won't work a second time," said Charlie, his mind somewhere else.

"Why not? It seemed like a pretty effective trick to me."

"Because Glen knows. Glen has been in the probe too. I can feel him."

CHAPTER 10

Nothing was said for the next several miles as Captain Webber tried to get his mind wrapped around the bombshell Charlie had just dropped on him. Charlie, for his part, was trying to anticipate all the bad things that could happen as a result of his revelation.

Webber started slowing the Yukon down to normal speed at about the time they passed the exit to Rincon, though he kept an eagle eye in his rear view mirror for the smoking monster that had almost killed them.

"Is there a chance you could be wrong?" asked Captain Webber bleakly.

"None. Glen was controlling Chip as he drove and wouldn't let him pull over even though the truck was going to self-destruct any second. He was also trying to get me to open my window so he'd have a better shot. He was in the probe before I was, but he's still not sure what's happening to him though he's starting to get the idea."

"Is he stronger than you?"

"His emotion is stronger than mine. He really hates me, and that's what's driving him. He knows now that the money I have in the credit union came from mining the gold up that wash, and he'll be convinced it belongs to him until the day he dies."

"You realize we can't let the local authorities try to take him in. To start with, they wouldn't even get close before he slaughtered them, and second, how could they contain him even if they got him under control?"

"I've been thinking the same thing. There isn't a pair of handcuffs, flex ties, or rope that he couldn't free himself from, and no jail cell lock he couldn't get through in a blink of an eye."

"This could easily get out of hand, Charlie. You're our best hope of working through the problem and getting this guy off the street before a lot of people get hurt."

As soon as they returned to Holloman Air Force Base, Webber called an emergency meeting of the security and base commanders that included OSI Headquarters on a scrambled line.

"How did this happen, Captain?" asked the two-star in Quantico, General Riley.

"General, we learned of this man's abilities quite by accident. He tried to shoot our subject while we were returning from Truth or Consequences. We knew he was after our man, but we had no idea he had developed the same telepathic and telekinetic abilities our man has. He must have been inside the probe before our man was and is only now beginning to realize the extent of his abilities."

"Can't we just dart him and keep him under sedation until we figure out a more secure way to hold him?" asked Colonel Whitehead, Chief of Security for the base.

"Charlie Perkins – our man - says that his body autonomically neutralizes any substance introduced into his body, be it biological or chemical."

"I'd like to see him neutralize about four nine millimeter slugs," growled Whitehead.

"That, of course, is our final option, Colonel," said the General, "I'm hoping you gentlemen can come up with a less permanent answer before that becomes necessary. Captain, do you think that psychologist, Captain Chase, would be of any help?"

"Very likely, Sir. Though this man is a whole different personality type than our man, she has a pretty good handle on why they're doing what they're doing, and would be in a position to anticipate reactions far better than anyone here right now."

"So how do we keep the local authorities from getting themselves killed?" asked the General commanding Holloman.

"We need to take this guy quickly and quietly out of the picture before anything else happens," said Colonel Whitehead. "My SWAT team is ready to roll at a moment's notice."

"Um, isn't bank robbery under the purview of the FBI?"

"Usually," said Colonel Whitehead, "but by the time they get a tactical team on the scene, it'll be all over."

"Something about a military operation on domestic soil, Colonel?" asked General Riley.

"Sir, I think we can argue successfully that this falls under the category of national security, which takes precedence over anyone's territory."

"Very well," said General Riley, "run with it Colonel. In the meantime, Captain Webber, I want you and this Captain Chase to put together a profile of this man."

*****

Glen sat seething while Chip put more oil in the smoking and heat-ticking pickup. *So Charlie has the touch, huh? We'll see who's toughest and next time I won't miss.* In the few seconds that their consciounesses melded, Glen saw Charlie in the probe, scared to death as the blue ring circled and circled like a shark getting ready to strike. Charlie seemed to be more aware of what was going on than Glen but there wasn't time to probe further to find out about the gold, where Charlie had been, and who he was with.

He had no idea how to go about finding Charlie Perkins except by watching the Black Range Federal Credit Union, which he didn't expect Charlie would be coming back to any time soon. There were too many other ways to get money out of an account without going to the home branch. As a matter of fact, Glen was getting close to using one – again.

When Chip got back in the pickup, he looked over at Glen. "Now what?"

"We get rid of this fucking piece of shit truck, that's what. Keep heading for Cruces. We'll find something down there."

By the time they got to Radium Springs, Glen had mellowed out some, but Chip's guard was still up.

"Pull into the WalMart parking lot on Lohman. We'll walk around until we find something. I'd jack something but it would call too much attention to the car, so let's just find something a little older that we can boost and get the hell out of there."

It didn't take them long to find a rancher's Ford F150 pickup, a later model than what they had, with the keys in it and nearly a full tank of gas. Glen jumped in and the pickup started right up.

"Okay, you follow me. We'll stash the Chevy somewhere in case we need it. We can find a cool plate somewhere and if we get stopped, I can talk us out of it."

The trip back to T or C was uneventful, and they found a side street behind the fairgrounds where they parked the old Chevy pickup, locked it, and drove away in the Ford. Glen drove them right to the Plugged Nickel.

"I need a beer and it's about time I got laid. Do what you want and I'll meet you back at the room later."

The minute they walked into the tavern, Glen saw his target. She was with two other young twenty-something girls sitting at the bar, drinking beer from the bottles. They appeared to be minding their own business, but each was fully aware of the effect they were having on the host of prospectors who were trying hard not to stare and talk among themselves. Chip walked over to his cohorts, but Glen walked over and took the stool next to the three girls.

"How you girls doing tonight?" he asked with a smile.

All three nodded and smiled. He picked out the short blond with the biggest tits and popped into her head, suggesting that she didn't really want to stay here slumming with her girlfriends and if this handsome miner asked her out, she would go without a fight. In the time it took for Glen to buy the girls another round and drink a beer himself, she was ready to go, and they left. They went over to his motel room and were out of their clothes in no time. Even though her tits were fake, they felt good, and he thought they had a pretty good time, considering she had no idea why she was rolling around on the bed with a stranger she had just met who smelled of body odor, cigarettes, and poor dental hygiene. But when he finished for the second time and fell asleep, she was aghast at what she had done and ran into the bathroom to shower. By the time she had finished, he was awake, up, and dressing.

"I'll run you home to your apartment, if you want," said Glen evenly as he looked at her naked body. She would never be able to explain to herself why she let him. He dropped her off without a kiss goodbye, and that was the end of it. The girl would never go into the Plugged Nickel Saloon again.

Over coffee at Denny's the next morning, Glen said: "I think it's time we freshened up the kitty. We're getting a little low. I thought this time we might go for a bigger bank – say one in Socorro – and see if we do any better than we did in Hatch. I'd still like to do that Black Range Credit Union but the highway is just too screwed up there to get away clean. At least we have a clean ride now. That should help."

Chip just nodded. He was happy. He got laid last night too. It wasn't with a twenty-something-year-old with big knockers, but she wasn't bad, in a crank whore sort of a way.

They filled the truck with gas and checked the oil – right up where it should be – and headed north. The endless greasewood-infested landscape was easy to ignore as Glen thought about how he wanted to up the ante a little, to force Perkins out of hiding if he was helping the cops. If he wasn't, then no harm done, but Perkins would have to come for him eventually, and it would be interesting to see just what the extent of his new-found abilities was.

They cruised through Socorro, checking out the banks, and finally choosing one near the south end. They sat across the street and watched for a while to get a feel for the amount of traffic coming in and out, and found that there was little stirring at opening time, so they parked around the corner and walked in. There were two open teller windows and two women sitting at desks behind and to the left. The women at the desks were busily typing away at their computers and when Glen "announced" the robbery, they stopped immediately and, per his instructions, put their hands palms down on the desktop.

He sent Chip behind the counters and ordered the tellers to fill Chip's pillow case with cash, but no dye packs or transmitters. He determined who the manager was and ordered her to unlock the gate into the open vault, and she did so without resistance. Chip forced her into the vault ahead of him and made her put packets of cash in the pillow case until it wouldn't hold any more. Chip took her keys and walked the other three into the vault He locked the gate tossing the keys onto one of the desks. They walked out of the bank to their truck as if they had just made a legitimate transaction.

As Chip drove away, behind the bank, two patrol cars, lights and sirens ablaze, came screaming into the bank's parking lot.

"Just be cool, dude," said Glen, laying a hand on Chip's arm. They don't even know we're here, and sure as hell don't know we're the robbers, so just relax and drive like normal, don't panic."

Chip nodded, but his heart was pounding and his breathing was heavy. He kept looking in the rearview mirror until he almost hit a pedestrian and had to lock up the brakes. A third patrol car appeared and turned down the side street on which they had parked. It went around the block as they had and pulled in behind them on the main road.

"Aw Christ, Glen, there's a cop right behind us!"

"Be cool," Glen ordered. "If he pulls us over, just go along with the program. I'll take care of it. Just don't panic and do something stupid, like pulling your gun."

Suddenly the patrol car's lights came to life, and Chip's heart leaped into his throat as he started to pull over. For a second, the car followed behind them, then abruptly did a u-turn and screamed back the other way. Chip realized he had been holding his breath, and let it out slowly.

"That was too close. I thought he was stopping us for sure."

"They're like farts in a frying pan after a bank robbery alarm goes out. They don't know which way to turn or who to stop and even if they did, they have no way of knowing if you did it, because they have no descriptions, thanks to me."

"Okay, fine, but let's get the fuck out of here anyway."

Glen was more than pleased. He discovered that he could control all four women in the bank at one time and, more importantly, was able to dissuade the cop from stopping them even before the cop radioed in their license plate number. His "powers" were expanding, and he was really getting to like it.

"Let's stop in San Antonio for lunch. There's a restaurant called The Crane. I hear the enchiladas are really good," said Glen casually as he put his arm up across the back of the seat.

"You want to stop and eat? Are you crazy?" said a dumbfounded Chip.

"No, I'm hungry. Robbing banks always makes me hungry. Go figure."

"You sure it's safe?"

"Sure. We'll stuff the pillow case behind the seat and go have lunch like regular people."

*****

Charlie Perkins was sitting in Pete's office waiting for Samantha to arrive.

"Ever since I learned that Glen had been in the probe, I've been wracking my brain trying to think of ways to combat his ability to dominate someone's consciousness and bend them to his will," said Charlie. "There's the question of when or if we tangle, what would happen, and whether or not I can fend off his onslaught, because that's what it would be. He would come full bore at me, trying to use his heightened emotional state to overwhelm my ability to block him. I have to come up with a way to redirect the force so it bounces off harmlessly, more or less. In figuring out a way to do that, I might be able to come up with a defense any of us can use. I'm hoping Samantha can help, because I'm not getting very far on my own."

"I've been doing the same thing, Charlie. If we develop a technique to fend off your telepathic suggestion, is there anything left to fight off a gun or a knife or a punch? I think we can assume that this guy is always armed. I don't even know how we can subdue him without killing him."

"I'm not worried about subduing him. If we get into it, it'll be a fight to the death. He won't quit until one of us is dead."

"No quarter, huh?"

"It's not my philosophy. That's the way Glen Ritchey wants it, so that's the way it's going to be. Just like on the freeway. He wasn't about to give us any warning, and if your Yukon crashed and you were injured, do you think he'd stop? Only to make sure I was dead."

"But what if you're not there? If he gets chased by the cops after, say, a bank robbery, and gets cornered, what then? Is there no way to contain him without killing him?"

"Well, we discovered that six guys rushing at me can put me down, but I didn't have a gun in my hand and wouldn't hurt anyone anyway."

Just then Samantha was escorted into Pete's office. Both men stood and Pete offered her a seat.

"Okay, you two, why am I here?" she asked without preamble.

"Charlie's telepathic and telekinetic abilities are getting stronger every day. They already saved his life and probably mine, when Glen Ritchey tried to kill us the other day. Oh, and Ritchey has the same abilities Charlie has."

"Whoa . . . wait a minute. Tried to kill you?"

Charlie explained the enmity between him and Ritchey and how the hate had ratcheted up to an obsessive level in the man. He detailed how Ritchey had tried to take advantage of an opportunity the other day to exact revenge, and explained why it didn't work.

"I realized that he had been in the probe too, and was showing the same signs of a higher functioning brain that I am. The difference is, he's a twenty-four carat bad guy. We were just sitting here trying to come up with a way we can counter his attempts to control someone without having to kill him, and so far we're not doing very well. We're hoping you can help. We've had a meeting with the big dogs, but it's still our responsibility to get this guy stopped."

Samantha was silent for nearly a minute as she stared at the wall.

Finally, she said: "Charlie, 'suggest' to Pete that he get up and open the door. Pete, fight off the suggestion if you can."

Charlie nodded and looked at Pete who, without blinking an eye, got up and opened his office door.

"I resisted as much as I could but he just bowled me over. I had no choice."

"Okay," said Samantha, "now this time, Pete, sit back down and start counting to two hundred inside your head, and don't stop for anything, no matter what. Charlie, when he's ready, 'suggest' he get up and close the door."

When it was clear that Pete was counting, Charlie looked at him but this time, though a little restless, Pete didn't move.

"Pete, stand up," said Samantha.

Webber immediately stood up.

"How far along are you in your counting?"

"Eighty-six."

"Okay, you can quit now."

Both men looked at her questioningly. Then Pete grinned, walked over, and shut the door.

"We all have certain behaviors programmed into us at an early age and counting is one of the basics. It's long been known that you can do something else while counting numbers and doing something else with the counting relegated nearly to the subconscious is possible for anyone. Apparently if you concentrate hard enough on one of your basic programmed responses, you can divert your attention away from Charlie trying to get you to close the door. I think with practice, you get better at it, but that was a very good first try. Pete, could you tell Charlie was working on you?"

"I felt it and just kept concentrating harder on counting. I could feel myself wanting to get up, but the urge wasn't strong enough to act on."

"Charlie, you didn't let him off easy?"

"No Ma'am, I was bearing down full force on him, well, concentrating hard but not hard enough to cause an injury."

"Unfortunately we don't have anyone who can 'suggest' something to you, so you might have to practice this on your own. Keep counting while you do something else that needs some conscious effort. We'll help you as much as we can, but it's going to be up to you to concentrate more-or-less on two things at once. Think you can do it?"

"If it means getting an edge on Glen Ritchey, you bet."

"I would suggest, Pete, that you brief your whole squad as you did me and get them all involved in this attention diversion exercise."

"They already know everything, except that Charlie isn't our only clairvoyant. We did some experimenting – like I described to you over the phone – and discovered quite a few interesting things about Mr. Perkins. For one thing, he likes to be at the bottom of a pile of people."

Charlie laughed. "Yeah, that was real fun, but it was good to know too."

"Charlie," asked Samantha, "we have a lot more testing to do, but for now, I just have a couple of questions regarding Glen Ritchey. Dare I assume that your abilities are equal?"

"That's probably true, except for the emotional level at the time that Glen tries something. He's obsessed with killing me, and the hate is almost palpable. I'm assuming this would give him an edge for a little while, but drains his energy quicker."

"Do you think you have the ability to kill someone without touching them?"

"I don't think so. I could probably suggest someone jump off a bridge or out of a moving car, but I couldn't just reach out, figuratively speaking, and kill someone. Telekinetically, I doubt I could lift anything heavy enough to do much damage. I'm much better at pushing than lifting."

"So we needn't worry about Ritchey unless he's armed?"

"I'd like to wait until we work on this counting thing a while longer before I answer that, but on the surface, I think you might be right. Damn Pete, she's here, what, half an hour and already has our problem solved?"

"Let's hope so. I'll get the squad together and we'll try some of this out, but we can't wait very long before we go looking for Ritchey. Any idea how to find him?"

"I don't know if I have that remote viewing ability you mentioned, you guys," Charlie replied, "but sometimes I see people at certain locations. I have no way of knowing if this vision is accurate, but I do see them. That's about the only 'extra-sensory' assistance I can offer, but right now it's more important to get the men up to speed on Ritchey and the attention diversion technique."

"Let me call Colonel Whitehead. He might be interested in running his people through this before they tangle with Ritchey," said Webber, picking up the phone.

"Colonel Whitehead," answered the brusque voice.

"Colonel, Captain Webber. We've just come up with something that might reduce Ritchey's influence on your troops so they can still function. We're just getting ready to run my squad through the training, and you're welcome to participate."

"Thank you, no, Captain, as I said before, my troops are already trained up and ready to go at a moment's notice. They don't need any distraction."

"But Sir . . ." was as far as Webber got before the Colonel hung up the phone.

He stared at the phone in disbelief for several seconds before slamming it down onto its cradle.

"That stupid son-of-a-bitch is going to get someone killed!"

"Why?" asked Samantha.

"My troops are already trained up and ready to go at a moment's notice, they don't need any distraction," Webber mocked. "They might be 'trained up', but I guarantee you none of them have a clue how to deal with someone like Glen Ritchey."

"Well, if the colonel says his men don't need any more training, then I guess we have to live with it but we don't with yours," said Samantha Chase.

Once again they gathered the squad in the hangar.

"Time for some payback for all the piling on," said Charlie with a grin, which was returned in kind. "As you know, I can suggest something to someone and they are more or less compelled to do it. We've discovered that Glen Ritchey has the same ability, and we've possibly come up with a method to combat it. I'm going to implant a suggestion in each of your minds, and you won't be able to resist it. When that's done, we'll show you what you can do to resist it."

They went through the first exercise and no one was able to resist taking off his shoe, unbuttoning his shirt, or handing his wallet to the man next to him. Then Samantha took over with the counting technique, and they tried Charlie's suggestions again. The results were mixed, but every man who failed wanted another chance to concentrate harder. They practiced all afternoon, and by the time they were done, no one was following Charlie's suggestions. Charlie practiced right along with them, but he concentrated more on how many of Pete's men he could occupy at one time. Not only did it save some time, but it gave him an idea how much stronger his ability was than last time, and where the cutoff was.

Pete's phone was ringing when they returned to his office.

"Captain Webber."

"You been watching the news?"

"Who is this?"

"Sergeant Ramirez, Sierra County Sheriff's Office."

"Sorry Sergeant, I didn't recognize your voice. What's that about watching the news?"

"Just turn on a television. They've been airing it about every fifteen minutes. Seems our bank robbers hit the same bank in Hatch, but this time a Doña Ana County Deputy got there in time. He had the front covered but when one of the robbers came out, the deputy holstered his gun, and the robber shot him. Somebody got it on video, and the television network is splashing it all over."

"Is he dead?"

"No, he took the round in the trauma plate of his ballistic vest. Knocked him ass over teakettle, and they were afraid there was some damage to his heart, but now they say he'll be okay."

"Good God."

"Reason I called is the shooter is, at least in my mind, Glen Ritchey. He's getting completely out of control, and we need to lock him down – now. We need to smoke him out into the open and your boy, Charlie Perkins, might be the way to do that."

"You mean use him as bait? How could we do that without endangering his life?"

"I thought we might get together and brainstorm this a little; see if we could come up with an idea or two."

"Let me check with Charlie and I'll call you back ASAP."

"Good enough," said Ramirez and the line went dead.

Both Charlie and Samantha looked at Webber questioningly.

"That was Sergeant Ramirez from Sierra County . . . well, hold on, let's get the TV on and you can see for yourself."

He turned the TV on just as the announcer was saying: ". . . breaking news. A Doña Ana County Sheriff's Deputy was shot during a bank robbery in Hatch this afternoon. A word of caution: the following video footage is graphic and very disturbing."

The image on the screen segued to a slightly fuzzy video depicting a Sheriff's Department patrol car parked in front of what appeared to be a bank. The driver and sole occupant was getting out of his car while drawing his weapon, then hunkered down by his door while looking intently at the front of the building. A tall, slender man dressed in dark clothing, sunglasses, and a ball cap pulled low, emerged from the building holding his hands about shoulder height. As he walked down the three steps from the building, the Deputy stood up and holstered his weapon. Suddenly the tall man reached around behind him, produced a handgun and fired one shot at the Deputy who was thrust backward off his feet onto his back as if he'd been slapped by an invisible hand. The tall man half turned and motioned for another man. They ran across the front of the bank and disappeared around the corner. At that point, the person shooting the video concentrated on the downed Deputy.

"There is no word yet on the Deputy's identity or his present condition. He was evacuated by air to Memorial Medical Center. The suspects escaped and have not been identified. There was no word on how much cash the robbers got away with. And in other news . . ."

Webber turned off the television and looked at Charlie "Is there any doubt in your mind who those two were?"

Charlie locked eyes with him and shook his head. "No doubt it was Glen and Chip. It's not clear exactly why the Deputy holstered his weapon, but there are two possibilities in my mind. Either Glen identified himself as a bank employee and told the Deputy the robbers were gone or he just 'suggested' to the Deputy that he put away his gun. Personally, I think the latter would be more Glen's style. What did Ramirez have to say?"

"Nothing we haven't already talked about. We need to get these two guys in custody yesterday. The Deputy's vest is all that saved him from probably dying at the scene. Ramirez wants to talk about using you to smoke Ritchey out into the open."

"Kind of like a sacrificial lamb, eh?"

"That's why he wants to talk. He knows I'm not going to let anything happen to you, so unless we can come up with a foolproof plan that will ensure your safety, he's out of luck."

"For what it's worth," said Samantha, "guys like Ritchey aren't going to quit. He has the taste of success and each time he's successful, the more powerful he feels, and the more risk he's willing to take to satisfy his ego."

"I'll help them any way I can," said Charlie, rubbing his face with his hands. "Right now I'm beat. It takes a lot of energy to do what I was doing this afternoon, and I'll bet it took a toll on Glen, too."

"Damnit, I wish we could tell Ramirez what Ritchey is capable of. Any cop who even does an innocent traffic stop on them is liable to get blown away and never get a chance to defend himself," Webber said in consternation.

"I say we call it a day," said Samantha. "Anybody want to discuss this further over dinner? Pete is buying," she added mischievously.

Over dinner, Charlie said soberly: "I can't stand by and let Glen kill someone, knowing that I could prevent it. I've got to do something."

"What did you have in mind, a gunfight at noon on main street?" asked Pete. He was frustrated, because he couldn't think of a plan that would neutralize Glen Ritchey without putting Charlie in harm's way. "Hell, we don't even have communications with the guy. How can we negotiate anything?"

"You can't negotiate with someone with Ritchey's mind set," said Samantha. "He is on a high and believes nothing can touch him. The only thing he might listen to is a direct challenge from someone like Charlie, whom he wants badly. The only edge Charlie might have is surprise, if we can introduce him into a scenario while Ritchey is distracted. I don't see how we can coordinate a civilian police operation, even getting Charlie in close, without having to do some explaining."

"And without Glen knowing I'm there," Charlie added soberly.

"That might not be that hard. Ramirez asked for Charlie's assistance. They know Charlie is with us, and we might have something to say that will influence what Charlie might do. If I arrange to produce Charlie when they need him, they might go along, no questions asked. Charlie, what do you think? Do you think you can hold him off long enough for us to gang up on him, or shoot him if necessary?"

"Glen won't be thinking very far down the road when he does something next time, but I just don't see how you can plan an operation without having some idea what the scenario will be, and it's painfully clear we're all drawing a blank."

*****

Glen Ritchey *was* riding high. Everything he touched or caused to happen was going his way. Life was good. The cop he shot didn't die. Not that it made that much difference, but because of it, the manhunt for him was growing wider. But he was immune to their efforts. No one could touch him as long as he or Chip didn't fuck up. Chip was sometimes borderline more trouble than he was worth, but Glen had become accustomed to having a gofer who no longer asked stupid questions.

And Glen had had a great idea, and this evening he was going to put it into practice. It was probably a lot safer than banks, and there was potential for greater hauls, considering no one could lie to him or refuse him anything. He just had to pick the right places which, with his talents, shouldn't be too hard.

He had chosen the manager of one of the grocery stores in town as his first victim. First he identified who that was, then followed him home. They waited until later in the evening, then walked up to the front door and rang the bell. A paunchy middle-aged man answered the door but merely backed out of the way a few steps when Glen and Chip barged in.

"Who else is in the house, asshole?" Glen asked, grabbing the man by the front of his shirt.

"Just . . . just my wife and daughter. What is going on, why are you doing this?" the man asked in a voice rising with every word.

"Nathan?" called a voice from deeper in house. "Is everything alright?" His wife emerged from a hallway and cried: "What are you doing? Get out before I call the police!"

Chip was in front of her in two long strides and slapped her across the mouth.

"Shut up. Keep your mouth shut and nobody will get hurt. Keep flapping your gums and somebody gets shot," he said as he waved his gun in front of her. Her eyes grew wide, but she had enough presence of mind not to scream.

"Take her into the living room and tie her up," ordered Glen, who still had a fistful of the man's shirt. "You, where's the money?"

"What money? What are you talking about?"

Glen let loose of the front of the man's shirt and backhanded him across the face. "Don't play cute with me, asshole, I know you keep cash here, and you're going to give it to me."

The man had turned a sickly fish belly white and began to shake, but said nothing. Glen stared at him, then began to smile. He slapped the man again and said: "Now I know you're lying. Where's your daughter?"

"She's upstairs. She's already gone to bed. She's a sound sleeper, she won't hear anything."

Glen grinned. "You say so. Let's go open your safe." He called to Chip: "Keep an eye on the old broad while we go open the safe." He could hear duct tape being stripped off a roll and a faint "okay".

The man turned and walked down the hallway from which his wife had emerged, then turned into one of the rooms. It was a nicely furnished den with a massive roll top desk, a couch, and one wall lined with bookshelves loaded with a vast number of books. The man walked directly to the closet, opened the door, and knelt to uncover the face of a floor safe. He looked back at Glen.

"Open it, asshole."

The man turned back to the safe and spun the dial then dialed in the combination. The lid to the safe popped open and the man stood and stepped back.

"What are you doing?" said Glen. He grabbed a WalMart bag off the desk, emptied the contents onto the desktop, then shoved the bag at the man. "Put the money in here, but first pick up that gun by the barrel with two fingers and hand it to me."

The man's shoulders sagged as he again knelt down before the safe, then reached in and extracted a small semi-automatic pistol by his thumb and forefinger.

Glen was sufficiently confident in his control of the man that he hadn't even drawn his weapon. He grabbed the gun from the man and checked to see if there was a round in the chamber. There was not. On his knees, the man had hesitated while Glen checked the gun but, when the robber glared at him, he began loading bundles of cash into the bag.

"No checks, change or any of that credit card shit. Just cash and all of it," ordered Glen as he stuffed the small gun in his back pocket. When the man finished, he handed the bag to Glen then rose and backed away from the safe so Glen could confirm that it was empty of cash.

"Okay, is that all in the house?"

The man nodded and Ritchey nodded in agreement.

"Okay, let's go find your old lady."

While Chip was trussing the man up and gagging him with duct tape, Glen slipped the small automatic into Chip's back pocket.

"That's a little present for you. I'm going upstairs to check on the daughter," he said with a hard glint in his eyes.

Both parents made to rise and started making noises through the tape.

"Shut up," said Chip, waving his gun in front of them, then cuffing the man alongside the head. He looked over at Glen and grinned. "Don't do anything I wouldn't do."

Glen slowly mounted the stairs until he reached the upstairs landing. He stopped and cocked his head, then smiled. He walked confidently down the hallway to the second door on the right and slowly opened it. It was clearly a girl's room, with lace curtains on the window, a canopied bed, and a small mountain of stuffed animals piled on top of a dresser. A young woman, her hair tousled, sat pressed hard up against the headboard, as far away from the door as possible. She had the covers pulled around her and clutched a large pillow to her chest.

Glen stood in the doorway and stared at the woman, who couldn't be more than eighteen, for a moment, then she lowered the pillow and climbed over to his side of the bed. She stood up and began to take off her pajamas. Glen watched for a moment before easing further into the room.

Later, after Glen and Chip had taken rooms at one of the local motels, they counted the money from the home invasion robbery. Both were pleased and not at all sure the family would even report the crime, considering the suggestions Ritchey had imparted to them before they left.

Yes, life was good, very very good.

CHAPTER 11

Charlie barged into Pete's office the next morning without knocking finding the captain at his desk and Samantha sitting across from him. Charlie's face turned bright red and he backed right out of the room.

"Charlie! Get back in here," yelled Pete.

Charlie opened the door and peeked in shamefacedly. "Sorry, I should have knocked."

"Whatever for? You've been barging in here every morning, what's different about today?" asked Samantha.

"The way sparks were flying in here, I thought I might get burned," said Charlie ingenuously. Now was it Pete and Samantha with bright red faces?

"Can we just move on?" asked Samantha with a slight smirk on her face. "Charlie, we were just talking about trying some remote viewing experiments, since Ritchey and Lakin seemed to have dropped off the radar grid."

"Okay, sure, as long as it's safe to be in here," Charlie replied, now intentionally needling the pair, who were trying very hard to maintain their decorum.

"We thought what we'd do to start with is have Pete go into one of the four interview rooms. You try to locate him, to 'see' him without really making this a guessing game, okay?"

Twelve rooms later, Charlie hadn't missed a one and Samantha was starting to get excited.

"Charlie, what's going on outside in the hangar where the probe is?" asked Webber.

Charlie stood up.

"No! Just sit there and try to let your mind go out there for you. Just ease out there in your mind and take a look around. Obviously we're not trying to catch the guys goofing off, but testing your ability to 'reach' a little farther."

"Well, four of the guys are trying to drill a hole into the hull of the probe with a carbide-tipped bit. One's actually drilling, another is holding bits, one is filming, and one is taking notes. One is in the can, and one is outside taking a smoke break."

Without a word, Pete Webber was out the door and into the hangar. He was back in sixty seconds with both thumbs up. "Right on, Charlie. Just as you described."

"Charlie, how many red cars are in the public parking lot out by the main gate?"

Charlie stared off into the distance for a minute then replied: "I can't see any red cars in the parking lot."

Webber called the front gate and asked the same question. Moments later, he received the answer he was hoping for.

"By the way, Pete," said Charlie, "they're going to move the probe over to Nellis sometime this week, before Friday."

"How do you know that?" asked Webber, surprised.

"When I was looking out there, it just came to me, just like what was going on in here when I first got here. It just came to me. I wasn't trying to read your minds, honest."

Through a faint blush, Samantha said: "What exactly was going on?"

"Out of politeness, I won't say. I will say it was coming from both of you."

Webber and Chase shared a look, then looked back at Charlie.

"Charlie, can you tell me who is on duty in the guard shack?" asked Pete.

Charlie thought for just a moment, then replied: "There's a Sergeant Blake and an Airman Tuttle."

Webber nodded. "Blake answered the phone and Tuttle was passing through cars."

"Do you think you could find someone on the base if we gave you a name?" asked Chase.

"Probably not, unless I've been there. I'm familiar with the hangar and the parking lot, and even the guard shack, but to search rooms I've never been in seems iffy. It's like I can tell you right now that there's no one but a coyote near the place you recovered the probe, and no one has yet cleared the rest of that cottonwood out of the wash, and probably won't ever."

Samantha looked at Charlie with raised eyebrows and asked: "You can 'see' that far away?"

"Yes, pretty easily as a matter of fact. I can also see that my old house has been rented by a young Hispanic couple who just got married. I think it has to do with the way I can unlock a door. If I'm familiar with the mechanism and know what needs to happen to make it unlock, I can do it, but if I'm not familiar with the mechanism, such as one of these electronic locks, I'd have a lot more trouble. 'Course I could always just force the door open too."

"You mean like willing something to come apart?" Webber asked.

"No, it's more like directing my telekinetic strength. You wouldn't believe how strong I am when I project that strength."

"So I suppose Ritchey can do the same things?" Pete mused.

"I don't see why not."

"I don't suppose you can cast your mind out there and find him?"

Charlie sat for several minutes just staring into space. Finally he said: "I'm not very good at that. I've already tried it a few times. If he's in a particular building that I know, like the Plugged Nickel, I probably could pick him up, but just to drift around, say, T or C and detect him is near impossible for me."

"So we won't be able to surprise Ritchey with your presence and vice versa?"

"That's right, unless one of us is heavily distracted. You know, like the guys gang tackling me?"

"What about if I showed you a picture of a place you'd never been? Do you think you could tell what was going on there?"

"Let's try it. Don't tell me where it is. I'll start with trying to figure that out, then, if that's successful, I'll see what I can 'see'."

Samantha laid down a black and white satellite surveillance photo of what was clearly a major naval base. Since it was overhead, no hull numbers or ships names were evident.

Charlie stared at it for several minutes, time enough for Pete to bring them all fresh coffee. "Do you have a magnifying glass?" he asked. Pete produced one from his top desk drawer, saying: "It's basic detective equipment," with a smile.

Charlie examined the photo with the magnifying glass for several more minutes. Finally he stood up and announced: "This is the Chinese North Sea Fleet Headquarters in Qingdao, Shandong Province. It looks like the aircraft carrier Liaoning, guided missile destroyers Qingdao and Harbin, oiler Taicang, and supply ship Weishanhu. They're preparing to leave port. Do you want the rest of the ships that are in port? There are quite a few."

Pete and Samantha were aghast. "Charlie, did you know anything about this place or these ships before I showed you the photo?"

He shook his head.

"One last thing, then we'll give you a break. Can you tell where this fleet is headed, or any of their plans, or gather any other operational data from the naval base?"

"They won't be at sea very long, because they are still having a lot of trouble replenishing while underway. They are just going out on maneuvers, not making any port calls that I can tell . . ."

Pete cut him off: "Okay, that's good enough. Charlie, are you sure of your information?"

"Yes," he said simply.

"You won't *believe* what the reaction is going to be in DC when they hear about this," said Samantha.

"I probably can't imagine, but I'll reiterate what I said before: I'm not going to DC. I don't care what the big shots want."

"I'll remember," said Pete

"Let's go have some lunch and table this for now," said Samantha. She was confident Charlie would not try to determine what she was thinking – he had promised – but she didn't want him to know how strong her doubts were that he would have any voice in where he wound up for further testing, or even for operational analysis, which looked like where he would be headed. His life as a prospector had pretty much ended. He just didn't know it yet.

Over lunch Pete admitted that in one way, he was glad to see the probe go. "We've done everything we can think of, and it would be nice to let my guys get back to their investigative assignments. I mean, significant crime investigation around this base has pretty much come to a halt thanks to you, Charlie. Base security takes care of the little stuff, but I have no fewer than a dozen major theft investigations open and I think some of them might be connected, which means we have some kind of black market theft ring working on base."

"Do you have any idea who the players are?" asked Samantha.

"I think we know some of the mid-level conspirators, but there has to be someone at the top giving orders . . . or maybe taking orders in this instance, but I just can't seem to tie them to a particular theft or to each other."

"Well Captain Sir," said Charlie pensively, "if you'd care to bring in about three of your suspects and put them in different interview rooms, I believe I could sap – figuratively speaking – the truth out of at least one of them and couldn't you play that one against the other two?"

Webber thought about the idea for a while over coffee and said finally: I'd have to make one or two of the suspects believe the others had rolled over by telling him in detail what he'd done and once he rolled the others would probably fall into place. Let me talk the idea over with my guys and we'll come up with a plan about who to bring in and what to say."

"I can see where you'd have to be very careful that Charlie's existence not come out, they'd blow you out of the water in court if that happened," said Samantha.

Webber called his squad in for a meeting. "Charlie thinks he can be of assistance in identifying the main players in the theft ring. He thinks he can just 'overhear' some of what the suspects are thinking and maybe come up with enough to play one bad guy against another. We'll call in three of the subjects we know are involved, and let them cool their heels in the interview rooms. We'll take our time going in to question them in order to let their minds wander, and see if Charlie can get a 'read' on what they know. Then we'll play it by ear how we go about interrogating them."

The plan went into effect the next morning. Webber called in two senior airmen and a staff sergeant believed to have knowledge of at least some of the thefts. Thus far they had not been cooperative, and insisted that they didn't know anything. They were seated in the first three interview rooms with a cup of coffee and allowed to stew. Charlie sat in Webber's office for a few minutes listening.

"None of them seem to know very much," he told Pete. "It's almost like none of them are trusted with the whole picture but it seems a pretty sophisticated scheme. Basically, there are three or four guys in the group who can vouch for a particular customer. The prospective customer is sent to the Four Winds Lounge, where he drops the name of the man vouching for him and tells the bartender what he's looking for. The bartender makes a call, and if the merchandise is available, he tells the customer the price. When the customer comes back with the money, he has to leave his keys in his vehicle, cash in an envelope over the visor, and come in and have a beer or two. Someone comes and gets the vehicle, takes it to the merchandise, loads it, and brings it back, leaving the keys under the seat. The customer then goes on his way with the merchandise he paid for never knowing from whom he bought it."

"One of your suspects, the staff sergeant, can vouch for someone. One of the senior airmen pulls the inventory, and the other one loads it in the customer's vehicle. None of them know who drives the customer's vehicle, but that individual has to get the loaded vehicle through the gate, so he's probably paying off a gate guard too. I'm afraid these are pretty small fish."

A light went on in Pete's head. "Why don't we try to buy something? Can you suggest to the sergeant that someone can be vouched for?"

"Sure."

"Can you tell where a good place to 'encounter' the sergeant might be?"

"He likes the Four Winds, if you can believe that."

"I figure if two guys go into the tavern and get to talking about needing a piece of equipment, say a generator or a big compressor, maybe he'll overhear us and one thing will lead to another. I'll probably have to do the undercover, since he's seen the rest of the squad. I don't know about a second guy, though. I could probably get someone out of security to go along for the ride. We'll have the rest of the squad set up for surveillance, but it won't be necessary when we first make contact. Only when it's time to get the merchandise."

"How about I go with you, Pete?"asked Charlie. "I'm a prospector by trade, so it would make sense for me to be looking for equipment. It would be helpful for me to be close enough to monitor what he's got on his mind. I could say I need a big powerful generator to run the equipment on my claim, and that wouldn't be far from the truth, by the time you get a vacuum, dry washer, lights and a pump running."

"That sounds like a good plan, actually," said Pete. "Charlie and I will go fishing this evening at the Four Winds. We'll deploy the squad around the base, just in case things happen faster than we anticipate."

That evening, in civilian clothes and driving an undercover Chevy pickup, they pulled into the parking lot of the Four Winds. The parking lot held seven or eight vehicles, which was pretty good for a weekday night. Sergeant Scott's Dodge Ram was among them. The bar itself had a fifties feel to it, with neon palm trees above the entry and white gravel accenting the concrete sidewalk leading up to it. A straggly ocotillo cactus and a couple of older barrel cacti were all the vegetation in the courtyard.

As expected, the interior was dimly lit and smelled of cigarette smoke and stale beer. A bar claimed the left wall, and booths were set along the right. There were tables scattered between them and most of the all-male crowd sat at the bar. Sergeant Scott, in civilian clothes, sat at a table before a large flat-screened television watching a baseball game. Pete and Charlie chose a table well within earshot of Sergeant Scott's table and ordered a pitcher of beer from the bored barmaid. She was well into her forties, wearing tight stretch pants and a low cut blouse under a vest.

While they waited for the beer, both men looked around the bar in a desultory fashion, then glanced at each other before gazing up at the television. "So how are things going in T or C?" asked Pete.

"Oh, not too bad," Charlie replied. "This latest claim is taking up a lot more time than it should, but it's showing more color than any of the others. I'd like to work it big time, with all my equipment but unfortunately, there's no power to be had and I can't afford a generator. Having to work everything by hand really slows me down and that's frustrating. There's gold in there, Pete, I can see it."

"Can't you borrow a generator from someone?"

"Few of the people I know have one big enough to do me that much good. I need something in the twelve to fifteen hundred Kw range, and that's a big, heavy generator. I could find help to unload a beast like that, but I just can't come up with the money they want for one. Hell, they run two or three thousand dollars for a good one. It looks like I'll just have to keep working the claim piecemeal until I can come up with enough money. I just hate wasting all the man hours when I know I can be doing it a lot more efficiently."

"So how're things over here?" he asked Pete. "I haven't seen you for a couple of weeks; you still framing that one house?"

"Yep, we're about two thirds done with it. What a big bastard. I don't know who the owner is, but he's putting a helluva lot of money into the place. The guy's got more toys than ten people ought to. Hell, he didn't even miss it when I helped myself to an eight thousand pound Warn winch he had buried under a huge pile of shit in his shop. Must be nice to be so rich you can afford to give it away without knowing it."

"He didn't even realize the winch was gone? What a dumb-ass. Too bad he doesn't have a big assed generator in the same pile. I'd make him the same offer you made on the winch."

They both laughed as the barmaid brought their beer. Pete poured for both of them and they sat back and looked at the television as they drank. "Who's playing," Pete asked a little louder than conversational level.

Scott replied: "Yankees and Red Sox."

"Yeah? That's usually a good game. What's the score?"

"Red Sox three to one in the bottom of the seventh."

"You know, with all the money the Yankees spend on players, you'd think their team would be invincible. Goes to show that money doesn't necessarily guarantee good performance."

Scott looked over at them. "Yeah, I know what you mean. They've disappointed me so many times, I quit rooting for them. Now they're all just a bunch of overpaid egocentric assholes."

"Yeah, there's a couple of exceptions, like Ichiro, but the A-Rods and Jeters are exactly what you described. I can't stand to watch them away from the field, but you gotta give them credit, they know how to play the game."

"Yeah, and take performance-enhancing drugs."

"Yeah, no shit."

"Hey, I heard your buddy talking about needing a generator. I might be able to help you out if you're not too particular where it comes from."

"If you heard him talking about needing a generator, you heard me talk about my five-fingered discount on a winch so, no, we're not too particular. Why? What do you have?"

"Well, I'm not sure. I'll have to call a buddy and see if his is still for sale and how much he wants for it. I think it's a real big one, and he just never used it, so he was talking about selling it. I know he got a *real* good deal on it, if you know what I mean."

"Works for me; how about you, Charlie?"

"Depends on how much, that's all I care about. I have some cash but not three thousand dollars."

"Yeah, I don't know what he wants for it, but I'm pretty sure he's not in it near that much."

"Well, then sure, make your call."

"S'cuse me a second," said Scott, as he walked toward the door, pulling out his cell phone at the same time. He was back in less than five minutes. "He says he's got a twelve-thousand five Kw generator he could let you have for fifteen hundred."

"No shit?"

"He says it's brand new, never been used. It's not the same one I was thinking about that he had used a little. He said he already sold that one, for a thousand even but it was smaller."

"It'll take me until tomorrow to get the money together. Should I just bring it here and give it to you or what?"

"When you get the money, just come back here and talk to Isaac, he's the bartender. Tell him I said it was okay. He'll make a phone call and arrange everything. Leave the money in an envelope above the visor and the keys in the ignition."

"God, that's fucking great, man. Let me at least buy you a beer."

"Yeah, sure. People around here call me Scotty. You're Pete and your Charlie, right?"

"Yeah, you got a good memory," said Pete, "so, do we pay you a finder's fee or what?"

"Nah, you don't have to worry about a thing. My buddy'll take care of me."

"Here, take the rest of the pitcher, I gotta go start getting some cash together. Fifteen hundred you said?"

"Yep," said Scotty, pouring himself a fresh beer from their pitcher.

"Hey, thanks a lot, man, you don't know how much you're helpin' me out," said Charlie as he bumped fists with Scotty. Pete just nodded as he and Charlie headed for the door.

As they got back in Pete's pickup, he asked Charlie: "How much did you have to 'persuade' him?"

"Not a bit. Everything he did, he did completely on his own hook. All I did was make sure we weren't doing anything that made him suspicious. He took care of the rest," Charlie replied with a grin.

"Now where, on base, would they have a new generator that big?" Pete mused out loud.

"Don't you have like a big warehouse full of stuff you need to draw from, from time to time?" Charlie asked.

"There's base supply, but I don't know where they would keep the generators. I'll make some calls when we get back. We're going to need to know for the surveillance teams tomorrow night," Pete replied, his mind already several steps ahead.

It was late, after ten, by the time Pete and Charlie returned to the base. Pete was on the phone almost from the minute they left the Four Winds, and seemed attached to the instrument for the next two hours. Charlie, with nothing to do, went back to the Inn after Pete told him he would be busy for a while.

At oh eight hundred the next morning the entire team was assembled in the conference room. Captain Webber outlined the plan and the assignments as best as they could be anticipated. This would be a buy and "slide". No one was to be arrested or in any way be aware that law enforcement was involved.

The operation was set to begin at eight that night, but everyone was on site or in position before then, ironing out little last minute contingencies. At eight, Pete and Charlie got into Pete's undercover pickup, and Pete made his first of many calls of the night. This call was to the base operations center, where remote piloting of Predator drones was conducted. He was immediately connected to his liaison officer, who would relay information between the team and the actual pilot of the drone.

"Okay, we're ready to leave the base and are approaching the main gate."

"Roger, Hardhat, just let us know when you actually pass through the gate."

Pete did as commanded, and the liaison officer confirmed they had a lock on him. The drone would remain locked on the vehicle until the operation was over. Pete drove slowly over to the Four Winds and parked, leaving an envelope with fifteen marked and recorded one-hundred dollar bills above the visor and the keys in the ignition. He and Charlie went in and took seats at the bar. Isaac was working and within seconds was assisting them.

"Um, we'll both have a Bud and my pickup is in the parking lot all set up the way Scotty told us to do it. It's a silver 2003 Chevy short wide 4x4. Is that okay?"

Isaac smiled and said: "Two Buds coming right up." Before he returned, Charlie saw him slip into the back as he pulled a cell phone out of his pocket. He was gone no more than thirty seconds, and returned with two ice cold Buds in his hands. "Got a pretty good ball game going on. You guys might want to get comfortable and enjoy the game."

Master Sergeant Jerry Glisan was the surveillance team liaison with the Predator. His radio crackled to life: "Hardhat Two from base. Target has arrived and is stationary at this time.

"Roger base, Hardhat team is in position."

The bad thing about surveillance is that bad guys don't often follow any kind of a schedule and get around to doing what they're going to do when they damned well feel like it. It was an endless source of frustration to Pete's surveillance team because it meant they had to wait, and wait, and wait some more. All kinds of fears emerged in the watchers' minds about what can go wrong with the operation: "Should I change to a different, maybe better location? Can the other team members hear me or me them? Did I make sure the flash is off on my camera?" and innumerable other small tasks that waiting causes to pop into one's head.

Finally, at about nine forty-five, Predator base reported the lights were on in Pete's truck and it was moving. Whoever was driving was playing it safe, remaining within the speed limits and using his or her signals, which made it easier for the Predator pilot. The pilot tracked the pickup through downtown Alamogordo, then onto Highway 70 heading south out of town. Finally, it signaled a turn into the main gate of Holloman Air Force Base.

"Hardhat Three confirms Primary has entered the base. There was a delay getting through security, but apparently it was resolved."

"Base to Hardhats, Primary seems to be just driving around some of the buildings as if making sure he doesn't have a tail. Recommend all units remain stationary."

No one moved, and when they saw headlights, they ducked down.

Fifteen minutes later came an update: "Base to Hardhats, Primary is slowly approaching the main supply warehouse."

"Hardhat Five, I've got him. He's backing up to the main door. It's opening and there's a forklift with the merchandise already loaded inside the door. Okay, the Primary is backing into the building and the guy that opened the door is on the forklift. Now he's loading the package. Primary is out and the big door is closing. Jeez that was fast!"

"Base to Hardhats, Primary is heading directly back toward the main gate, stand by."

"Hardhat Three: Primary is through the gate. He hardly even slowed down before someone waved him through."

"Base to Hardhats, Primary is back on Highway 70."

Five minutes later: "Base to Hardhats, Primary has pulled into the original location's parking lot and is now stationary. Lights are off."

"Roger, Base from Hardhat Two: see if you can pick up the next vehicle out of the parking lot and take him home."

"Base, Roger. There's a vehicle pulling out now."

"Hardhat Two to all units, maintain position until Base puts the vehicle to bed and we hear from Hardhat One."

Another half hour elapsed before Base came back on the net: "Base to all Hardhat units, secondary vehicle has pulled into an apartment complex and parked. Hardhat One is on the phone and has the location of the secondary vehicle. Hardhat One orders all Hardhat units to proceed to HQ."

The operation was over and from the looks of things, successfully. The debrief would determine that Hardhat Three, atced the base gate, had obtained good photographs of the driver of Pete's truck both coming and going, but was not able to visually identify the driver. Both gate guards had been identified and would be interviewed in due time. Hardhat Five, at the warehouse, was also able to get good video of the driver and of the man who had opened the door and operated the forklift. Hardhat Four had driven through the apartment complex and acquired a license plate number. The vehicle had an enlisted base sticker. A digital copy of the Predator's track was forthcoming and the "merchandise" was secreted, along with the pickup, at a storage facility off the base. They were lucky, very lucky. Webber had guessed right in his anticipation of where his vehicle would be driven on the base, and it got them the identification of whomever had opened the warehouse door and loaded the merchandise. The only unknown was who Isaac had called when Pete and Charlie spoke to him at the bar and Charlie could probably help them with that. If not, they could always write a search warrant for Isaac's phone and records.

CHAPTER 12

The next morning, Charlie and Pete were discussing the evening's operation over coffee in Pete's office when Samantha tapped on the door, then walked in. "Hi guys, didn't want to interrupt your discussion, but we might have a problem. Seems Washington is sufficiently interested in Charlie from our remote viewing exercise that they want to send out a team of 'experts' to duplicate the tests I've conducted and to do some of their own, instead of bringing Charlie to DC."

"Why is that a problem?" asked Charlie.

"I was afraid it might hinder your working with Pete on the big criminal case."

"It won't be a problem. Most of that stuff is happening in the evening anyway. Who are these experts?" asked Pete

"As far as I can tell, CIA, FBI, DIA, DARPA and NSA are sending representatives. Charlie, when you show them what you can do, they're going to exert a lot of pressure on you to come back to DC with them."

"You know how I feel about that, Samantha. It simply isn't going to happen."

"I hope you realize they're going to consider you a national asset and are going to want to protect you from getting snatched by some foreign government or terrorist group."

"They can protect me from here or Nellis just as easily. I really mean it, I'm *not* going to Washington, D.C. even for a visit."

"Okay, I understand. I'm just trying to give you an idea of what you're going to be up against."

"Yeah," he said slyly, "but don't forget I have my ways of ameliorating the situation in my favor."

Samantha laughed. "Really? I would never have guessed. So how is your case going?"

"Very well, I think," said Pete. "JAG wants us to make at least two more buys before we start gathering co-conspirators. Then it's going to be like a domino game with a lot of bad guys knocked over before it's all said and done."

"Good, nothing like arresting bad guys who are really deserving."

"We can't be sure, of course, but it looks like these guys have been ripping the Air Force for better than a million dollars' worth of equipment for over the past year. It's time that stopped. Thanks to Charlie here, we can do that."

"Are you using him on any other cases?"

"I've been sorely tempted, but I thought until we get him established in the courts, I'd better not risk the integrity of any more cases we can work another way. This one was just at a dead end and we only needed a break to get our teeth into it, and as it turned out the bad guys gave us everything we needed after Charlie pointed us in the right direction."

"Which brings up a question I've been meaning to ask, Charlie," said Pete. "Is the per diem we're giving you taking care of your expenses, or are you losing money by being here?"

"If I was drinking like I used to, I'd be broke all the time, but so far things are okay, though at some point I'd like to see something a little more lucrative than just expenses."

"I've been thinking about that too," said Samantha. "At some point you're going to be considered a consultant and should either negotiate a contract for a consulting fee or become a Government Schedule employee. I lean toward the latter because it gives you a benefits package that includes retirement, insurance, stuff like that. Unless, of course, you'd like to join the Air Force?"

Charlie laughed. "No, I think I'm too set in my ways to join the military, but I kind of like the idea of providing a service the government can use, and getting paid for it. I don't know if we're talking a career here or what, but I'm still not going to Washington, D.C. I guess that's one more reason not to join the military, isn't it?"

*****

"Glen," said a pensive Chip Lakin, "I've been thinking."

"I thought we agreed that's not a good thing."

"Yeah, well I've been thinking that maybe we should take some of the cash we've been making and buy a good-producing claim and start working again as prospectors. Seems we've been really lucky stayin' away from the cops, but our luck is bound to change. Maybe it's time to lay low for a while, you know, until things cool off a little anyway."

"I thought I told you, our luck is never going to change. Don't you remember? I'm *making* our luck by making people do and say what I want them to. It's as easy for me to make someone forget what we look like and what we're driving as it is for you to tie your shoe. How can our luck change if nobody recognizes us or can give the cops a description of what we're driving?"

"It stands to reason that they know who we are, and more and more people are going to be after us, especially after you shot that cop."

"Have we even come close to getting busted?"

"Well, no, but the odds . . ."

"Fuck the odds, we've got a great thing going. What, don't you like the way we're living? Nice hotels, nice restaurants, and decent clothes?"

"Well sure, but . . ."

"But nothin'. You can bail out any time you want but just remember, you're as wanted as I am, and nobody but me can protect you from gettin' arrested. Keep that in mind if you decide to go."

"I wasn't thinkin' of splittin' up, Glen, I just thought . . ."

"See what happens when you go thinkin'?"

"Yeah, okay."

"We're getting low on cash and it's time to do another job. That home robbery did pretty good, but there aren't that many houses out there that have that much cash in them. We got lucky - the dumb bastard had the days' receipts at home, and we cleaned him out. I've got an idea for a really big score, but we have to wait for the right opportunity. Let's take a ride over to Alamogordo, just to see what we can see."

Chip drove them to Alamogordo and they cruised through the downtown streets looking and discussing the pros and cons of hitting various businesses. Chip almost slammed to a stop when Glen exclaimed: "There!" He pointed at an armored car that was just pulling away from a bank.

"Now?"

"Hell no, not now, but I think that will be our next score. Lag back a little. Let's get an idea what their route is, so we can pick the right time to hit them."

"But Glen, those guys have guns, and they're locked in the truck."

"Yeah, so? The cop I shot had a gun too. Fat lot of good it did him, right?"

"Yeah, right, but now there's three of them."

"Maybe just two if we hit one that's on a routine route. We need to find out when they're bringing money into a business and when they're taking it out. No sense hitting an empty truck. Slow down, slow down, I think they're getting ready to make a stop. Okay, pull over there. Let's just watch to see what their routine is."

When the armored truck pulled over, the driver stayed in the cab, and a guard jumped out of the back and walked empty-handed into the store. He was back in less than ten minutes carrying what looked like a heavy bag. He opened the back door, climbed in with the bag, and the truck pulled away. Chip and Glen followed the truck all over Alamogordo, then back to its base in Las Cruces. Glen was satisfied with their surveillance. They could do this!

They followed the truck from the armored truck company for three days, noting the different routes. The truck made the rounds of the banks first, picking up and delivering money, then made the business circuit where their routine was the same. On the fourth day, Glen declared that they were ready.

He decided to pick off the truck as it was finishing its last bank. It was still relatively early, and traffic was light as their target arrived at the last bank. The guard jumped out with a bag and headed into the bank. Glen immediately got out of the pickup and went up to the driver's door of the armored truck. Suddenly the driver had an overwhelming urge to open his door.

Glen stuck a gun in his ribs and said: "No gun, no alarm, no radio and no phone. You behave, you live, you try to be a hero over some money, you die." He didn't even bother to strip the driver of his equipment before he went to the back of the truck. Within seconds, he was inside and had closed the door again. He kept reminding the driver of his orders, and the driver just sat there.

When Glen heard the key in the lock, he pulled his weapon. As the guard with the money bag entered the back of the truck, he too felt the gun in his ribs and got the same admonishment. Glen ordered the driver to drive around into the alley behind the bank, where Chip was waiting.

When they stopped, Glen immediately opened the back door and told Chip to cover the driver. He pulled the guard out of the truck, relieved him of his equipment, then had him lay face down on the asphalt. Chip brought the driver out and they did the same thing with him.

"Okay, keep 'em covered. If either one tries to be a hero, shoot 'em."

Luckily neither the driver nor the guard could see how badly Chip's gun hand was shaking.

Glen climbed back into the truck and began sorting through the locked bags of money. He was able to open the locks without effort and sort through the cash, winnowing out the change, paper receipts, and anything that looked like a tracker. He transferred all the paper money into two bags, which were surprisingly light when full. After he finished, he ordered both men on the ground into the back of the truck.

"Our other partner is going to be watching the back of the truck through a scoped rifle for the next twenty minutes. He sees a head pop out, he'll blow it apart like a ripe watermelon. We'll throw all your shit in the front and lock it. We don't want any kiddies getting ahold of those guns, do we? You won't remember what really happened except you were robbed. You can't give much of a description of us or our car. Have a nice day."

In twenty minutes they were well over halfway back to Las Cruces, but Glen kept an eye out the back of the pickup for any kind of pursuit. No one paid them a second glance, and they were back in their hotel in T or C an hour later. They put both money pouches in a black garbage bag and carried it up to their room. Once inside, Glen emptied the two pouches on the bed, and the two men looked at each other with big grins on their faces.

"See? I told you we'd score big! There's gotta be thirty or forty thou here, and nobody's the wiser. Still want to go prospectin'?"

Chip's grin was kind of sheepish. "No Glen, you were right. They can't touch us."

Glen threw a couple of bundles of hundred dollar bills at Chip. "Okay, I don't want to hear any more about that, got it?" Chip nodded but said nothing.

"Now let's party! You go get us some more beer – or champagne if you want – and some munchies, and I'll find us some pussy."

Both wound up being successful and a hearty party ensued. Glen had discovered that if he wanted to get drunk or high or both, he could. He just had to adjust his body's metabolism. They laughed, danced, and fornicated all night long until dawn was starting to break. Finally the girls – two *putas* from Juarez – decided it was time to leave but the men still were raring to go since both were high as kites on meth. Glen looked around the room and decided that dawn was probably a great time to check out considering the mess they had made in the room but he was happy. It had been a good party and he looked forward to the next one.

The hotel manager wasn't as impressed when he saw the state of the room. Trash, including syringes, food wrappers, soft drink cups, condoms and contents of ashtrays littered the floor. Both beds not only had the linens completely torn loose, but the mattresses were half laying on the floor. The shower curtain was pulled down off the rod, two drinking glasses were broken, and a hole was even punched in the wall behind the door where someone had slammed the doorknob through. The key was nowhere to be found, and two towels were missing. He had just about decided to call the police but, at the last minute, decided they probably would never find the perpetrators and decided to write the repairs off as a bad debt.

*****

Pete Webber got another call from Sergeant Ramirez later that second afternoon. "They hit again, this time in your backyard. Took off an armored truck at one of the banks in Alamogordo. Nobody was hurt, but there's an awful lot of unexplained behavior on the part of the two armored truck employees. The driver opened the door of the cab of the truck and neither man even tried to pull his weapon. Without an explanation, their actions seem almost criminal; you know, like the other robberies. People doing completely out-of-character things and not knowing why. I'm asking again, Captain, what is there about these guys you're not telling us?"

"Sergeant, I don't know what to say. No one is more sensitive to the danger your people are in than I am, but I'm caught on the horns of a dilemma. No one wants to help you more than I – we – do, if you could get a line on where they are, we'd be more than happy to take the point on taking them into custody. That's not to say that we'd necessarily do anything different than what you'd do, but we're willing to do what we can to help. We want these guys off the street as badly as you do."

"So you're not gonna tell me anything, right?"

"I can't tell you what I don't know. I have no way of knowing how to find these two; if I did, it would already be a done deal."

"I suppose Perkins is still with you guys, and he doesn't know anything either?"

"Charlie is his own man. If he could help, I have no doubt in my mind he would."

"I still think there's something – maybe something classified – that we need to know about. You won't be offended if my Sheriff goes to the governor, who will go to the commanding general of the base to see if we can find out what that is, right?"

"Be my guest, and I hope you get all the cooperation in the world. In the meantime, if you get a whiff of where these guys are, please don't hesitate to call us. I have a fully equipped SWAT team available and . . ." he almost said too much, ". . . we'll do anything we can."

"I believe you would, but I'd much rather know the rest of the story."

"For what it's worth, I'll take the matter up with my superiors, maybe we can come to some kind of an accommodation."

"Goddamnit, you just admitted in so many words there's more. Can't you see that lives are at stake? Does a cop have to die to get that across?"

"I did no such thing. I'm sorry if you interpreted it that way. I was going to go to my superiors and see if I couldn't get the SWAT team made available on a fulltime basis."

"We don't need another SWAT team. We need information about what's going on with these guys. That's the only thing we need."

"We were wondering if a joint task force would be a good idea. We'd certainly be willing to chip in men and equipment. Charlie has no objection to us bringing his Jeep back over to T or C and parking it around town with surveillance in hopes Ritchey or

Lakin takes the bait. I know that sounds like the granddaddy of all fishing expeditions, but what else do we have to work with until they make a mistake? I'm afraid a scenario like the one where the deputy was shot will reoccur, or some unwitting cop will pull traffic on them and get himself blown away."

"I hope you're being straight with me about not knowing anything more. If it comes out in the end that you did, the press will hear about it, and it will go beyond the governor to the Senate."

"Fair enough. How's Darrell Cunningham making out as a material witness?"

"I think he's still scared enough, after hearing what happened to you and Perkins, to be quite happy to be right where he is."

"That doesn't surprise me. Please call if something comes up or someone has a harebrained idea of how to grab these guys that we can help with."

"Later," was the brusque reply, and then there was only dial tone.

"He wasn't very happy with me," said Webber to Charlie and Samantha.

"I can't say as I blame him," said Samantha, "especially if someone does get hurt. Couldn't we tell them that Ritchey and Charlie here are under the influence of some kind of intoxicant that we can't identify and it has made them able to do what they do? We don't have an antidote or any way to know what they might be able to do next, but we have discovered a way to somewhat combat their ability to control people's actions."

"You mean like they're wacked out on 'peyote on steroids'?" Pete asked, with a smile at Charlie.

"Something like that."

"Well, I have to do something. Why don't you two continue your testing, and I'll make some phone calls."

Webber was halfway through his first phone call – to OSI Headquarters – when Samantha reappeared. She waited patiently while he finished his call.

"The director is going to call the base Commanding General and they'll discuss it. I'm sure that'll get the ball rolling in a hurry," Webber said with a grimace.

"More good news," said Sam as she sat down. "The team from Washington? They're here, at my lab at Nellis that is. We're supposed to proceed there ASAP."

"At least they have the probe there to ooh and aah over until we get there. Are we going commercial, or taking the regular shuttle?"

"The shuttle leaves in an hour and forty-five minutes; that should give us enough time to get Charlie packed. He already knows, and is probably over at the Inn by now, so if we can get a car, we'll just meet him there. Will that give you enough time?"

"Yeah, I'll meet you guys. I've been pretty much expecting something like this and am already about packed. I just need to get my notes and laptop together then swing by to get my luggage. We don't know how long this will last, right?"

She shook her head. "My guess is that we'll zing right through the duplicating of my preliminary tests then they'll get to what they're really looking for. I know there's a rush background investigation going on so as soon as there's a provisional clearance, they're going to want to show Charlie some classified photographs and see what he can tell them that they can or have verified another way."

"Do you think that's all they really want from him? His remote viewing capabilities or do they want to use him for counter-espionage purposes too?"

"There have been so many parapsychology studies, it's hard to know. What's hot right now compared to twenty years ago? I would hate to think they'd ignore his help when they know there's a mole at CIA or something like that, but all that is way above my pay grade."

"Still, no one knows him as well as we do and what his capabilities are. I'm just glad I've been ordered – and the General reiterated this on the phone just now – to stay with Charlie through everything and look out for him."

It was past eleven o'clock by the time the shuttle dropped them into Nellis Air Force Base and Samantha got Charlie and Pete settled at the Nellis Inn. She was grateful to get home again and went right to bed. She knew she'd need her rest, because tomorrow would be stressful, though she didn't want to share that thought with the others.

CHAPTER 13

The morning did not disappoint. Charlie, Pete, and Samantha had breakfast together at the Nellis Inn. It was a quiet, tense meal and they took their second cups of coffee over to Samantha's office, arriving just after seven-thirty. At precisely eight o'clock, they met with three men and one woman in the nearby small conference room. Introductions were made and the visiting quartet were identified as Robert Schneider, Central Intelligence Agency; Lieutenant Colonel David Orr, U.S. Army, Defense Intelligence Agency; Special Agent Denise Ratcliff, Federal Bureau of Investigation; and Commander Peter Hampton, U.S. Navy, National Security Agency. The representative from the Defense Advanced Research Projects Agency was detained, and would not be here for the initial meeting.

It almost felt like a Congressional hearing: four representatives from the Defense and Justice Departments were on a fact-finding mission to see if Charlie was the real thing or not. Charlie sat between Pete and Samantha and prepared for the worst. He could sense a lot of cynicism in the air.

"Mr. Perkins, as you know," said Robert Schneider, we're here to try to replicate Dr. Chase's test results. If we find merit with the results, we will conduct some other, more specific, examinations. Do you have any questions before we start?"

"No Sir."

"Dr. Chase, as you know, the series of tests you performed are mostly straightforward and boilerplate in nature. I'd hate to waste your and Captain Webber's time since Mr. Perkins will need to complete them on his own."

"Yes, Mr. Schneider, I know, " Samantha replied, "but I also know that Charlie will blaze through them in just fractions of the time we're used to. Don't forget, not only can he influence people's actions without their realizing it and move things with his mind, but his brain is functioning at an exponentially higher capacity than ours. The medical tests Charlie underwent proved that conclusively. We don't know how this happened, only that it did. Therefore, I thought it best that I remain in case there are questions or any confusion about what Charlie does. Captain Webber is under orders to remain with Charlie throughout his examination, and those orders come from Major General Riley, OSI Commander, in Quantico."

As Captain Chase had warned, Charlie was done in less than three hours with all the tests, and the panel was astonished. Lieutenant Colonel Orr sniffed, "We'll see how well he did before we're properly impressed."

It took the panel the rest of the day to compile the test results, so Charlie, Pete and Samantha gathered alone at lunch. "They're sure out to prove that this is a hoax," said Charlie. "The only one I sense any support from is the FBI representative, Agent Ratcliff."

"Think of it another way, Charlie. What they determine about your abilities will begin to affect our national defense. They'd better be right."

"I suppose, but they don't have be so damned superior about it. I really don't like their attitude, and it's going to cost them."

"What do you mean?" asked Samantha.

"I mean they're going to be sorry they didn't come into this with more of an open mind. I'm going to make sure they're convinced within the first hour that we're back together."

"Now Charlie, don't go doing something we'll all regret," said Pete.

"Oh, I won't. I just plan to make a big impression on them tomorrow morning."

Charlie thought about what he was going to do all afternoon, weighing the pros and cons. He wanted these people on his side, but he could already tell he was going to have to overcome some earnest resistance.

The next morning, everyone gathered in the same conference room ostensibly to announce Charlie's test scores and then to conduct further examinations. Before it started, Charlie stood up. "Lady and gentlemen, I have some opening remarks before we get down to business. First, as you have undoubtedly noticed, I did better on these exams than I did on Captain Chase's. I remembered the questions from the first time, because I have total recall. What I see, what I read, and what I experience, I never forget."

"Two of you are assuming already that I cheated and studied for the re-test, but that's not true, and the onus is on me to convince you of that. Mr. Schneider, you are a career intelligence analyst currently assigned to the North Korean desk. You have yet to personally see any useful intelligence come out of the parapsychological studies that have been conducted over the years and though you're hopeful, you're skeptical. You prefer people to call you Robert, hate it when they call you Bob, but allow your mother to call you Bobby. You are currently concentrating on gathering and collating intelligence about the death of Jang Song Thaek, Kim Jong Un's uncle and second in command of the country. You have information that conclusively confirms that Jang and five associates were thrown into a pen full of ravenous dogs and eaten alive. That the manner of death is confirmed is of secondary importance to the mental health of Kim Jon Un and his stability in the international arena. You are looking for signs of psychotic behavior, but thus far have only determined that he is a full-blown sociopath bent on consolidating his power."

Schneider blanched. "That's classified information. Where did . . ."

"Unfortunately we cannot turn off our brains and when you're thinking about your job, you're emanating intelligence – at least to me – that no one else can gather. You personally believe that Kim Jong Un will be dead within five years and that's based on your analysis, not on wishful thinking. Even now, there is a growing tide of resentment and resistance to Kim's governance and unless his counter-espionage apparatus can roll up the entire resistance organization, his days as leader are numbered. Obviously if I could get close to this particular Great Successor, I could tell you exactly what's on his mind just as I have done for you."

"Lieutenant Colonel Orr, it hadn't occurred to you that I might have cheated or studied for the tests you helped administer yesterday. You lead an analytical team concentrating on Al Qaeda in Sudan, and particularly on the information being gleaned from Abu Anas Al-Liby, who was captured back in March of 2013 and turned over to us. I won't go into the details of that information, but at this point, you believe you're still in the process of peeling back the layers of the onion that are his lies. You are married and can't wait to get home to your two young children, Jenny and Emily, who take center stage even above your job, though sometimes the conflict between the two can be stressful. You have a beagle named Jake, which is the same name as your favorite dog when you were a child growing up in Indianapolis. If I could get close to Abu, I could tell you easily if he's lying or not and what information he gives you is the truth."

"Special Agent Denise Ratcliff, you have been assigned to counter-intelligence for the past seven years. You're not quite sure why you're here, since parapsychological research is nothing you have had any experience with. You were just told to be present and represent the FBI as appropriate. Your primary assignment is to collate intelligence information and prepare a daily brief for your director and his staff. It's not a very rewarding assignment and you'd much rather be in a field office. You're not too particular who knows this, but your boss thinks you do a terrific job and is resistant to losing you, even though you've applied for transfer more than once. I don't know how much I can do for you except convince your boss it's time for you to get out of Washington, D. C."

"*Rear Admiral* Peter Hampton, you are the biggest skeptic on the panel, having worked in parapsychological research for the past seven years. You personally think it is an enormous waste of money and manpower, and the assets could be better used for human intelligence-gathering pursuits. You've seen several allegedly potential 'psych' candidates come and go, and believe that about half of them were intentionally trying to defraud the government, while the other half were just trying to be good citizens and believed they had a gift, which they did not. You are here specifically because of your prejudice in an attempt to cut this short and let all four of you get back to work. You had huevos rancheros and coffee for breakfast this morning. and the mild sauce used on the eggs isn't sitting too well. To be honest, my 'remote viewing' abilities have still been undetermined unless you count the photo Pete and Samantha showed me of the Qingdao shipyard a little while back. No one could ever tell me if I was correct or not."

"Oh, you were correct, all right. Every ship in the task force was only out for a few days before returning to port," said Admiral Hampton. "First, I guess we can all agree that you did, in fact, do better on these tests than you did on the previous ones, and I won't even try to find an explanation. Your statement that you just remembered the questions is as valid as any, but we've never seen scores like that in the past and certainly not at the speed at which you completed them. You're also right about what I had for breakfast, but I have to point out that huevos rancheros is a far cry from convincing any intelligence officer worth his or her salt that you're legitimate. Seeing through the subterfuge of my rank was a step in the right direction."

"Fair enough," said Charlie. "Unless there's an aberration in the previous tests that you'd like to explore, shall we go ahead with your other examinations?"

"Mr. Perkins . . ." Agent Ratcliff began.

"Could I impose on you all just to call me Charlie? When you say Mr. Perkins, I automatically think I'm in the principal's office."

"Very well, Charlie," Agent Ratcliff continued, "when you watch television, can you tell what the speaker is really thinking, as opposed to what he or she is saying?"

"If it's a live broadcast, depending on how strongly they're emoting their thoughts, I can pick up some of what they're thinking. It's much better live and in person. That's something else I should mention. I can read your thoughts as easily as my own and I did so when I gave my opening statement, but I won't do it again unless invited, or unless you generate an emotional spike I can't ignore."

"How long does one of your suggestions last once you've instilled it in someone?" asked Orr.

"That depends on the circumstances. If, for example, I wanted you to raise your arm," Lieutenant Colonel Orr watched his right arm raise up above his head, "it only lasts until I put your arm down again." Down went the arm. "If," he said, looking at Agent Ratcliff, "I was to try to impose a suggestion that lasted, I have to say I don't know. We haven't tested that."

"How far away can someone be and still be subject to your suggestions?" asked Schneider.

"We only tested to the perimeter of this building, which was successful; I don't know if I can successfully suggest something to someone at the main gate and have it work."

"Can you anticipate certain future events with any degree of accuracy?" asked Lieutenant Colonel Orr.

"I haven't tried, but I think there's a situation brewing in New Mexico where I think I should try."

"What's that about?" asked Orr.

"There is, apparently, another man who has been subjected to the probe," said Captain Webber. "At least we think so. We know he has been in the area where we found the probe, and he has been cutting a helluva swath across southern New Mexico committing robberies where the victims inexplicably do precisely what he tells them to do, up to and including a police officer holstering his gun just before the suspect shot him in the chest. Luckily the officer was wearing a ballistic vest with a trauma plate, and it saved his life. No one seems to be able to give a description of the suspects that's anything but hazy, and we've yet to get a vehicle description either."

"And what would you do about that, uh . . . Charlie?" asked Lieutenant Colonel Orr.

"I'd love to be able to pinpoint where he is, so he can be neutralized."

"Neutralized?" asked Admiral Hampton.

"I don't know if he can be arrested. He had me as a hostage for a while and in handcuffs, but I was able to just unlock them, and they fell off my wrists. I'm assuming he can do the same thing, and I worry about what he can do to a squad of officers with regard to mind control before they can subdue him. We tried some of that here and discovered that I could keep at least three people at bay, but any more than that could overpower me."

"So you're actually saying shoot this man?"

"I wish I could come up with a better idea and I've racked my brain for a scenario where I could combat him and get him peacefully into custody."

"This guy hates Charlie," said Captain Webber. "He already tried to shoot us on the freeway coming out of T or C one day."

"Why?" asked Orr.

"He believes I stole his gold from a claim up in the Black Range. He had killed his partner then abandoned the site, so I worked it for almost five weeks, and pulled out quite a bit of gold."

"And you can't just find him by casting your mind out to different places you know he's been?" asked Admiral Hampton.

"Not so far. I did notice one time when I drove by a tavern we used to frequent, that I could feel that he had been there recently but I knew he wasn't there then. I had no idea how long ago he had been there, but it hadn't been long."

"We've been discussing with the Sheriff's Office in Truth or Consequences the possibility of using Charlie's Jeep as bait with a surveillance team on it to see if they bite but no decision has been made that I know of."

"So you can sense a particular presence from at least a little distance away?" asked Admiral Hampton.

"Yes, most of the time."

"Why do you want to come to work for the government?" asked Mr. Schneider.

"I don't know that I do," said Charlie.

"We kind of had to pull his abilities out of him like pulling teeth," Captain Webber explained.

"So he didn't come to you saying what he was capable of doing?" asked Admiral Hampton.

"No, quite the opposite," Webber replied. "He came to us with some photos he took of the probe and asked us if we wanted it; because he didn't think it was from around there. He offered to take us up there. Obviously he was right."

"So you don't know anything about the probe?" asked Colonel Orr.

"No Sir, not more than what I've already told Captain Webber and Captain Chase. I do know I don't want to go back in it for anybody," Charlie replied soberly.

The questioning went on for the rest of the day about what happened to Charlie in the probe and what he could and couldn't do. He was exhausted by the time they quit, and so were the panelists. They seemed to have a better attitude toward him now though. Admiral Hampton, especially, seemed to have warmed up after he learned that Captains Webber and Chase had had to pry Charlie's abilities out of him.

The same kind of questioning began the third day. "When you look at a photograph of someone, what do you know about the subject?" asked Agent Ratcliff.

"Generally, I can tell who they are and what their recent history is, depending on what was in their conscious mind at the time of the photograph. Sometimes I can tell where the photo was taken but I have no idea where they are currently or what they've been doing since the photograph was taken, so if your photograph is old, you won't get much. As I said, live and close to face-to-face or the equivalent is best."

"Do you know from where your information came that the Chinese task force wasn't going to stay out very long?" asked Mr. Schneider.

"You mean from which individual? No, only that it was obvious that the group of ships wasn't going on a long voyage."

"Can you overhear a phone conversation?" asked Admiral Hampton.

"Yes, if I'm close enough. Sometimes I can tell who the caller is and where the call originated, unless it's one of those multi-transfer kinds of set ups."

The barrage of questions lasted through the rest of the day. Once again, Charlie and his board of inquiry were drained at the end of the day but not too tired to get together for a drink after the day's questioning was done.

"You probably know what we want to do next . . ." Admiral Hampton began.

"No Sir, I don't. I told you up front that I wouldn't intrude on your thoughts past that introduction, and I meant it. I'll do so with your permission but not on my own. I think that's unethical," said Charlie, then took another sip of his iced tea.

"Fair enough," said Admiral Hampton, "we want to run you though some exercises to maybe get an idea what the limits of your abilities are; you know, things that haven't been tested yet."

"Do any of you still have any lingering doubts about Charlie's abilities?" asked Samantha.

The quartet looked at each other and shook their collective heads. "Our only question is where his limits are."

There were a few last minute questions the next morning, but everyone on the panel seemed anxious to get to the practical exercises. Each member of the group became the guinea pig for various experiments. Lieutenant Colonel Orr was sent to the main gate and Charlie was asked to suggest the officer raise his arm then unbutton his tunic, both of which he did.

"Charlie," asked Agent Ratcliff when Lieutenant Colonel Orr returned, "is there any kind of barrier that you've discovered that blocks your attempts to suggest things?"

"Just distance so far," he replied.

When Samantha's phone rang in the next room, Charlie said: "That's Dr. Hickman calling from Administration. He wants to remind you your monthly report is almost due." As an aside, he added: "He's also upset that one of his daughters, Kimberly, wants to change her major at UCLA even though she's about to finish her third year of majoring in philosophy. Do you want to know what else is on his mind?"

"Now that you know where Dr. Hickman is, Charlie, could you glean this information without the phone contact?"

"No, he's too far away."

"Where's the Administration building?" asked Agent Ratcliff.

"On the other side of the campus," said Captain Chase.

"Charlie, can you remotely start any of the cars parked outside the building?" asked Mr. Schneider.

"I don't think so. Partly because most of them are too far away, and partly because I'm not familiar with the starting circuits on the newer cars. If it was an older car subject to being hot-wired I could probably do some of them, but unless I'm familiar with the mechanism, I'm not much good at unlocking things."

By mid-afternoon, they had a pretty good idea what the extent of Charlie's abilities were and what his limits were. They gathered in the conference room after a late lunch.

"Charlie, I think this is the last phase of our examination. We want to show you a series of photographs of various subjects, and see if you can at least identify them and tell us when and where the photo was taken. I assume you can also tell us how the photo was taken and by whom?"

"Probably, but I've never tried that."

Mr. Schneider laid down a photograph of Kim Jong Un with his uncle, Jang Song Thaek.

Charlie identified the image and suddenly looked surprised.

"What?" said Schneider.

"Jang really was planning a coup!" Charlie announced.

Schneider didn't look particularly surprised. "What can you tell me about 'The Great Successor'?"

"He's a thug, immature, and on a huge ego trip. He has no particular talent for his position and no long term agenda, except to consolidate and maintain his power and increase his notoriety on the world stage. But he's sane as you or me, just sociopathic."

Schneider pursed his lips. "And that's all from the photograph?"

"Yes. I would love to be nearby when someone is talking to this guy."

"Why?"

"Because – excuse me Agent Ratcliff - he's an asshole and he's easy to read, but he's dangerous as hell. His arrogance will be his downfall."

Schneider raised his eyebrows, then sighed. "And he has nuclear weapons," he said dryly.

Next, Lieutenant Colonel Orr showed Charlie a mug shot of a man of Middle Eastern descent.

"That's your guy Abu Anas Al-Liby shortly after the Sudanese handed him over to you. He's as treacherous as a black mamba and twice as aggressive. Don't ever turn your back on him. His real name is Nazih Abdul-Hamed Nabih al-Ruqai'I and he's actually from Libya, though he's been active in several African countries, including Kenya, Egypt, and Sudan. He's a computer whiz, even though he's fifty years old. He has a long and active association with Al Qaeda and he has been held and interrogated so many times he's con-wise as hell. Assume he'll withhold some information until he dies, but he'll give up some things just to convince you you've broken him."

Agent Ratcliff dropped a surveillance photo in front of Charlie of a white male coming out of some kind of business. "That's Keith Roark, but his real name is Mikhail Sevelyev. He's a computer programmer at Java and he's been laying very low since the arrest of the Illegals, the ten Russian spies the FBI rolled up in 2010 and traded back to Russia. He knew Igor Sutyagin and Anna Chapman, who were major players, but at the time Roark was only a low level gofer. Now he's trying to keep Java as porous as it's been these last several years in order to allow others in his group to hack into other sites. Roark is pretty complacent because he thinks he's under the radar after the Illegals roundup. He was with a man named Mark Simpson who also works at Java. Roark is cultivating him. Simpson is not a player yet but he's thinking about it.

Admiral Hampton looked at his associates with raised eyebrows. All three nodded.

"Well, you scored a hundred percent, Charlie," he said with a smile, "and told my associates a little more than they knew about the pictures they showed you. Now they have to work for a living!"

Amid the laughter, Hampton continued: "You've made the best of our test subjects look like rank amateurs, Charlie, and that's saying something, because some of our people are pretty damned good. I can't begin to imagine how valuable you can be to the intelligence and counter-intelligence gathering organizations of this country. Without question, your existence will be classified TOP SECRET and Compartmented with Eyes Only access. You are now a very big headline in the intelligence community, and face time with you will be as hard to get as unscheduled time on the Very Large Array radio telescope in your home state of New Mexico. I think my associates have several more photographs to show you, and then we'll wrap this up. Is there any way you know of to spoof you?"

"Odd that you mention that, Admiral," said Pete. "One afternoon we took Charlie out into the hangar at Holloman and tried a few ways to overcome his unique influence. Captain Chase came up with the idea of merely counting as you went about your work, and it kept Charlie from taking over our subconsciouses."

"Yes, we've tried that, and the problem with it is that a subject like Charlie can tell you're counting and given enough time, can work around it. We've found that strict mind control training, and forcing your mind to concentrate in just certain areas, works the best. That's what we teach our people, and that's what I did with Charlie."

"Care to try again, Admiral?" asked Charlie with a smile.

"I don't think so. Let's get these questions out of the way and get back home. Charlie we want - no, we *need* - you at NSA. All the branches will have access but I think it will ultimately be determined that your home is at NSA. How do you feel about moving to Maryland?"

"That's the one problem, Admiral," said Charlie slowly, "I don't want to move. I don't mind being over here, but I was born and raised in New Mexico and feel no need to move away, even if you wash your hands of me. I suppose I could be available for consultation here in Nevada, but no way am I coming to the Washington, D. C. area, sorry."

Admiral Hampton nodded. "Yeah, a little birdie told me that would be your position and I can't really blame you, but understand my predicament. Right now there are few people in the world that know of your existence. Those with that knowledge will increase, and eventually there will be unauthorized access, and the bad guys will know you exist. Once that happens, a helluva lot of people are going to want to at least get their hands on you, or even eliminate you. Now that I have met you and seen you at work, I feel responsibility for your welfare. How can we reconcile your desire to stay out west with the cold hard facts?"

"Let me give that some thought, Admiral, and I'd like to confer with my advisors," he said with a smile, first looking at Pete then at Samantha.

"Fair enough. Let's get on with the rest of the pictures."

That evening, after the panel had returned to Washington, Charlie said over dinner: "I meant what I said about not going to Washington, but if I absolutely have to go, there's one thing I have to do first. We *have* to get Glen Ritchey off the streets."

CHAPTER 14

Chip Lakin was worried. He had just awakened after crashing for fourteen hours and Glen was still sitting at the table, a beer in front of him, brooding. He had suddenly quit partying about nine last night, paid off his whore, who left, leaving Chip still in bed with the other one. Knowing Glen was watching made Chip very self-conscious, and it wasn't long before the other girl slipped quietly out the door.

"Hey," he asked, "what's going on? What's wrong? You sick or something?"

Glen was a long time answering and when he did, his voice was deep and hoarse. "It's that fucking Perkins. Here we sit, trying to get by with the law down on us everywhere while he's sitting pretty with my money in the bank. That's not right, and I'm not gonna let him get away with it."

"What are you gonna do?"

"I don't know yet, but I'll think of something."

Chip knew better than to try to continue the conversation; it would only piss Glen off, and that was the last thing he wanted, so he went back to bed and fell asleep.

The next afternoon when he awoke, Glen was still brooding. Chip knew that the man was strung out and needed sleep, but his partner had this idea in his head and wouldn't let go of it.

"Hey man, why don't you get some sleep? We're good here for another couple of days, and you've been up three days already. Get some sleep and maybe you'll come up with a good idea when you wake up. I'll keep an eye on things. You don't have to worry about nothin'."

To his surprise, Glen nodded, got up from his chair, and laid down on the bed, his right forearm draped across his eyes. "Maybe you're right, but I'm not letting him get away with my money and all the shit he's done to me."

Predictably, Glen crashed - hard - this time for eighteen hours, and when he awoke he was rocky. Chip handed him a handful of aspirin and a beer to chase them down. Glen lay back on the bed and closed his eyes. Chip thought he had gone back to sleep until that deep, hoarse voice said: "No more dope until we get Perkins. I wanna be straight when I see it in his eyes that he's dead meat." Then he dozed off again.

When next he awoke, his eyes were bloodshot as he got up and staggered into the bathroom. Moments after hearing the toilet flush, Chip heard the shower running and knew that Glen was up, at least for a while. When the bathroom door opened again, Glen was still nude, and drying his hair with a towel. He stopped at a bag on the counter, tore open a package of jockey shorts, and put a pair on. Then he opened a stick of deodorant and haphazardly ran the stick across his armpits a couple of times. He took the rest of his clothes back into the bathroom and when he emerged, he was dressed and brushing his longish damp hair back with his fingers.

"Got any more of those aspirins?"

Chip held out the aspirin bottle and retrieved a bottle of beer from the ice chest he had brought in the night before. It was still cold even though it was mostly water in the bottom of the cooler.

Glen shook out a small pile of aspirin and handed the bottle back to Chip then chased the pain killers with half the beer.

"Talk about being fuuucked up," he said with a rueful grin. "You hungry?"

Lakin nodded and they went in search of someplace to eat.

While they ate, Glen said: "I meant it about Perkins. I'm gonna get that guy, or this is gonna eat me alive. And no more dope until we finish the job. Then we can celebrate."

"Sure, Glen. You know I'm with you a hundred percent." What he didn't say was that little niggling doubt had returned, and he was concerned that they were approaching the end of their run. They had been too lucky for too long, and that streak had to end sometime, didn't it?

"Do you have a plan how you want to take Perkins out?" Chip asked.

"Not yet," said Glen, "but when the time comes, I'll know what to do."

They drove around El Paso for a while, eyeballing the girls and discussing different places that might be a good target for their next job. Glen hadn't liked the armored car. He said that controlling the two guards so closely was a huge drain on his energy, and he didn't want to risk it again. He thought that maybe a bank on the east end of El Paso would be a good hit then they could head back toward home, but for now they were flush and didn't need to rush it.

They passed an El Paso PD patrol car that had someone pulled over, and Glen studied it intensely when they slowly drove by. "Turn around," he ordered suddenly. "I want to go by again." This time he didn't stop staring until they were a block past the traffic stop. "Let's go get a beer," was all he said.

Glen was quiet when they entered the strip club and sat down near the front. A big-breasted girl, down to her g-string, with bright red hair was onstage making love to a pole, and Chip watched with avid interest. Glen stared at his beer and didn't say a word, even when the topless waitress brought back their change.

Finally, the redhead finished her routine and went backstage to a smattering of applause. Chip leaned over to Glen and asked: "What about a place like this? They haul in a ton of cash after a good night."

"Nah, too big a chance somebody besides us will be packing heat, and we'd wind up in a situation. I don't want no shooting unless we got no choice, and hitting a place like this is just an invitation for that. There's too many people for one thing, and too many punks thinking it's cool to pack some kind of piece. Let's go back to the room. I want to lay down for a while."

Chip drove them back to the motel and Glen stretched out on the bed that had been made and the room tidied up. "The fucking maid has her hands full with us around," Chip joked once they had noticed how tidy everything was.

Glen didn't say anything, just closed his eyes and appeared to drop off.

The next day they cruised through east El Paso and hit a small bank in a new shopping center. It wasn't the most lucrative job they'd done, but it was the easiest, since there were only two employees inside.

Glen chose a motel on the north end of T or C as their next center of operations. They had stayed there early on in their spree and hadn't left so much of a mess that the management wouldn't let them return. Glen made sure they got a room on the back side, with direct parking lot access. They cruised around town, just in case Glen might catch a scent of Charlie Perkins, then they stopped for a pitcher at the Plugged Nickel. There were a few familiar faces there and, of course, Glen had to play the big man and buy a round for everyone. No one had seen Charlie Perkins in what seemed like weeks, and some had just assumed he had moved on, but Glen knew better. He knew the sniveling coward was in hiding, and God help him when Glen found him.

They had dinner and were back in the motel room with a cooler full of iced beer by nine that evening. "Don't get too beered up," Glen warned his partner, "we have plans for later tonight."

"Yeah? Did you already scope us out some girls?" Chip asked as he picked a scab off his face, a common side-effect from methamphetamine abuse.

"No, tonight we start my plan to root out Charlie fucking Perkins, and I don't want any fuckups because you were too drunk to understand what you have to do."

"What do I have to do?"

"Just do what I tell you when I tell you, and things will go smooth."

"You say so, man."

Glen rousted Chip from his bed at eleven. "C'mon, we're gonna go cruise around."

"What for?"

"It's part of the plan, stupid. First thing we gotta do is get a different plate for this pickup, one that's cool if we get stopped."

"But it won't be registered to us and we don't have insurance or any of that shit," Chip protested.

"Don't start thinking on me, Chip. I have it all figured out so let me do the thinking and the worrying, okay?"

"Whatever you say, Glen, I was just sayin' . . ."

Glen cut him off brusquely: "I know what you were saying now let's get going."

They cruised around Elephant Butte until they found what Glen was looking for, a similar pickup that looked like it hadn't been driven in a while. He sent Lakin to retrieve the rear plate then, when they found a quiet spot, had him replace the plate on the pickup with the stolen one.

"Okay, now we go cruising for a cop, preferably one from the Sheriff's Office."

Chip opened his mouth to speak, thought better of it, and closed it without a sound.

They drove around T or C for nearly an hour before Glen looked at his watch. He told his partner to drive over to the courthouse and find a place to park where they could watch the back of the building, where the Sheriff's Department parked their cars. They waited about fifteen minutes until a young deputy, Mike Emmerson, emerged from the building and sauntered out to one of the marked patrol cars. When Emmerson pulled out of the parking lot and came to a stop at the traffic light, his turn signal indicated a left turn south through town. Glen had Chip fall in behind the car at a distance of a couple of blocks until they got clear of downtown. Then he sped up to about fifteen above the thirty-five-mile-an hour speed limit and passed the deputy.

Predictably Emmerson started to pace him and as they were nearing Williamsburg, he activated his overhead lights. Chip nearly panicked. "Glen, he's stopping us. I told you he would! Now what are we going to do?"

"Just go on a little more around the curve then pull over," Glen said grimly, about half disgusted with his partner.

Chip pulled the pickup over, and the patrol car followed suit. "Are you going to shoot him?" he asked, almost hysterical.

"Goddamn it, SHUT UP!" Glen hissed through clenched teeth as Emmerson approached the passenger side of the pickup. Glen rolled down his window and didn't even let Emmerson open his mouth before he froze him with a thought then got out of the pickup.

"Get in," Glen ordered, "leave your gun and radio in their holsters, and scoot over into the middle." He crowded in beside Emmerson and slammed the door. "Okay, Chip, drive to the interchange, then north back toward the motel. You, Deputy, just sit there nice and quiet, and nobody gets hurt." The deputy didn't say a word, just sat there as if he was in a fog and didn't realize what was happening.

Chip was almost sobbing as he drove the pickup back along I-25 to the motel. At Glen's direction he drove at a normal speed, took the north exit off the freeway into North T or C, then into the motel parking lot and all the way to the back in front of their room.

"Okay, Deputy, we're going to walk into that motel room, and you're going to be just as peaceful as you can be. You do what you're told, and no one has to get hurt."

Chip's head was swiveling 180 to 180 left and right as they made their way to their room, but Glen looked straight ahead, his hand gripping Emmerson's bicep. Chip unlocked the room and quickly closed the door after Glen guided the deputy in and sat him down on a chair near the table.

"Okay, Chip, pull the deputy's handcuffs out and cuff him through the back of the chair, then tape his feet to the legs and his chest to the seat back. Can you do that without fucking it up?"

Chip was shaking as he retrieved a pair of handcuffs from Emmerson's duty belt and ratcheted them into place.

"Now take his gun and radio and put them on the bed." Then he leaned down until his nose was less than an inch from Emmerson's. "I could kill you just like that," he said with a snap of his fingers, "but I think you'll convey a better message alive than dead. You tell your bosses that unless they produce Charlie Perkins, I'll be taking another deputy – maybe even you – and this time the deputy won't be so lucky. You got that? I'm taking your radio and in two days – at noon on the third day – I'm going to call on the channel it's set on and there had better be an answer. It had better be the one I want"

Emmerson nodded, still not appearing to be completely lucid.

"Okay, Chip, put some tape over his mouth, dump the chair on its side, and we're out of here."

As they drove away, Glen could see that his partner was brimming over with questions but was afraid to ask them. All he asked was: "Where to?"

"I think back to El Paso. It's big enough we can lose ourselves. We'll have to come back here when it's time to make the call but until then, I think it's best to be out of the hot zone."

"Hot zone! Jesus, Glen, that's the understatement of the year. Cops all over the state are going to go ape shit when they find that deputy's patrol car abandoned."

"The bastards should be grateful he's alive with all his fingers and toes. Listen, Chip, if it's getting too hot for you, now's the time to say so. I can't have somebody at my back I can't trust to stay there. You're acting pretty shaky, and I'm starting to get the feeling you can't handle the heat."

"I'd a been a lot better if I had known what you were going to do, but to drop it on me like that . . . that's not right. How would you feel?"

"Yeah, okay, point taken. But you gotta get some backbone, man, because once I off Perkins, it's gonna be twice as bad. I think it'll be time to make a move to someplace like L.A. or Vegas once I put that fucker out of his misery. We can start over fresh, maybe go up into northern California and try prospecting up there. Or grow dope. They say it's pretty easy and there're a lot of growers up there already."

"What the hell, why don't we just go now? Perkins ain't worth dyin' over, and even you are gonna be outnumbered if they ever find us."

"Go ahead and go if you're so scared, Chip," growled Glen. "This is my thing with Perkins and you don't have to be involved. But I'm gonna get him if it's the last thing I do."

*****

"One Sierra Ten, calling One Sierra Ten," called the dispatcher over the main Sheriff's Office frequency.

The silence lasted no more than five seconds but felt like an age. "Sergeant, we've been calling Deputy Emmerson every five minutes for the past twenty with no response."

"How long has he been out on traffic?" asked the Watch Commander, Sergeant Burnum.

"Fifty-three minutes."

"Where's the closest unit?"

"Cuchillo."

"Damn these guys when they forget to clear after a traffic stop and then turn their radio down."

Just then the phone rang and the dispatcher picked it up. "Sheriff's Office Dispatch, do you have an emergency?"

"I don't know. There's a police car parked out on Broadway near the Veteran's Home. It's been parked out there for almost an hour with its lights on and everything, and there's no one around the car."

"He might be in one of the houses in the neighborhood on a call, Ma'am," said the dispatcher, motioning to the Watch Commander.

"I don't think so. We're the only house on Broadway in the area and like I said, the Veteran's Home is on the other side of the street."

Without even thinking about it, the dispatcher took the caller's name, address, and phone number, then hung up. She turned to the Watch Commander and told him about the call.

"Okay," said the grim-faced Sergeant, "I'll go out there myself."

The scene was as the caller had described. Emmerson's car was all lit up, keys in it and running, but there was no deputy. Sergeant Burnum called in all available deputies and reserves to do a search of the area, but that came up almost completely negative too. They did find Emmerson's notebook and flashlight on the opposite side of the sidewalk from the street, about thirty feet ahead of the patrol car. There were no signs of a struggle and, thank God, no traces of blood.

Burnum notified the chain of command above him and the Sheriff himself responded and ordered the area searched and canvassed again, but the results were the same. The car was towed in for processing, and the flashlight and notebook were sent in for fingerprint analysis.

BOLOs (be on the lookout for) and ATLs (attempt to locate) were sent out over the states of New Mexico, Arizona, and Texas, but there were no takers. Deputy Emmerson had vanished without a trace.

Morning came with a fresh troop of young Explorers doing a third grid search over the same ground in the vicinity of the car, but still no one found so much as a fresh cigarette butt.

The license number Emmerson called in on the truck was found to belong on a 1994 Ford pickup registered in Elephant Butte. A check of the residence revealed the truck parked with weeds growing around it and a registered owner who was left scratching his head at the sudden onslaught of questions.

The FBI brought up a mobile command post from El Paso and parked it in the parking lot at the Sheriff's Office. The Sheriff's Office telephone system was patched through the command post in case a call for ransom or any other tips came in. A hotline was set up and press releases made but still there was no sign of the missing deputy.

Finally the call came from the motel. A maid had gone in to clean the room, taken one look at a body taped to a chair, then threw up her hands (and towels), and ran screaming from the room. She returned with the manager, but refused to go back in the room. When the manager found that the body was very much alive, he called the police from the room and stood by until a multitude of law enforcement types responded and took over not only the room, but most of the parking lot.

Emmerson was unhurt save for his pride, and he was embarrassed by the magnitude of the response to his disappearance. He had the luxury of an understanding audience when he explained that when his abductor told him to do something, he found that he had no will to resist. They had heard it all before, too many times in the preceding weeks. When he gave them Ritchey's message, there was no doubt in the room that it was a threat they should take seriously. Sergeant Ramirez was on the phone to Captain Webber immediately.

"You heard about the missing deputy?" he asked without preamble.

"Yes, how's that going?"

"We found him, trussed up like a Christmas goose in a room at a motel in T or C. Seems he was kidnapped to emphasize the message he carried from none other than Glen Ritchey. Produce Charlie Perkins, or the next time, a deputy won't be so lucky."

"And you're sure it was Ritchey?"

"Oh yeah, right down to the inability to resist."

"Got any ideas? We can't throw Charlie under the bus."

"No, but could you at least bring him over so we can talk about it?"

"Yes but we're in Nevada. It'll take some time to arrange a flight to get there."

"We'll be waiting."

*****

It was after six when Pete and Charlie got back to T or C. Pete had called Ramirez the minute they arrived at Holloman to let him know they were on their way. As they pulled into the parking lot behind the courthouse, they looked at each other.

Pete spoke first. "I suppose we'd better assume Ritchey is close by and watching. That means we take no chances with you. I'll pull up next to the door, and you duck in and wait for me there while I park the car, okay?"

Charlie sighed. "Okay."

Once Webber joined him in the entry, Ramirez led them through the security door and through a maze of hallways to one of the smaller courtrooms. It was nearly full of law enforcement officers ranging from T or C PD to the Border Patrol, since no one knew where or whom Ritchey would strike next.

They found chairs near where Ramirez was sitting, but the Sergeant said: "Don't sit down yet, let me introduce you and let folks get a good look at you, Charlie."

"Folks, this is Captain Webber from the Air Force and Charlie Perkins, the man who is unintentionally causing all this uproar."

Both men nodded as they scanned the room, then sat down quickly.

"This, by the way, is the victim of Glen Ritchey's abduction, Deputy Bob Emmerson," said Ramirez, indicating the man in uniform sitting next to him.

"I know him," whispered Charlie to Pete, "we went to high school together."

"Have you come up with a plan of any kind?" Webber asked, looking at Ramirez.

"We've been brainstorming like crazy since we got Bob here back, but none of us has been in circumstances quite like this. We were sort of hoping you could fill us in on what exactly this Glen Ritchey is capable of."

Webber had anticipated this and had pressured his boss in Quantico into authorizing a partial release of the manifestations of being in the probe.

Webber stood. "Are there any media types here?"

Ramirez answered for the group: "No, these are all card-carrying law enforcement officers."

"Good. What I'm about to tell you is TOP SECRET. I'm asking on your honor as law enforcement officers that it goes no further than this room." There were nods around the room, and a couple of officers scooted forward on their seats.

"Charlie and Glen Ritchey were exposed to the same unknown source of contamination. We still don't know what it is and the only way we know that much is that they are both displaying the same symptoms, increased brain activity manifested in the ability to control people and a lesser ability to move things with their mind. Charlie can't stop a speeding bullet if that's what you're thinking, but he can turn off the lights in this room, prevent a weapon from firing – which has already saved our lives – and he could probably nudge a firearm off target."

"We have done extensive tests on Charlie which gives us the what, up to a point but not the how or if there's a why. He can, for example, control the actions of up to four men simultaneously but any more than that, his concentration breaks down and he can be overcome. We've experimented with ways to minimize this and found that if one subconsciously starts counting while doing something else, if he concentrates hard enough, he can prevent Charlie controlling his actions. It's not easy to do and takes practice but counting while doing something else apparently fills part of the sub-conscious with activity which Charlie's mind cannot invade. It only takes a momentary lapse and Charlie is back in and once he's in, he's there to stay until he voluntarily withdraws."

"Bob," Pete said, looking at Emmerson, "I hope you're not beating yourself up over being controlled by Ritchey. You had no idea what he could do, and he had you before you even had a clue. From then on you were in his hands. I'm only glad that he chose to send his message with a live messenger."

"People, do not contact with Ritchey assuming you can fend him off by counting. You have to really work at it, and the people we experimented with were paying attention only to that. They didn't have other things on their mind to distract them from the counting. From what I can see, our best defense is to overwhelm him or give the green light to a sniper who has escaped his notice. Charlie and Ritchey can sense a presence from at least as far as two or three blocks away, but they can be distracted which would limit that range of detection."

"So Charlie or Ritchey can't overwhelm you and render you unconscious or some other way *hors de combat* with his mind?" asked an FBI agent.

"Well, controlling your actions puts you out of the game, but as far as knocking you out or killing you, we don't think so."

"Who's stronger, Ritchey or Mr. Perkins here?" one of the officers inquired.

"Ritchey was exposed first, but I think we've exercised Charlie's abilities more and have a better idea of his limitations than Ritchey does. In a *mano a mano* confrontation, we don't know. There are too many variables. Ritchey does meth – or at least we assume he's continuing to use meth – and if he's strung out, the odds are with Charlie, but if Ritchey is straight, it's anybody's guess," Pete added.

"Do you know of any way to get him under control short of shooting him?" asked the Sheriff of Sierra County.

"Not a for sure way, no. And there's the issue of keeping him in custody. Ritchey at one point had kidnapped Charlie and held him handcuffed in a cabin in Hillsboro; when Charlie saw his chance to escape, he simply released himself from the restraints and ran. Charlie tells me that if he understands a mechanism, he can manipulate it. For example, a door lock, all he has to do is push the bolt back with his mind and the door will open. The same with handcuffs. If someone has a different type of restraint with an uncommon locking mechanism, that might restrain him physically, but won't hinder his ability to control those around him which, of course, includes getting someone to release him."

"What about a dart with a soporific charge in it?" asked a Border Patrolman.

Charley answered that. "I can neutralize anything introduced into my system – or not – as I choose. If Ritchey injected himself with meth, he automatically would neutralize its effects but he can consciously amend the drug's effect to 'enjoy' it. He will automatically neutralize a drug dart and I don't know how many you'd have to hit him with to overwhelm him but then there's the danger of overdosing him. And remember, the first four or so men who shoot him with a dart will be under his control, and you can imagine what he'd do."

"Jesus," said a deputy from another jurisdiction, "why don't we just have Captain Webber call in an air strike on the guy?"

Charlie took the question seriously. "The pilot would be in jeopardy of coming under Ritchey's control. More likely than not, if that happened, there would be a catastrophic crash."

Ramirez stood up. "So what are we going to do? We have about thirty-six hours before we have to turn Charlie over to Ritchey." Ramirez looked at Charlie as he continued: "That isn't going to happen, Mr. Perkins. As we see it, you in no way got yourself into this situation and we're certainly not going to sacrifice you. We appreciate your cooperation, and you're giving us more information about the guy than we had before. Still we need a good idea about how to take this guy down."

"I wish I could give you that, Sergeant," said Charlie sincerely, "but I just don't know. The idea of overwhelming him has merit, except the first several men to get to him will be at Ritchey's mercy."

"What about this guy who's with him, this Chip Lakin?" asked another sheriff.

"Lakin is just a guy who has latched onto Ritchey like a remora to a shark. He's just a gofer and not a very good one but you can't ignore him or he'll probably shoot you in the back."

Several officers wanted to see firsthand Charlie's ability to control someone and interject a suggestion. He obliged by causing several of the officers to take off their jackets and even put them on backward. It didn't take long before Bob Emmerson was getting a lot more sympathetic looks than before.

Pete had one last question for the group, but looked at Emmerson. "Does anyone have any fresh intelligence on these two? Where they have stayed, what they're driving, with whom they are associating?"

Emmerson stood up. "When I stopped them, they were in an old ninety-four Ford pickup. I'm not sure of the color because we were under the sodium vapor street lights, but the truck had seen better days. Obviously I was more interested in who was in it than what it was. They're both carrying revolvers. Lakin seems like he's willing to do anything Ritchey tells him to do including helping take a cop hostage."

"One last time, before we adjourn," said Ramirez, "does *anyone* have an idea or a plan that will neutralize this man without getting Charlie or a bunch of officers hurt?"

Ramirez grimaced as he continued: "I assume, Captain Webber, that you have provided suitable secure accommodations for Mr. Perkins on the base?"

"Yes, I think Charlie feels as safe there as anywhere else?" he asked as he looked at Charlie, who nodded.

"Okay," said Ramirez, "I suggest we re-convene tomorrow morning, here, at oh seven hundred."

People started to get up and gather their gear. A low murmur of talking broke out, and Emmerson walked over to Charlie and held out his hand.

"A long time, Charlie, since high school."

"Yep, Bob, a long time. Sure glad you came out of this okay."

"Thanks for demonstrating. I had the feeling a lot of people just didn't believe what I told them until you showed them."

"What's your gut tell you about Ritchey?"

"He's a stone cold psychopath. He wouldn't have had any qualms about shooting me, and the only reason I'm alive is because I was worth more giving the message alive than dead. I'm sure the next officer won't be so lucky."

"I wish you were wrong, Bob, but I completely agree with your assessment."

Pete and Charlie reversed the procedure for getting Charlie back in the car and Charlie kept a vigilant eye on any vehicles around them, which were few at that time of night. There was little conversation in the car as Pete drove them back to Alamogordo.

When they pulled up in front of Pete's office instead of at the Inn, Charlie looked up in surprise.

"Come in for a minute, will you, Charlie?" he asked casually as he got out of the car.

They walked into the office and Pete unbuckled his belt and stripped off a holster containing a .40 caliber Glock and sat it on the desk. He withdrew two full extra magazines from his jacket pocket and laid them beside the holstered weapon. "This is my personal weapon, not Air Force issue, and it's my favorite of all the weapons I've handled. I have to go use the men's room and then I'll drop you off. I'll meet you out front. Oh, and lock up for me, will you?" he said as he walked out the door leaving the weapon and magazines on the desk.

  Charlie's thoughts crystallized as he stared at the weapon. He was familiar with guns from his cowboying days, though an automatic wasn't as familiar as a revolver. He hefted the piece, then shoved it and the ammunition in his jacket pockets and locked the door behind him.

CHAPTER 15

Charlie didn't really have much of a plan. All he knew was that he didn't want any law enforcement officers to lose their lives over him. He needed to find a way to take on Glen himself. He ran his belt through the loops on the Glock's holster and made sure all three magazines were loaded and there was a round in the chamber. Then he left the Inn and hiked up to his old blue Cherokee still in the visitor's parking lot near the main gate. It started right up and no one even gave him a second glance when he drove through the gate and off the base. Now he would try to find the man who wanted to kill him, and neutralize him any way he could.

As Charlie drove back toward T or C, he considered how he could close with his quarry without unnecessarily endangering other people. It was a tall order, and he finally decided that he had probably better locate Ritchey before trying to come up with a way to defeat him. When he arrived at the Williamsburg exit, he opted to head for the high ground, which would be at the next exit into town, up near the water tower. From there he hoped, as he looked down over the city, he could get a "whiff" of his adversary. He knew it was a lost cause to locate his man without being located himself but that was just too bad.

From the water tower Charlie let his consciousness flow down over the town, alternately concentrating on different areas as his senses glided above the surface. At this hour, as most people slept, their conscious thoughts were in neutral but there was a strong undercurrent of thought and emotion Charlie had no problem detecting. It was easiest to detect strong emotions – domestic squabbles, sexual release, and flaring tempers – but the smoldering malignancy that was Glen Ritchey was nowhere to be found. That didn't mean he wasn't there and was, for a time, distracted by something else, but Charlie could not sense him anywhere within the town.

Up close, Ritchey would be easy to pick out, but from a distance, not so much. He wasn't surprised he hadn't sensed Ritchey from this distance. He drove back down into town, cruising through areas he knew Ritchey and Lakin frequented, ever cognizant of vehicles around him, lest that pickup suddenly appear. He slowed down when he approached the Plugged Nickel, debating whether to go in or not. He stopped at the entrance then pulled in, knowing that the moment he came out, he would be a target if Ritchey was around. He made sure the Glock was not visible under his jacket when he got out of the Jeep and walked into the bar.

There were only a couple of customers left and the reason became apparent when he approached the bartender. "Sorry," the young aproned man said, "but we've already had last call and are getting ready to close up for the night."

"That's okay," Charlie replied with a smile, "I was just looking for some prospector friends of mine, Glen Ritchey and Chip Lakin. Seen them around lately?"

"I saw them about three nights ago. They were in and had a couple of beers."

"Damn! I missed them again. I don't suppose they happened to mention where they're hanging their hats these days, did they?"

"Not that I heard, but I don't talk to customers much who don't sit at the bar, the barmaid takes care of that."

"Okay, well, if you talk to them, tell them Charlie was looking for them."

"Will do. Have a nice night."

Cautiously, Charlie returned to his Jeep and pulled out of the parking lot, his head swiveling in all directions, but no gunshot pierced the quiet of the night and no pickup bore down on him. He continued his rounds of all the taverns and all the motels, but still came up empty. It didn't look like Ritchey was in town, even though his deadline was fast approaching. When Charlie could think of no place else in town to look, he decided to take a chance and head up to Hillsboro. Ritchey and Lakin had already shown a preference for the area, and maybe he'd get lucky - if locating a killer dead set on doing the same to him was considered lucky.

He allowed his senses and his muscles to relax a little as he drove. He was amazed how tense he had become, then decided that tension was trying to save his hide. He noticed for the first time that his senses had sharpened. He could see better at night than before, and his hearing seemed more acute. That meant that Ritchey's was too, and that put Charlie that much more on his guard. With a loose cannon like Ritchey, he could appear any time, any place and if Charlie wasn't on his guard, Ritchey would kill him with no more regard than stepping on a bug. Charlie knew this was a fight to the death, and he didn't know if he could arbitrarily shoot Ritchey down if he had the chance, but he damn sure knew that if Ritchey had the same opportunity, he wouldn't hesitate.

Just after he steered through the curve near the entrance to Copper Flats, Charlie saw headlights coming down the mountain ahead of him. As the vehicle came out of the curves and onto the straightaway, Charlie was sure of two things: it was Ritchey in the vehicle, and the man knew he was here. The vehicle's lights were on bright and as it came closer, Charlie could see that it was over halfway into his lane. He figured Lakin was driving, as usual, and Ritchey was urging him to run Charlie off the road where, hopefully, he would crash. *That wasn't going to happen!*

Charlie squared his shoulders, set his mouth in a grim line and gripped the wheel with both hands as he accelerated toward the oncoming vehicle. *I'm either going to die in a head-on collision, or Lakin is going to flinch.* When they were close enough that Charlie could clearly see the front of the pickup, a long band of flame erupted across the hood from the passenger side of the pickup. Ritchey was already shooting, and with something heavy, because the muzzle blast extended nearly the width of the pickup's hood. Charlie forced himself not to recoil as he heard the second round hit and punch a hole through the window behind him. Finally, Lakin abruptly swerved back into his own lane, just milliseconds before the two vehicles would have been reduced to scrap metal. As Charlie's Jeep flew past the pickup, he could see Ritchey gesticulating wildly, while Lakin swerved viciously back and forth in his lane, trying to correct his over steer while nearly rolling the truck.

Charlie had to make a decision quickly where he wanted this showdown to occur. He could just pull over and take the only cover available behind his Jeep, continue up to Hillsboro to make his stand, or surprise his pursuers and head back down toward T or C. He opted for Hillsboro. He wanted the cover of more than his Jeep, but wanted to keep the fight away from more populated areas. As he accelerated away from the near collision, he called nine one one on his cell phone: "This is Charlie Perkins. Glen Ritchey and Chip Lakin are chasing me on Highway 152 up toward . . ." The phone cut out – he was out of range! He hoped his message got through. He didn't want Pete thinking he had just bailed on him.

*****

"Goddamn you, you chicken shit!" bellowed Glen when Charlie barreled by them headed for Hillsboro. "Get this piece of shit turned around and catch that bastard! Goddamn it, if you hadn't flinched, we'd of had him off the side of the road, shot full of holes with no one the wiser."

Chip didn't say anything. He was too shook up. That had been close, if Perkins's Jeep would have had a wider outside rearview mirror, it would have impacted with his own. They had been that close when they passed each other. He did a sloppy three-point turn and headed back for Hillsboro as fast as the old pickup would go – which didn't seem very fast to Glen when viewed from a dead stop. The pickup got up to speed at about the time they met the curves at the top of the grade going down into Hillsboro, so he had to slow down for some of them. Every time he hit the brake, Glen would yell "fuck!" and pound on the dash.

When they finally got through the curves, Chip gunned the truck through town, both of them looking left and right for any sign of the Jeep. When they didn't see it, they continued on through town and all the way to Kingston before turning around.

"Great! Now we lost the fucker. Turn around. Maybe we missed him in Hillsboro."

Chip did as he was commanded. When he reached the outskirts of town again, he slowed to a crawl and they crept through town, looking carefully for any signs of the blue Jeep or dust hanging in the air to suggest a car had pulled off on one of the gravel side streets. Once through town, they raced toward the freeway, in case Perkins had doubled back on them.

After their near-collision, Charlie figured he had maybe a thirty-second head start on his pursuers, and accelerated through the curves as fast as he could, barely holding the Jeep on the roadway. His adrenalin was starting to make him shaky as he dashed for the relative security of several unoccupied buildings toward the middle of the nearly abandoned mining town. He made a hard left onto a bridge that took him over the creek bed. He tucked his Jeep in between two abandoned buildings and got out, drawing the Glock. He ran behind the uphill building and crouched down, peeking around the corner at his Jeep and waiting for the pickup to skid to a stop somewhere behind it. Instead, he heard the unmistakable rumble of the pickup approach then roar by the side street as it continued through the sleeping town as Charlie's mind counted slowly and deliberately to a hundred.

Charlie decided to get closer to town, where his cell phone would work and he could call in some back up. He ran back and started the Jeep, then headed back the way he had come through town, his foot mashing the accelerator to the floor.

Then he had second thoughts. What if they didn't continue back toward town? What if they had pulled off the road and were waiting for him to go by? He still didn't want a shootout where innocent people could get hurt. Finally, he made a decision and turned around toward Hillsboro. He would go back to his original hiding place and wait. If they found his Jeep, they would settle it once and for all, but if they continued on toward town, Charlie wasn't sure what he would do.

He parked his Jeep again and made himself as comfortable as he could at the corner of the building, his ears attuned to every passing sound; after all, it wasn't inconceivable they would walk back through town searching for him. An hour went by, then another. Charlie was beginning to wonder if Glen and Chip had just gone back to their hideout when he heard the rumble of a V-8 pass slowly by his side street. Charlie couldn't see the main street from his vantage point, but he could hear anything passing by. Because it went by so slowly, he was pretty sure the vehicle belonged to his pursuers but he couldn't sense Ritchey's presence. He stood and strained to hear the last of the vehicle as it continued down the main street in the direction of I-25, some sixteen or seventeen miles distant. He was confident it had not stopped.

Now what should he do? He weighed his options back and forth for several minutes before, in a pique of frustration, asked himself why he was the rabbit and not the hound? Who said he had to run while Glen Ritchey chased? The more he thought about it, the angrier he got, until finally, he stood up and walked back to his Jeep, then headed back toward the freeway. He would go slow to avoid an ambush, but he was tired of being the one chased. *Let's see how Ritchey handles being the one on the run.* He had tried to shoot Charlie twice, now, Charlie didn't have any qualms left about shooting back.

As he drove cautiously through the curves coming up out of Hillsboro, he was startled at how many places one could lie in wait and get a clear shot at a passing car before the driver could react. When he reached the open straightaways he was relieved. Now he could see miles ahead. Clearly the duo had continued down to the freeway, unless they were waiting at the interchange, which would be a smart choice. His flashpoint receded to caution as he approached the interchange. Sure enough, there sat a dark-colored pickup backed perpendicular to the highway, and Glen was in it.

Charlie saw no way to turn the pickup's position to a tactical advantage and stomped on the accelerator, knowing that Ritchey would have a shot at him if Chip didn't move too soon.

But Chip was already spinning gravel in his eagerness to get behind Charlie. Still, there was a muzzle flash, and Charlie felt the thump as the bullet hit his door then, moments later, he felt a sting on his lap, and something warm trickled down his legs. But that was the least of his worries as he accelerated under the interstate and down to the old two-lane highway that ran parallel to it. He didn't slow down as he turned hard left toward T or C, tires squealing. He floored it again and went over the rise and down onto the Caballo flat. At the church, Charlie could see that the pickup hadn't made it to the top of the grade yet. He did a fishtailing one eighty in the gravel parking lot before gaining the pavement again, then headed back in the direction from which the pickup would appear. Just as he got back on the pavement and accelerated, the pickup cleared the rise.

Charlie hit the high beams and aimed right for it and Chip took the shoulder versus the impact and slewed sideways down the side hill until his tires caught. He rode the shoulder nearly to the bottom of the hill before wrapping the driver's side of the pickup around a power pole. Charlie saw the crash and immediately turned around and pulled in behind the pickup, smoke and dust filling the air. He didn't know how Chip could have survived the impact so he worked his way along the soft shoulder to the passenger side and peeked in. Glen was slumped over, blood running from several cuts on his face caused by the collapsed windshield. Charlie tried to open the door, but it was stuck, so he holstered the Glock to put both hands on the handle and give a heftier pull.

Just then, Ritchey gave the door a huge kick, forcing it open and sending Charlie staggering down the soft gravel hillside almost to the bottom. Glen didn't hesitate and flew out of the pickup, plowing his way through the soft gravel down to Charlie. Ritchey had lost his revolver in the collision, but saw Charlie's Glock slip from his holster and cartwheel down the hill ahead of him. Glen made a dash for the weapon and was mere inches from it when Charlie tackled him at the knees. They went rolling the rest of the way down the hill, punching and scrabbling for a purchase. Glen outweighed Charlie by thirty pounds and had a four-inch reach advantage, but Charlie was quicker and wound up on top. He punched Glen twice in the face before Glen was able to buck him off. Once again they rolled around on the ground, each trying to reach the Glock first. Charlie had been bucked off in the direction of the gun and almost reached it when Glen dragged him back and punched him in the kidney. Starved for breath, Charlie hesitated, and Ritchey dove over the top of him toward the gun, his fingers brushing against the barrel but unable to gain a grip.

Charlie punched Glen in the back of the head, then crawled up his back and ground his face into the rocky soil as he grabbed the Glock by the barrel. Glen grabbed Charlie's wrist holding the gun and tried to twist, succeeded in making Charlie drop the gun momentarily. He managed to scoop it back up, this time by the grips. Glen tried again to twist it out of his grasp. Charlie slammed the base of the grip down onto Glen's forehead. Dazed, Glen released his hold on Charlie's wrist, but grabbed for his crotch with his other hand. Charlie shoved the barrel of the gun down toward Glen's torso and fired twice in rapid succession. Slowly, the man's resistance waned until he lay limp beneath Charlie.

Charlie could only lay there breathing heavily, trying to gather his strength. Finally, he managed to roll off Ritchey and get up on his knees. Ritchey didn't move so Charlie reached over to check for a pulse, finding a weak one. He struggled to his feet and started to make his way back up the embankment when he heard a noise above him and looked up. Chip stood on the shoulder of the road swaying from side to side. The left side of his face was covered in blood and his left arm seemed to be out of alignment as if broken. In his other hand Chip held a small revolver that he raised and pointed it at Charlie. Charlie dove for the ground just as Chip fired, and he felt the bullet enter the right side of his chest. Without thinking, he emptied the Glock's magazine in Lakin's direction then slumped to the ground, waiting for the shot that never came. Chip collapsed and lay still with his head pointing down the embankment.

CHAPTER 16

When Charlie woke up, he didn't know where he was, but he was still too deep under the anesthesia to react. All he knew was that he was groggy, his throat was dry and raspy, and everything around him was bright and mostly white. A lady kept coming over and talking to him every time his eyes would close and he still didn't know what she looked like. He vowed the next time he'd be ready for her, but he was not.

Eventually he was able to stay awake longer and finally caught the kind, middle-aged face of the woman who kept talking to him. He found it difficult to talk and his limbs felt incredibly heavy.

"Mr. Perkins? Can you hear me? Time to wake up."

Who the hell put me to sleep in the first place?

"How are you feeling, Mr. Perkins? Are you in pain?"

Charlie mumbled something about being okay and tried to ask where he was, but the face had taken off again. *That woman doesn't stay still for anyone!*

Finally she came back. "Okay, Mr. Perkins, we're going to take you to your room now. You're just going to take a little ride and before you know it, you'll be tucked in your own bed."

The ride was nothing to write home about; he just passed under a host of light fixtures and couldn't really see anything on either side of him.

The same woman, along with a male orderly, maneuvered him into a room bright with sunlight and quickly transferred him to another bed with cool sheets. He missed those warm blankets they had put over him. Another face, this one attached to a woman's body, came in and fussed with a pouch near the foot of his bed.

"What's that for?" Charlie croaked.

"That's just a saline solution to keep you hydrated. As soon as you feel up to it, you can have something to drink and maybe later, when you're more awake, we can find you something to nibble on."

"Where am I?"

"You're in the Sierra Vista Hospital in Truth or Consequences, New Mexico."

"The last thing I remember, I was alongside the road and . . ."

"Shh, don't try to talk too much just yet, you're still groggy from the anesthesia. Just go with the flow and try to sleep, okay?"

The sun was lower in the sky when Charlie woke up again. This time he felt more awake, and saw that there was a rolling table nearby that temptingly held a cup with a straw sticking out. He was thirsty enough that he reached for the cup and immediately winced from the pain shooting below his neck and across the front of his thighs. The nurse must have heard him moan and she was there seconds after he reached for the cup.

"What's wrong with me? Why do I hurt?"

"It usually happens that way when you get shot a couple of times," said Pete as he and Samantha walked into the room behind the nurse. The nurse ignored them and but asked Charlie if he needed anything.

He looked over at the cup and asked: "Is that water?"

She nodded, picked up the cup and held the straw to his lips. He drank slowly, afraid he'd aspirate some of the liquid. That would make him cough, and *that* would make him hurt some more.

The nurse freshened up around Charlie's bed, then left the room. The captains walked closer to the bed and leaned down with smiles on their faces.

"He doesn't look all that bad to me, what do you think?" Pete asked Samantha.

"He's as white as the sheet and clearly in pain," she protested softly.

"How do you feel, Charlie?" Pete asked, concern supplanting the smile on his face.

"I guess I feel okay," he said, somewhat mystified. "You said I got shot a couple of times?"

"Yeah," said Pete, "but let's not get into that. It would spoil Ramirez's fun, he'll be along shortly. For now we're just here to see for ourselves that you're okay"

"You mean I was in danger – other than from Ritchey and Lakin?"

"They weren't sure about your wounds until they got you here and got a good look at you. The doc says you were very lucky that your wounds are not life-threatening, Chip's round clipped your collar bone and traveled down the outside of your rib cage before exiting at your belt line. Glen's round went through the Jeep's door and grooved the fronts of your thighs. I have to make a report to my bosses explaining how I let you go cowboying after a couple of bad guys with no help. You scared the hell out of me, pal."

"Don't mind him," said Samantha as she elbowed Pete in the side. "He's just hoping he isn't in trouble for losing track of you. I think everything will be fine, so don't worry about it, okay?"

"Yeah . . . uh . . . what about Ritchey and Lakin?"

"Let's let Ramirez get into all that, okay?"

"Can you at least tell me if I'm in some kind of trouble?"

Both officers laughed. "No, Charlie, you needn't worry about being in trouble."

Just then Sergeant Ramirez walked in. Charlie saw him smiling for the first time. "Hey *amigo, cómo estàs?*"

"I guess I'm doing okay, Sergeant, but these two aren't telling me much."

Ramirez pulled up a chair, and sat down next to the bed. Charlie noticed he had a portable tape recorder in one hand, along with a notebook.

Webber spotted the recorder and asked: "Uh, Sarge, do you think it wise to record the statement of a man still under the effects of an anesthetic?"

"Oh, I guess you're right. Charlie, I'd like to ask you about what happened today, if you're up to it and I'll try to answer any questions you might have. Captain Webber is right about tape recording though. We wouldn't want you to space out into the ozone and start talking about being kidnapped by a UFO or something, so I'll just take notes. That way any errors or inconsistencies are my mistake, not yours."

Ramirez turned to the two Air Force officers. "Are you going to stay for the interview?"

"If you don't mind, Sergeant, we'd like to."

"I guess we'd better round up a couple more chairs and get started then."

Ramirez skillfully walked Charlie through his actions from the time he and Pete left the meeting at the Sierra County Courthouse the previous evening. He asked Charlie to clarify the acquisition of the Glock.

"Captain Webber was showing it to me and left it on his desk when he went to the can. He asked me to lock up and he'd meet me at the front door. I just borrowed the weapon, knowing I might wind up in a gunfight. Did you find the gun at the scene?"

"Yes, you apparently dropped it when you collapsed. It was right beside you, empty with the slide locked back."

"Yeah, I just emptied the clip at Chip after he shot me. He had the advantage of being above me so I just sprayed the rounds hoping I'd hit him or scare him off. Did I?"

"As a matter of fact you didn't. He died of a small tear in his aorta which we assume occurred during the crash so no, you didn't kill him. I meant to ask – why didn't you use your ability to control his actions to keep him from shooting you?"

"It didn't even occur to me. By then I was exhausted from fighting with Glen and I was too busy trying to survive to try something I barely had learned to do."

"And against Glen?"

"We both tried that, but he couldn't get the edge on me and vice versa, so it was a draw. It just turned into a matter of fighting to survive with whatever effort I could bring to bear. What about Glen? Is he in custody?"

"Your two rounds killed him. They went down into his chest and hit most of the major organs before exiting from his abdomen. We never did find the slugs."

"I was so tired. I knew that if he got me by the balls, the fight would be over and he'd finish me off; I didn't see as I had much of a choice."

"No one is doubting you, Charlie, especially considering these two's propensity toward violence. No, even the fact that you went looking for them doesn't sound so bad when you factor in that they were out looking for you too."

"I just couldn't let a bunch of innocent people go in harm's way for something that was apparently my responsibility. Glen was obsessed with the idea that I had stolen his gold, and wasn't about to be dissuaded."

"Next time keep in mind that that's our job, okay? That's what they pay us for."

"Where's my Jeep?"

"It's here at the impound garage. They'll probably finish processing it before you get out of here, so it'll be waiting for you. You're going to have to get that rear window replaced and patch the bullet hole in your door and the opposite arm rest where we found the slug but otherwise I think it's good to go."

"So how much trouble am I in?"

"The DA will take the case before the Grand Jury to determine if the deaths are justifiable homicide or not. I don't think you have much to worry about."

"Should I have a lawyer?" Charlie asked.

"You're entitled to one if you want one, but under these circumstances I think it would be a waste of your money." Ramirez replied with a shrug.

"I thought the State had to provide an attorney at no expense," said Charlie.

"Not under these circumstances. If you were formally charged with a crime and couldn't afford an attorney, one would be appointed, but since you're not charged with a crime and probably won't be, there doesn't seem to be much sense in getting an attorney involved."

"Okay, if you say so." Charlie didn't seem as convinced that he was out of the woods as Ramirez did, but he was willing to trust someone who knew far more about the system than he did.

Before Ramirez could ask another question, Charlie yawned hugely and his eyes drooped.

"I think we're overdoing it a little," said Samantha, nodding toward the sleepy patient.

"Yeah, I think that's enough for now," said Ramirez. "Charlie, is it okay if we talk again?"

"Anytime, Sergeant," Charlie said sleepily, the anesthesia and pain meds still having their effect. "Sorry I'm pooping out, but I just can't stay awake any longer," he apologized, then closed his eyes.

As the three officers walked down the hall from Charlie's room, Captain Chase asked Ramirez: "He really doesn't have anything to worry about, does he?"

"Not as far as I'm concerned, and if the DA sees it any way but justifiable homicide on both counts, I'll be very surprised. Those of us in law enforcement see what he did as heroic. Even though he had his own agenda, his first thought was for the welfare of others. I'd put him in for a medal if I could. I'll let the civilians and politicians wrangle over that; I'm going to have the Sheriff send him a glowing letter of commendation and appreciation."

Charlie's doctor saw no sense in keeping him in the hospital once it was clear he had sustained no infection from his wounds. He was released the next day with his right arm in a sling due to his broken collar bone. Pete was there to collect him. They made arrangements to leave Charlie's Jeep at the Sheriff's Office, then stopped by the prosecutor's office to accept service of a subpoena for Grand Jury. It was set sufficiently in the future not to cause unnecessary hardship for the star witness.

As they left the prosecutor's office, Pete asked his charge: "I guess you need to tell me where to go next. Do you want to stay here in town, or go back to Holloman with me?"

"What about your gun? I don't want to see you lose that weapon just because I borrowed it."

Webber smirked. "We both know the truth of that, so don't bullshit a bullshitter, okay? I've already arranged to get it back once the Grand Jury returns a 'No True Bill' on your case. Ramirez's case will be closed, and evidence disposed of, including the Glock which will be returned to its rightful owner, yours truly."

"I've been meaning to thank you for your foresight. It saved my life."

"You're welcome, but I should have been there to help you."

"In answer to your question about where I want to stay, I guess it depends on what the Air Force's position is on me. Are you through with me or what?"

"Charlie, nothing could be further from the truth. Remember Admiral Hampton from that board of inquiry? You sold him a hundred percent and he wants to put you to work yesterday. He knows you've been slowed down for a little while, but as soon as you're ready he wants to talk to you about fulltime employment with the government."

"Doing what? Do you know?"

"Not specifically because I don't have the need to know. My guess is that they'll start you slow so the first cases you see will be low-key and not major issues of national security. The Admiral, of course, really wants you to move to the DC area as soon as possible."

"Now that's where I have to put my foot down. I've told him and anyone else who cares to listen that I don't want to move out of the southwest. After a lot of consideration, I am willing to compromise by going to DC occasionally on a temporary basis but I'm not going to subtly get sucked into living there fulltime. I'll work for 'em fulltime if they want but most of the work has to come to me here. That sounds pretty egotistical, doesn't it?"

"Depends on your perspective. I can't say that I blame you for wanting to stay here. Let's face it, though, much of your work will originate from DC so it makes sense to have you close by. But if you can't work there, if it distracts you or stresses you too much then you're not much good to anyone."

"Well, for now, let's head back to Holloman and the Inn, if that's still an option."

"It is and we're on our way as of now."

"Where does Samantha fit in to all this?"

"She would like to make you a lifelong study if you and the Air Force would allow it. When you're not working for the intelligence community, she'd like to do some long term studies of what goes on in your head when you're functioning at that higher level. She sees great potential in using what she learns from you for autism research, among other things."

"What about you? What's the future going to be like for you? Are we going to finish that theft case?"

"That case is already well on its way to the prosecution phase. Once we had the framework and the mechanism, it didn't take much to break into it on our own and we made another buy last night. You made the difference on that case but unfortunately it'll have to be a difference that forever stays silent. I doubt the Defense Department and Homeland Security are going to want to share you for criminal cases for us but until I'm told differently, I'm still your gofer for lack of a better word. I can't say protector since I failed miserably at that."

"Now don't start on that again. I didn't give you a chance to do your job, and I already apologized for that. I surely would have liked to have you along, but I couldn't get over the idea I might have jeopardized your life for something that wasn't your responsibility."

"But you know better now, right?"

"Yeah," Charlie said with a sigh, "But I still can't get used to the idea that I'm considered a national asset and need to be protected twenty-four seven."

"Get used to it, pal, because you are! Something else I've been thinking about, now that it's on my mind," said Webber.

"What's that?"

"I think I know why whoever made that probe eliminated anything less than subjects with a certain intelligence."

"The bodies would be piling up for one thing."

Pete laughed. "Yeah, that too, but can you imagine a bear or a mountain lion with the expanded brain functioning you have?"

"It's scary enough with Glen and me but yeah, I see your point."

As they passed through the main gate at Holloman, Pete said: "Why don't you take it easy the rest of the day and go see that everything is okay at the Inn. I'll come get you for breakfast in the morning if you're up to it, but I think you'd better relax and give yourself a chance to heal from all you've been through. I mean, not only have you been shot twice, but Ritchey roughed you up pretty good when you were scuffling for the gun. You're bound to be sore for a while, so just kick back and cool it for a while. You'll get busier than you can handle soon enough, so enjoy the calm while you can."

The next morning Charlie called Pete and cancelled breakfast. He was just too sore and stove up to want to jump in a car and drive to breakfast. He would have something brought up if that was okay – which it was.

The enforced idleness started to take its toll on the third day and Charlie called Pete" "I'm bored spitless, isn't there something I can help with?"

"Not really but there's something you can do to help yourself. If you're up to it, go get a haircut and get all shipshape. Admiral Hampton's coming in tomorrow just to see you."

"He's probably going to try to con me into coming to DC with him. I just won't do it, Pete. Like I said, I'll compromise and visit once in a while but that's it."

Admiral Hampton flew into Holloman late the next day. Pete and Charlie met him for breakfast at the Inn and, over coffee, Admiral Hampton asked: "How does it feel to know you can save the lives of uncounted people and save millions of dollars in property damage?"

Charlie smiled and looked down at his coffee. "Admiral, I think that's stretching it a little, don't you?"

"Oh, I don't know, Mr. Perkins – can I call you Charlie?"

"I wish you would."

"Why don't we continue this conversation somewhere a little more private. Captain, is your office secure?"

"Yes Sir. Let me get the check and we can head right over there."

When they were settled in Pete's office and coffee served all around, Admiral Hampton continued: "As I was saying, Charlie, two of the last photographs Mr. Schneider showed you when you were with us at Nellis were unknown associates of his main target, Abu Anas Al-Liby. Turns out they were in the U.S. but no one could identify them, but you pegged them as Al Qaeda operatives and closely associated with Al-Liby. They weren't here on vacation. Agent Ratcliff ran interference for Mr. Schneider with the FBI's counter-terrorism folks and they put a tail on the two men you identified. When they connected with a really radicalized mosque in Philadelphia, they knew something was up."

"To make a long story short, the two operatives were the catalyst to kick off an attack against an anti-Al Qaeda, Hebrew-language magazine in downtown Philadelphia. They were going to gun down everyone then use thermite grenades to incinerate the spaces of the magazine and as much of the city block as they could. So you see, you're already in the win column."

"How were they detected?" asked Charlie.

"That's classified, Charlie, and I doubt the counter-terrorism guys want to discuss it."

"The nation owes you a debt of gratitude. Unfortunately, since it's all classified, mine are the only thanks you're probably going to get. Maybe this will make it feel a little better," he said as he handed Charlie an envelope.

In it was a U.S. government check for ten thousand dollars. Charlie was speechless.

"We both know that's a drop in the bucket compared to what you saved the government, but it's all I could squeeze out of the cheap bastards."

Everyone laughed until Admiral Hampton came back to topic. "I also have a contract – an employment contract – that I'd like you to look over. It's clean so you could even show it to an attorney, so long as you don't tell him exactly what kind of services you'd be performing for us. It's a five-year contract that starts you out as a GS-12 step four which, with cost adjustment provides you with about a $75,000-per-year salary plus the usual government benefits package. That also makes you an assimilated O-4, which is a major in the Air Force so, technically, you would outrank Captain Webber, though I have a feeling that won't be for long."

"The contract provides for twelve visits per year to the nation's capital at no extra salary, each visit to last no more than a week, plus another twelve visits to other undesignated locations in the United States under the same pay circumstances. After that there is a scale for overtime and comp time which hopefully will compensate you for extra hours. As I said, have an attorney peruse it, then call me and tell me what you think. We'd like to have you on board permanently as soon as possible, so please don't take too long with your attorney."

Suddenly Pete's phone vibrated and it made him jump. He looked embarrassed but said: "Excuse me, Admiral, that's a priority page. I'd better answer it."

He got up and went outside to take the call, but was back within thirty seconds and even interrupted Admiral Hampton: "We need to get Charlie to Nellis as soon as possible. They're spooling up a plane to take us right away."

Admiral Hampton sighed with irritation. "Someone thinks he has a case out there he can't solve without Charlie?"

"No Sir. The probe has apparently become active again. The ramp is down and it is demanding communication with either Charlie or Glen Ritchey."

ACKNOWLEDGEMENTS

No one can write a book alone. Just as "no man is an island" there are other people behind the scenes who, one way or another, have contributed to the birth of this work. They all deserve my undying gratitude and approbation for their efforts and contributions that made this book possible.

First and foremost is my ex-wife, Barbara, for her staunch support in allowing me the time to write and for her never-flagging interest and willingness to critique my efforts.

To Dave and Gayle for their unwavering faith and technical assistance. Jeez Dave!

To the host of others who have taken the time to read (some pretty bad drafts) and remain honest about their reactions. This includes but is not limited to both Bills, Dennis, Carol, and Jim. Thanks you guys, but for you this would have remained a dream.

AUTHOR'S BIO

Terry L. Shaffer grew up near Oregon City, about twenty miles south of Portland, Oregon. He graduated from Oregon City High School and Clackamas Community College before moving on to Portland State University, majoring in Political Science. Between high school and college, Terry spent four years in the United States Navy, and was assigned duty stations in Long Beach, California, and Naval Intelligence billets in Washington, D.C. and Alameda, California, from where he sailed to the Western Pacific aboard an aircraft carrier and earned both the Vietnam Service Medal and the Vietnam Campaign Medal.

During his college days at Portland State, Terry joined the Clackamas County Sheriff's Department where he was assigned a variety of positions including patrol, detectives and narcotics. He retired in 2000 after twenty-five years' service. After writing thousands of pages of police reports and search warrant affidavits, he likes to say that he has twenty-five years' experience writing in the true crime genre.

Terry began his writing career in fiction shortly before he retired and has been at it ever since. He lives full time in his motorhome and divides his time between his home in Colton, Oregon, and various locations in the American Southwest where he spends his time writing and exploring. Terry travels with his two miniature Dachshunds, Maggie and Emma, and enjoys off-roading, photography, reading and, of course, writing.

Made in the USA
Middletown, DE
07 June 2021